Bake
Wars

Julia,
You rock my
world! Your support
+ friendship means the
world.

D. M

Julian

You look m[e]

You'll know

happy

c'mon [illegible] support x

D.W

xx

Bake Wars

book one

by D.M. Tregaskis

Message from the Author

In my wildest dreams, I wish for a rating system for books. That might sound weird, but if you're like me, you fantasize about reading but struggle to pick up new books because you don't know what's lurking in the pages. It's okay if we're nothing alike.

I understand that I might turn readers away at times with full disclosure, but I would rather you have an amazing experience because you're aware of the content.

Here is what you will find in Bake Wars:

Trigger Warnings:
Some discussion and elements of suicide, gun violence, and death (minimum blood)

Steam level:
Kissing only

Language:
Instances of crap, pissed, hell (location only)

I hope this guide helps you have an enjoyable read.

xo, D.M.

ISBN: 978-1-63203-673-5 (paperback) | ISBN: 978-1-63203-672-8 (e-book)

Dedications:

Taylor, you know why. This book would have died without you.

And to all the women in the world named Karen:
may this story redeem you.

And to those of us derogatorily labeled as "a Karen,"
at least we know how to get the job done.

chapter one
One Gun. Two Paws.

Bridge O'Niall hocked her spit into the rusted tin can next to her customer's shiny dress shoe. That was for turning his nose up at her. Sure, her repair shop looked like a bomb had littered tools everywhere, and her skin glistened with sweat from the muggy heat, but if something had moving parts, Bridge could make it as good as new. There was nothing to get snooty about.

The man in the suit cradled his three-in-one juice extractor, citrus squeezer, and smoothie maker. A glance on Amazon said he'd spent over a thousand bucks on it.

"Are you sure you can fix it?" he asked.

Bridge bit back a smirk as she tied her curly, red hair into a ponytail. The sin of questioning her skills would cost him extra. Before she could answer, the front door opened, and the landlady for her apartment marched in, carrying the New Jersey heat with her. Mrs. Crampsus was a heavy-set woman, probably twice Bridge's age of twenty-six, with sharp eyebrows and two skill sets: looking peeved and ticking people off.

"O'Niall, that clicking sound is coming from your apartment again," Mrs. Crampsus said, her voice nasally like usual.

If Bridge wasn't putting her brother through dental school, she would buy her own place, eliminating the need for a landlord. And she'd have more space than her cramped studio apartment with a full kitchen to bake whatever she wanted, whenever she wanted. Delectable maple-buttercream scones. Decadent Sacher tortes. Tongue tantalizing rose and raspberry meringue tarts. The list was endless.

Bridge took the juicer and inspected it instead of making eye contact. "Sorry, Mrs. Crampsus. I'll fix it after lunch." There was nothing broken in her apartment. She knew exactly the sound her landlady was referring to. But it could wait.

"You can repair the dryer for my inconvenience of coming all the way over here." Mrs. Crampsus gave her a side-eye. "I consider lunch to be noon, so if that tapping isn't gone by—"

"Yeah, I got it," Bridge said through clenched teeth. It was one thing if Bridge offered to give help, but when people demanded it…She swallowed down a biting retort. "One p.m., not a moment longer."

Mrs. Crampsus gave her signature harumph and left the shop, the door banging behind her.

"Give me just a second…" Bridge unscrewed the plastic housing of the suit's precious appliance. The problem was simple—sheared wires. Most likely the juicer had been knocked off a counter, the cord severing as it held the heavy weight. "I just need to solder these wires to the board, and you'll be good to go."

She applied pressure to the ends with her gloved hand like she was staunching blood flow from a wound—something she unfortunately had experience with—and dabbed with her soldering gun.

"You seem proficient," the suit said, changing his snooty tune. He was slightly handsome, maybe a little old for her, though she didn't have time for a relationship. "What got you into fixing things?"

Bridge gave him a challenging stare. "I was tired of destroying other people's lives." She cranked up her playlist to drown out the possibility of more conversation and focused on her work. Bruno Mars sang about loving someone the way they were. If only she had time and could attract a guy who had that mindset. With her past, the only type of man Bridge would appeal to was someone like her, and she'd rather live lonely forever than fall down that hole.

Thieves could never be trusted.

Bridge finished fixing the glorified juicer, demonstrated to the suit that it worked as good as new, and gladly took his payment—twelve percent more than she would have charged if he'd kept his haughty looks to himself. After he left, she tidied her work area and locked up for lunch.

Outside, the clouds blocked the sun, making the heat slightly less stifling in her torn jeans and greasy t-shirt—the greasy part thanks to her job. Her apartment was a block and a half away, an easy distance to cover in two minutes if she hurried. But she wasn't in the mood to rush. The clicking sound in her apartment meant a message from her dad about the family business.

He was supposed to be retired.

A new poster hung in the Family Food Coalition's window, seeking volunteers for the next fundraising season. It caught Bridge's eye. She patted her ledger, a tiny black book she kept in her pocket. If she helped enough, she might justify marking off an item or two on the pages. After scanning the QR code, she filled out the quick sign-up form, and hit submit.

The nose-wrinkling scents of acrylic nails quickened her steps past a salon, but she paused in front of Lane No.5, a clothing boutique with its sophisticated, faceless mannequins. If she could go back in time—if she could rewrite her story—she'd be dressed like the women who shopped here—the types that made appointments with friends to get their nails and hair done. And she wouldn't have her creepy family crest tattooed on her wrist, which she kept hidden under a bandage at all times. It would crush her dad if she ever had it removed. During the holidays in her fantasy world, she'd wear sweaters, and in the summers, she'd vacation to Cape Cod or settle for a week at Lake Winnipesaukee—mostly because she loved What About Bob and Winnipesaukee was fun to say, though Lake Chaubunagungamaug in Massachusetts was a close second. With her friends, she'd carry shopping bags in one hand, an Italian soda with extra cream in the other.

At home, she'd bake every extra waking moment. She pictured herself delivering caramel-stuffed snickerdoodles to her elderly neighbors, white-velvet sugar cookies to kids, and she even had a dog biscuit recipe. Maybe she'd get her own fur baby. And of course, she'd live in a supportive community where everyone knew each other's names—just like in her favorite movies and TV shows.

An old beater drove past, belching fumes and bringing Bridge back to the present in her grungy outfit, where her life revolved around her family's choices. She swallowed the bitter taste on her tongue and forced herself to the apartment building and up the worn steps toward her room, the air thick with the smell of cigarette smoke and cat excrement. Her key slid in easily after five years of use—five years of living like this. She slipped inside to the sound of the telegraph machine. The device sat on her multi-purpose table that filled the roles of dining area, desk, and workstation. At a previous location, it had held plans—none of which were legal.

"Okay, okay," she said as the tapping continued, fraying her nerves. She could understand what Mrs. Crampsus had felt, though the sound was muffled by the floor between them.

Bridge sat, plugged in her headphones, and concentrated.

Dah, dah, dah. She wrote down *O*. Dit, dit, dah, dit equaled *F*. *T*, *O*, *W*, and *N* followed. The message finished with the word *STOP* and repeated, starting at the beginning. Her hand shook as she wrote down the rest—*GETOUT*—putting it all together for "Get out of town."

It was the message she hated, the one she'd hoped to never see again. A year had passed since the last one. Promises had been made then to ensure it never happened again, but they were clearly broken.

Her heart sped up as she replied. "How long? How far?" Back when they'd made thievery their lives, the O'Nialls often left for a few days until things cooled down and they ensured their true identities weren't blown. But they weren't supposed to be in that business anymore.

Bridge slammed two outfits into her suitcase, followed by toiletries and her throwing knives. Couldn't her dad think of anyone else besides himself? Tomorrow was Saturday, her busiest day. She'd have to eat the costs of a trip *and* the loss of business, even though he would probably offer to compensate her. But his money was tainted, not earned. She wouldn't accept his help and never had.

A response tapped through the machine. "Weekend. Take a plane."

"Tom Hiddleston," Bridge cursed. Normal people profaned their gods, but movie stars were the closest to deity she'd ever get. She returned the blades under her pillow on the bed—the TSA might get a tad upset upon finding them in her carry-on.

After washing up and changing into layers that were too hot for her comfort level, she packed her real driver's license and passport, just in case. Other items went into her bag including her lock-picking kit, a few recipes she'd been pining over, and charging cables for her phone—she planned to get drunk on movies on the plane. Quietly, she pried back a floorboard and pulled out documents and credit cards to use with one of her aliases—Esty Ryan from North Dakota. Bridge had picked the last name based on Meg Ryan from *Sleepless in Seattle* and *You've Got Mail*. The alias looked exactly like her, without any criminal activity tied to it. With all the other names, she'd used a wig and wax to distort her face.

A fresh bandage went on her wrist, covering her family crest tattoo, and she slipped out of the apartment, stepping in just the right spots where the floorboards and stairs wouldn't squeak. She didn't need Mrs. Crampsus knowing when she'd left in case anyone came looking for her. And her landlady would probably demand Bridge fix the dryer right then. Leaving without repairing it was one thing she didn't feel guilty about.

Bridge put in her earbuds, leaving the sound off, and walked to the subway like she was grooving to some sick beats. She scrolled on her phone during the train ride, but she rarely looked at the screen. Instead, she took note of everyone around her. The only thing that caught her attention was a dude with a foot-long hot pink beard—and that was only because she'd never seen one quite so big and colorful.

At the airport, she ditched her jacket in the bathroom, letting a flowery dress tumble down over her leggings—at least her ensemble was enjoyable, closer to resembling the life she wished for. She feigned a laid-back persona, casually making her way to the ticket counter where a handsome clerk greeted her. He was a few years older—thirty at most—with dark hair and a widow's peak.

"How can I help you?" He glanced Bridge over with his hazel eyes, pausing at her empty ring finger.

"I'm celebrating, and I want to take an adventure. What's the destination of the next plane leaving?" She passed her fake driver's license over the counter. So far, she'd noticed zero tails since leaving the apartment, but she was smart enough to keep her guard up.

A smile lifted his lips as his eyes did another sweep over her. "What are we celebrating?"

Bridge leaned ever so slightly across the counter, playing into the charade, her grifting skills easily coming out. "A huge promotion." If anyone was looking for her, they probably pictured a tall woman who kept to the shadows with her former grifting disguise: sleek black hair, tight clothes, and an arm full of fake tattoos. No one would suspect this redheaded flirty granola in a flowy dress.

The ticket agent clicked through the options on his screen. "And what do you do Mrs. Ryan?"

"*Miss* Ryan," she bantered back for the sake of maintaining her false identity. And honestly, it was the only flirting she'd had in months. No, scratch that. Probably all she'd had since the last time she was forced to leave town and had to convince some guys to float her some cash when her credit card had declined. Of course, she'd paid them back.

"That is need to know only." She flashed him a practiced, scandalous smile and leaned even more. "Where can I fly? I'd love to leave as soon as possible."

"I've got Milwaukee, New Orleans, and Omaha taking off within an hour, but if I can make a suggestion, I'd wait for the Portland flight in two hours."

"Oh?" she asked, though she would rather leave sooner than later. "Why is that?"

"There's something different about the West Coast. I swear, it's cooler."

Bridge could appreciate a temperature change. And if she were looking for an adventure, taking a recommendation from a stranger would make her story seem legit. "Book me to Portland, please." She handed over Esty Ryan's credit card, calculating how long it would take to pay the "trip" off. Even though the bills had no ties to her, she'd pay every last cent—it was the honest thing to do.

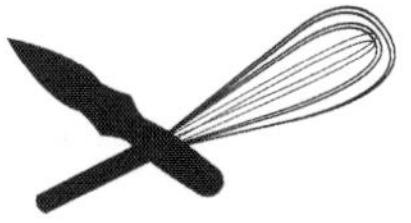

During a layover in Chicago, Bridge booked a car and a single-bedroom cottage in Pilpil Bay along the ocean. It was past eleven when she parked at the top of the hill, the house a hundred-foot journey down a gravel path below. Waves crashed nearby, the cool air filled with salt. There wasn't a neon sign anywhere, and the only other building in sight was another rental property, identical to her own, thirty yards away. She could get used to a setting like this.

Exhaustion spilled out of her fingers as she punched her code for the bungalow. The light stayed red. She tried again. Red. Again backward. Forward. Followed with a star, a pound sign. The lock refused to budge.

"Tom Hanks," she cursed. If she were at home, she'd be curled up with a pint of Tillamook watching a romantic suspense or comedy—her preferences depended on the day. But thanks to her dad, she was stuck here without even a bed.

She scrolled through her welcome email and found the host's name was Karen. "Zachary Levi," Bridge swore again, imagining how the woman—with that name—would react to a late-night call. She dialed and reached the voicemail.

"I'm sorry to bother you, but I'm trying to get into my accommodations, and the code won't work." She hung up and shook her head at the lock. If she hadn't called, she could have picked it. Except the lights were on in the other cottage. Someone might see.

With the moon at her back, Bridge hopped in the compact car to go somewhere to eat. But as she reached the single commercial street of Pilpil Bay, all the lights were out, giving off ghost town vibes. There wasn't even a gas station anywhere to be seen.

"Crackers it is." Bridge pulled out the unopened bags she'd swiped on the plane, the guilt for stealing them momentarily swallowed in necessity. Still, she pulled over to add it to her ledger and downed half the snacks before she considered water. She didn't have any.

By the time she made it back to the rental, she was so thirsty her tongue practically stuck to the roof of her mouth. A quick drink from inside her bungalow wouldn't take long. And the light next door was now off, so no one could see her break in. Bridge pulled her lock-picking set from her backpack, glanced all ways, and got to work on the door. Four. Three. Two. Click.

No one in her family could ever beat her time, and Bridge smiled knowing those skills were still intact. But was she still quieter than a mouse? Even though there were no dangers, she pretended the house was full of skilled marksmen with a pile of cash or a famous painting hidden inside.

Bridge's eyes adjusted quickly to the dark as she entered and took in every detail. A combo umbrella stand and coat rack stood near the door. Framed art hung on the hallway wall. Rugs lay at her feet. An overpowering linen smell covered a faint moldy odor. The tick tick ticking of an analog clock sounded nearby. Her feet glided silently into the kitchen where she took a long drink from the faucet and snagged the welcome basket off the counter. It had better have some decent food.

Exiting as quietly as she'd entered, she yawned and lugged her treasure with her. The moon shone overhead, lighting her path. She climbed into the car and tried to get comfortable, but the headrest was all wrong, the lumbar support too rigid. With less stealth than before, she went back into the house and nicked a pillow off the couch. She turned to leave and froze when she noticed a pair of men's loafers against the wall.

The hairs on the back of her neck rose.

A fearful trip across the room led to a peek in the bedroom where a sleeping form lay on the queen mattress. Her heart rate spiked as she crept closer, taking in details she wished she could unsee.

The handle of a forty-five poked out from under the pillow, and a pair of K9 paws shifted on the floor.

chapter two

Karen & the Other Meal

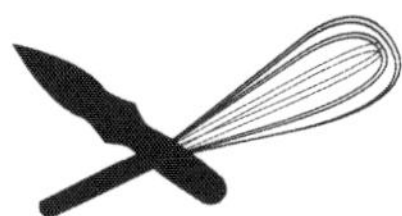

A medicine bottle next to the bed was probably the only reason the sleeping man hadn't roused. Or maybe he was faking it, waiting to strike. Soft snores came from the dog, but anything could wake a beast.

Bridge measured each breath, taking only the necessary amount needed to stay conscious. She backed out of the master then crept through the living room, down the hallway, and out the door, closing it softly behind her.

With each step up the gravel driveway, she was sure the man or the dog would attack her, but the only sounds were her heartbeats and the waves crashing in the distance.

Who was he? And was he there for her? It was possible someone intercepted the plans she'd made on her phone. Her brother could have hacked that information at seventeen, before she'd made him promise to never misuse his skills again. Or, there had been that creepy guy who'd slithered close when she was booking her rental during her layover. Anyone could have hired a local to keep tabs on her. Or worse.

As soon as Bridge got inside the car, she locked the doors and pulled up the rental contract on her phone. She glanced between it and the house, making sure she wasn't followed. The email listed three nineteen as her cottage number, and they were technically the numbers displayed on the fence at the top of the hill, but the nine hung beneath the other numbers like it was living far below its potential.

Her heart continued to pound as she drove to the next cottage and 319 stared back at her. More than likely, the top nail holding the six in place at the other cottage had given out, and the number had swung, making it appear to be a nine. After a quick surveillance of her surroundings, she got out and tested the code. The door unlocked, releasing another slightly moldy odor.

"Richard Dean Anderson." If she were as smart as MacGyver, she would have figured she was at the wrong place before picking the lock. With a groan, she set the gift basket she'd swiped next to an identical one on the entry table and found a welcome packet. There was a sticky note on top, detailing the programmable lights would stay on until midnight or until she pressed the reset button on the code next to the door. That's why the lights had been on.

Her fears waned, though they didn't disappear altogether. If her neighbor was out to get her, he didn't seem to be in the mood tonight. For now, she was safe.

Thoughts of sleep weighed her steps as she searched every inch of the place, logging possible weapons and escape routes into her sluggish brain. More than anything, she wanted to curl up in bed, but she laid a trap at each viable entrance with dishes from the kitchen and placed an arsenal of knives under her pillow. Bedtime prep had been her mom's rule, and it had saved Bridge's life more than once.

If only there had been a rule about not trusting outsiders. Maybe then her mom would still be alive.

She made the sign of the cross, knelt beside the mattress in the bedroom, and repeated her version of the Virgin Mary's prayer.

"Oh blessed Mother of Jesus, if possible, please assist in the forgiveness of my sins, though they are many. Help me to find Harley Rossi. Spare me from hellfire, or at least from coals and lava. And although I'm not fit for Heaven, help me lead others there."

Bridge's eyelids drooped as she climbed into bed, the sheets scented with lavender. Thoughts of finding and saving Harley Rossi fluttered through her head, keeping her awake like usual. Her conscious state allowed her dad's rules to infiltrate her mind and gnaw at her. He always insisted on making a plan.

"Wake early," she mumbled. "Run surveillance on the neighbor." Her words came out slurred and low. Since she'd arrived after the man with the gun, he had to be a local hire. But maybe stumbling upon him was a coincidence and he was an innocent bystander on vacation. She needed more evidence to know for sure. "Find more to eat."

An angry knock woke Bridge, and one glance at the windows told her the sun was already too high. Her senses kicked in as she gripped a paring knife and tiptoed to the door. Three scars littered her forearms from one of her first knife fights when she'd thought larger blades gave more protection. In reality, they were a greater liability, giving her attacker more leverage.

Bridge lifted a blind slat to see a sixty-something woman with a mess of hair domed on her head that was so gray it seemed blue.

"Marge Simpson," Bridge swore. It had been ages since she'd fought another female, and this one was taller and wider, but if she had to, she would.

"Can I help you?" Bridge asked as she parted the door. Usually, she'd open it all the way so her attacker had no room to hide anything from view, but the dishes still littered the floor.

"I got a call from you about not being able to get in." The woman crossed her arms over her chest.

"Oh, Karen." Bridge's shoulders relaxed.

The woman's eyes narrowed. "Excuse me?"

"Isn't your name Karen?"

"Oh, right." The woman laughed and patted her hair. If it were taller, the beehive-shaped dome would seriously compete with Marge Simpson's. "The name's Gertie. I just put Karen down to scare people out of calling." She peered through the door's opening. "Why do you have two gift baskets?"

Bridge didn't want to lie, but she also couldn't share the truth. "They were here when I woke up."

"Hmm…" Gertie said, her expression more cross than pleasant. "Where are you from?"

One question was fine, but two made Bridge nervous. "North Dakota. Is there anything I can help you with?"

"How long are you staying?"

Bridge placed a hand on the doorframe. "Just one more night." Maybe less if this Karen of a caretaker didn't back off. Or if surveillance found her neighbor was there to attack her.

Gertie glanced at Bridge's wrist, her expression twisting.

The bandage that hid Bridge's tattoo was gone—probably having fallen off in her sleep. "Sorry, it's a little disturbing." Bridge clenched her jaw and dropped her arm behind her back, hiding the crest of a spider eating another spider with a sword piercing both. She didn't like people seeing it.

"Yes, yes it is," Gertie said, her words long and drawn out. She shifted her focus, staring so intently at her tenant's features that Bridge took an uncomfortable step back and knocked over a glass cup. It made a dull thud, drawing Gertie's attention to the string of dishes on the floor. "Is that where Midwesterners keep their crockery?"

"Oh um, I saw a…" She was going to say spider, but she didn't want to conjure another troubled expression from the woman. "Will that be all? I need to pee."

"Of course. Enjoy your stay, Miss…" She glanced at her phone. "Ryan. I'm sorry for the interrogation. My therapist says I'm too gruff. I'm a work in progress."

"No apology necessary," Bridge said and closed the door, her heart pounding. She watched Gertie journey behind the next house and along the beach. Hopefully that was Bridge's only interaction the whole weekend. If the guy next door was simply a tourist, her plan was to buy ingredients and bake some new recipes. Sinless chocolate meringue cookies, caramel toasted coconut cake, and lavender shortbread were at the top of her list.

After using the bathroom with the knife still in hand, Bridge added a new bandage to cover her tattoo. The morning slipped by as she ran surveillance, watching the other cottage for any signs of life. Nothing. Wearing joggers and a t-shirt, she left and pretended to go for a run, taking in all of her surroundings on the empty beach. Where was everyone? If this was the East Coast, the area would be flooded with people.

Hangry that she had zero answers and only crackers in her stomach, she collected a handful of rocks and systematically pelted the clapboard siding of rental number three-sixteen. No one came to the door, so Bridge moved closer, inspecting tire treads near the house. She glanced around, noticing a worn road. These were all details she should have accounted for yesterday.

She gave the door a quick tap then a pounding knock before picking the lock and entering. Two bowls sat on the floor, one with water and the other with kibble dust. In the bedroom, she read the label on the medicine bottle on the nightstand. Unisom. The bed was unmade, and the room was empty of anything personal. In the bathroom, she found a knapsack on the floor and inside were a couple changes of clothes, deodorant which smelled of slightly intoxicating cologne, volumizing hair powder, toothpaste, floss, a toothbrush, and an unused shaver. If the man had any information on her, he'd taken it with him.

Exiting the way she'd entered, Bridge walked away as if she owned the place, though she glanced around, looking for watchful eyes and found none. Her stomach grumbled. She went back to change into a flowy dress and then hiked to her car at the top of the hill before driving into town. In the daylight, it was alive with shoppers. Open signs hung from each business's door except for two. Bridge parked in front of the vacant side-by-side buildings and peered inside both windows. One had counter space with covered glass shelving that made her think of a bakery, and when she craned her neck to see the back room, there was indeed a wall of ovens. The other was smaller with a kitchen as well. What she wouldn't give to open up her own shop in a place like this. But not until she'd made enough rights to cover her wrongs.

The rest of this side of the street held a bank, a mortgage company, a law firm, a boutique with clothes meant for much older women, a kitschy gift shop, and a bougie art gallery. Bridge crossed at the corner and found a store front with the door wide open and a worn sign that read Gertie's Cuts. Her host sat in a salon chair, reading a glamour magazine. Bridge knew better than to tiptoe past. The awkward speed would draw attention, but she found herself doing it anyway.

"Want a cut and color?" Gertie asked, waving Bridge over.

Bridge's summer dress swished as she neared. "Nah, I'm good." She wanted to rush past, but inside the salon, shelves of cat figurines lining the wall drew her gaze. Some were life-sized and furry. Others miniature and porcelain. Every inch of space housed felines with beady eyes and faux paws, ready to claw someone's face off.

"Robert De Niro," Bridge swore. The shrine was hideous.

"What was that, dearie?" Gertie stood and walked to the doorway.

"It's a beautiful day." Bridge looked away, but not before she'd noticed a jade green cat tucked into the corner. It was about ten inches tall and positioned with only one foot on the ground, the body already mid-pounce. The details were so intricate that if it were made of real jade, it would probably be worth a small fortune. And somehow, it looked familiar, but Bridge couldn't trace the memory. "I'll see you around," she said, though she hoped to never view the woman and her creepy cat wall again.

The next two shops held little interest—a seashell store and The Essential Oil Bazaar—but the rest of the street did. She passed by a DVD rental store, a massage parlor, and a grocery store with a direct view of the baking supplies aisle. If her neighbor with a gun wasn't after her, she'd bake the weekend away. Then this would feel like a vacation, not a waste of time and money.

Last was a diner called Leftovers. As disgusting as the name sounded, Bridge was too curious and hungry to pass it up. Inside, sparkly high back vinyl booths lined the walls with tables and chairs in the center. A bar held a row of swivel stools and an old-fashioned soda tap.

Promising, Bridge thought.

A single waitress worked the mostly empty dining room, wearing a poufy-sleeved dress covered by an apron that transported the whole place back to the fifties. The woman noticed Bridge and gave her a wave that meant she'd be another minute.

"Table for one?" the waitress asked when she approached with "Karen" on her nametag. Her permed, shoulder length hair was mostly blond except for a few stray grays.

Bridge held in a groan, hoping the woman didn't live up to her name. "Just me."

Karen led her to a booth with a view of the entire dining room. A family of four sat in one corner with twin toddler girls. Three men with gruff, white beards laughed in the middle, and exactly across from Bridge a man bowed his head low.

"I'll bring you a Coke with lime and a shot of coconut and cream. Or would you prefer raspberry?"

"Uh," Bridge wasn't expecting that offer, and her senses went on high alert. "How did you know my favorite drink?"

Karen grinned and slipped into the seat across from her. "I took this online waitressing class to improve my tips. Did you know that nine out of ten women in your age category prefer that exact combination? They call it a dirty Coke."

"A waitressing class?" Leave it to money grubbers to convince people they needed extra training to do mundane jobs. If Bridge found the perps, she'd track them down and exploit them. That could maybe cross off something in her ledger.

"Yeah, and my professor talked about the power of suggestion and how it can increase tips." Karen frowned. "But now I've probably blown it by telling you."

A professor of waitressing? This Karen was adorable. Bridge leaned across the table. "Sorry, you'll have to forgive my daydreams. I got lost after I ordered a dirty Coke with lime."

"Ah." Karen tapped her nose, grinning. "I see what you did there. I'll be right back."

While she waited, Bridge watched the room instead of focusing on her menu. The twins were busy eating french fries off their parent's plates, not the broccoli on their own. One of the men in the group was telling some tale, his hands doing more talking than his lips, and the lone straggler still had his head bent. Either that was an awfully long public prayer, or he was having a bad day.

He looked to be about her age with a yoked frame, thick brown hair, a few days of stubble, and strong facial lines. But without seeing his face, the verdict was still out on whether or not he was as handsome as his profile. Not like Bridge had time or ability to be interested—she was leaving tomorrow. Besides, if she were staying, her ledger took first priority.

"Here you are," Karen set down the drink on a tiny napkin.

"Why the name Leftovers?" Bridge asked, finally looking at the menu of American fare.

Karen laughed. "It prevents snooty folk from coming in and leaving nasty reviews. We prefer curious customers like yourself."

Bridge mulled the answer over. "I like it. What's your favorite thing here?"

"Ooh, suggestions are covered in next week's course, so I hope I don't screw this up. My favorite is the dill weed burger. I tried it because I thought the name sounded funny, but the flavor is out of this world."

"Sold. I'll take a dill weed burger, sweet potato fries, and a side of mayonnaise." She leaned forward. "You don't need waitressing school."

Karen beamed as if she'd received The Nobel Prize. "Coming right up." She disappeared into the kitchen, and Bridge went back to observing.

The man sitting alone had barely moved. When Karen brought him his sandwich and fries, he turned to thank her, his eyes rimmed red, his expression so hollow that Bridge understood exactly what he was feeling. She was positive he'd recently suffered loss. The same look had stared back from her own mirror after her mom's death. If she wasn't careful, it sometimes still did.

Karen went back to the kitchen and Bridge continued to watch the man's shuddered breaths as he attempted to eat. His toes tapped. He had difficulty swallowing. If she had to guess, the loss was recent, probably within the last few days. When Karen brought out the food, Bridge asked to borrow her order pad and pen and scribbled out a note.

Can I pay for that man's order? And will you add a milkshake for him too?

If there had been any baked goods on the list, Bridge would have picked one of those so he could take it with him, but a milkshake would have to do. She handed Karen the note and ate faster than normal to make sure she could leave before he got his bill. But it wasn't hard to beat him. He struggled with each bite.

"How was it?" Karen asked as she slipped the check for both meals with a wink.

"This burger probably made my top five favorites, which is impressive. I've eaten a lot of diner food." Bridge placed Esty Ryan's credit card on the bill.

Karen beamed. "I'll tell the chef." She returned a moment later with the receipt. "Do you live around these parts?"

"I wish." The odd, small town vibes intrigued her, even the cat lady. "I'm just visiting."

Karen's shoulders fell. "That's too bad. We need more people like you to revitalize Pilpil Bay. If you ever need to relocate, consider our small town."

Bridge added a generous tip to her total and signed Esty Ryan. "I'll keep that in mind." In three years, she would be done supporting her brother Liam's sorry butt through dental school. She'd promised her mother to steer him onto the right path. After that, he could take care of himself. And maybe then she would move away to wherever she wanted—if she'd paid enough for her mistakes. Other than an occasional family dinner, there was nothing tying her to New Jersey.

Bridge fingered the black ledger in her pocket as she stood, but she wouldn't cross anything off for buying the extra meal. Human decency didn't count for forgiving debts. She gave the grieving stranger one more sympathetic glance, handed the signed receipt to Karen, and left to buy ingredients.

Without an imminent threat, she was going to bake.

chapter three

Paying it Forward

Cowen Amaratti watched the redhead walk away, a grateful smile parting his lips. If only the woman could understand what he was going through and how much her gesture meant.

"I love stories like this when people pay for others." The waitress cleared his half-full plate. She'd picked up on his grief and thankfully made small talk instead of probing him with questions. "Especially when their paths cross later on." She said it with certainty like she had the direct number for fate. "That girl is definitely gorgeous. And smart as a whip, too. Are you single?" She stacked the silverware on top of her pile. "This could be one of those destiny things."

"Single, yes." The weight in his chest made conversation next to impossible, but he appreciated she was trying to distract him. "If *you* see her again, tell her I said thanks."

"Oh, son of a biscuit eater, I wasn't supposed to tell you it was her." The waitress held her forehead. "If you see her, definitely don't mention it. And I'm sorry for whatever you're going through," she said before whisking the dirty dishes away.

He left a generous tip for her kindness and exited the diner, his stomach still as twisted as when he'd entered. Outside, he failed to lift his eyes to see the momentary break of sunshine through the clouds, even though he felt it. His FBI partner's German Shepherd, Jasper—now *his* German Shepherd—whined from inside his open top Jeep. "Hey, old boy." Cowen scratched behind the dog's ears and gave him a treat from his pocket. He reached for the door handle and dropped his hand, his cruel mind expecting to still see blood. Without Cowen's permission, his thoughts rehashed the images from three days before of an assignment gone wrong.

Two bodies had left the scene in black, zippered bags. Noah, his FBI partner and best friend was in one. Cowen's first kill, Antoine Benoit, was in the other. Cowen gripped the top of the side mirror for support and heaved the small amount he'd eaten.

Jasper whined and nuzzled Cowen's hair.

"I'm okay," he said, even though he wasn't. He hopped in and drove to the stop sign, the bloody scene starting over in his thoughts. He'd told his partner to wait for backup, but Noah rushed into the mansion they'd been surveilling. Then, everything had gone wrong.

A honk sounded through Cowen's morbid daydream and he punched the gas, turning onto the street that led to the cottage. But the scene had barely begun. He parked on the shoulder, cradling his head in his hands. Gunfire had erupted from the balcony, and Cowen counted three perps. He'd aimed to distract, to get them to give up. But when Noah collapsed beside him, blood pooling on his chest, he'd changed tactics. With one bullet, he'd shot out the kneecap of the biggest aggressor. The others had continued firing so he took out the shoulder of the second. The last man wouldn't give up, so Cowen had aimed for the right side of his chest, but the man had dextrocardia like him, taking the bullet straight to the heart.

He'd never intended to kill anyone.

His phone rang, and he fumbled to pull it out of his pocket. "Hey, Mama."

"Hey, baby." She didn't have to ask how he was doing—somehow she always knew. "Is it raining there?"

Figuratively, the guilt was pouring down on him. "Not yet."

"Have you been eating?"

"Yes," he said, though nothing was staying down.

"I see. Are you sure you don't want to come here for your leave?"

Two weeks of paid time off didn't feel fair for what Cowen had done. "I'm fine, Mama. Really. I'm not gonna interrupt your honeymoon."

"You're never an interruption, and it's really not a honeymoon since we're at home." She paused as if waiting for him to accept her invitation, but he didn't. "How about baking? You remember my chocolate chip cookie recipe?"

He watched a flock of seagulls fly by, their numbers so large that anyone would stop to take notice. Though Cowen had zero memories of Noah and birds, he couldn't help thinking how his friend was missing this. And all because Cowen had used warning shots at first, not wanting anyone to get hurt. He should have taken the gunman down sooner. He should have—

"Cowen?"

He cleared his throat. "I could never forget your recipe."

"Your rental has a kitchen, right?" she asked, probing in her way that meant she wouldn't stop until she got what she thought was best.

"Yeah." He knew exactly where this was leading, and she was probably right.

"So bake. Use it to get your grief out, and keep baking until you can get back to life." Her voice softened. "But maybe think of a new career while you're at it? I don't ever want to lose you too."

She'd spoken the words he was already considering. The idea of returning to work without Noah filled his stomach with lead. But finding a new job was like ripping out his heart and tossing it off a cliff. All he knew was investigating. His dad had trained him since he was big enough to shoot a gun, and all he'd wanted was to follow in his footsteps. Putting away criminals was his way of adding order to the world, of making things right and keeping others safe. What good was he if he couldn't do that?

"I'll consider it," he said with a goodbye and hung up. And he *would* think about a change because the idea of ever taking another life…Cowen opened the door and puked again.

"Let's walk," he told Jasper, not wanting to break down while driving again. He clipped the dog on a leash, and together they returned to town, passing an empty storefront with a kitchen in the back. For a moment, he paused, imagining all the things he'd make if he had his own bakery. His mama's salted chocolate chip cookies, of course, but also key lime pies, fresh berry cake rolls, and caramel toffee brownies.

Jasper barked, directing his attention to the road as the red haired woman drove past in a dark blue compact. Somehow, someway, he wanted to pay her kindness forward.

He tied Jasper's leash to a post in front of the grocery store and came out ten minutes later with everything he needed to make his mama's cookies. As soon as they returned to the rental, he turned on classic rock to drown out his thoughts. Survivor and The Moody Blues seemed to know how he felt.

Jasper sniffed an invisible trail on the floor and prodded his bag in the bathroom.

"It's home for now, buddy," he said, as another wave of grief hit. The dog's life would never be the same without his owner. And neither would his own. Killing someone hadn't been part of the plan. He'd trained harder than anyone to make sure he never took a life. But he hadn't planned for all the variables. He'd made a mistake in shooting Benoit's chest.

Cowen sniffed, wiping his eyes as he got to work adding one cube of softened butter and two handfuls of brown sugar to a bowl. He stirred with a wooden spoon until creamy before adding more ingredients. A slosh of milk. A slight pour of vanilla. Another labored sniff. Another chest pain. One egg.

After blending the ingredients, he added a tiny bit more milk to make the mixture perfect. Then he grabbed a clean mug and scooped some flour, pouring it into another bowl until it looked about right when everything in his life felt so wrong. A few shakes of baking soda came next, and he poured salt into the palm of his hand, selecting the amount he needed and tossing the rest in the sink.

Fifteen self-loathing minutes later, the timer dinged, and he pulled out perfectly golden cookies with gooey insides. But he wasn't done. With his body bent, barely able to stand upright, he sprinkled the tops with coarse salt.

The clouds hung dark like his mood as he took a plate outside, planning to force feed himself on the porch. Before he sat down, he noticed the redhead on the beach, her toes in the sand. A glance around showed her car on top of the hill by the other cottage.

What were the odds she was his neighbor? The waitress's assumptions about Cowen seeing her again came back to him. Was this fate? He shook his head. He wasn't good company, his thoughts centering around the lives he'd stolen that horrible day. Only one of his bullets had killed, but he hadn't protected Noah. Cowen might as well assume responsibility for his death too.

The woman shifted on the sand. He'd probably never forget her kindness, a selfless gift that acted as a lighthouse on one of his darkest days. She deserved to have a little of that thoughtfulness back. With shaking hands, Cowen returned inside and found some tin foil in a drawer, wrapped up several cookies, and grabbed the notepad next to an old cordless telephone. What should he say? He wasn't supposed to know she'd paid for his meal, so he pulled up Google and asked for uplifting messages to leave strangers. The top results were not what he expected and probably all written by Gen Z.

Your aura makes everyone vibrate.

Here's hoping this makes you feel as good as you look.

I didn't realize until today that I was waiting for you.

Cowen wanted to thank the woman, not creep her out. He scrolled some more and settled on *Everyone deserves a plate of cookies*, that way she wouldn't suspect he knew about the paid bill if their paths crossed.

She was still standing on the sand when he walked to her back porch. Scents of something buttery and sweet drifted through the door. Could she have baked something too? He shrugged off the thought—it was probably an air freshener like the one at his place, though he would have preferred a baked goods scent like hers. He left the cookies, returned to his kitchen, and ate three, swigging back a glass of milk.

It was the first thing to stay down in days. Like always, his mama had been right. Baking made everything better.

His phone rang with a call from Director Spandy at the Portland office, and he shuddered. Unbeknownst to his boss, they had something to discuss. Something Cowen had failed to bring up. But today, he still didn't have the energy for it. Maybe he never would.

"What town did you say you're staying in?" The director was always direct and to the point instead of asking what people needed. *Hey, are you surviving? Do you need to talk? How are the suicidal thoughts?*

Those had definitely crossed Cowen's mind, though he didn't let them stick.

"Pilpil Bay," he said, finding his voice.

"Good. Good. I need you to stick around for a bit. We just got a lead in a decade-old case. Someone in Pilpil Bay made an internet search for the Foxfoot Thief."

chapter four

Frisking

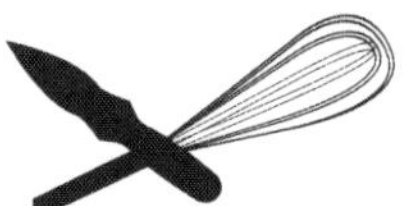

Bridge pulled her sinless chocolate meringues out of the oven, eyeing the cookies her neighbor had brought. They sat in a mangled heap on the counter, still warm. Of course, she'd checked them for a wireless bug, and although she hadn't seen any razors, she wouldn't rule out poison. They would sit in their gooey mess until she figured out what to do.

When she was on the beach and her neighbor had delivered them to her porch, she might have looked relaxed, but she was always on high alert and aware of her surroundings. She'd immediately recognized his shirt as the man's from the diner.

But what did he want with her? If he were there to watch or attack her, he was doing a terrible job of surveillance or intimidation. And what if he wasn't after her? What if he was just a normal guy, bringing his vacation neighbor some cookies?

Was that *normal* behavior? She kept circling back to that thought, stirring her suspicions. She'd spent so little time around men, other than her brother and dad, to know how they should act. But according to movies, guys didn't give things to girls unless they wanted something in return. Even Harold Crick, played by Will Ferrell in *Stranger Than Fiction*, gave "flowers" when he wanted Ana Pascal's forgiveness for being a life-sucking IRS agent who had to collect her back taxes.

She glanced at the cookie mess again, needing to know why her neighbor had brought them. Her mom had always said, "Keep your friends close and your enemies closer." And maybe it would be good to test out her fighting skills—if it came to that. With a paring knife in hand, she marched outside below dark and menacing storm clouds—just the way she liked them. The air held a bite, the wind blowing the nearby ocean waves. Her hair flew like a banshee as she stepped onto the wraparound porch at the back of her neighbor's bungalow and lifted her free hand. Her knock elicited an immediate bark, and she set the knife on the armrest of the porch swing right before the door opened.

"Why did you leave me cookies?" she asked, taking in every detail she could while still maintaining some semblance of eye contact. Her neighbor had a smidge of flour dust on his jeans and t-shirt, circles under his eyes despite the sleeping pills she'd found, and a surprised expression. Beyond that, he was nice to look at *and* he smelled like cookies—a dangerous combination.

The dog padded past him, sniffing her all over.

"Sorry, about Jasper," the man said. "He's friendly."

Jasper looked up at her expectantly, his tail wagging, and she scratched behind his ears until he'd had enough. He shuffled to the edge of the porch and curled up next to a post.

"The cookies were supposed to be anonymous, but since my cover is blown, I might as well say thanks for paying my bill," he said, his voice filling with emotion. "What you did meant a lot. I'm going through a—"

"Loss of someone close." Either that or he was an incredible actor. "How long has it been?" With enough questions, she'd get the truth out of him. Either that or she could always torture it out. But if he wasn't acting...

His chest rose and fell three times before he could say, "My partner." He quickly amended his statement with, "FBI Partner."

"Is that why you're packing?" Maybe he was telling the truth. Maybe he wasn't. She'd apologize for her lack of sympathy later.

The man's eyebrows lifted slightly before he understood what she meant. "Oh, this—" he reached behind his back.

In a swift motion, Bridge grabbed the knife, pointing it at him.

"Whoa, easy," he said, pulling his gun out and backing up to put it on the coffee table. "Do you not get out much?" he asked as he returned to the doorway, his hands up. He eyed her skeptically like he could easily thwart her attack.

She held her ground, analyzing his muscle mass for weakness, the knife still raised. If it came to a fight, she'd go for the neck. "I don't trust people."

"You don't say." His breaths came out naturally as if he wasn't threatened by her. If only he knew what she could do. "How about you put the knife down and we can sit on the swing and watch the storm roll in? You can ask me whatever you want."

"Sit on the swing together?" She eyed him up and down. If he was simply a nice-looking guy with a chestful of sadness, his offer was sweet after how rude she'd been. But if he were her enemy, the seat could become a kill box. "What other weapons do you have?"

He tilted his head as if finding her somewhat amusing. "If you put down that knife, you're free to check for yourself."

"Fine." She crouched and left the blade in the sand off the porch so she could kick it into her hand if necessary. "Hands on your head."

"Oh, you're serious?" He seemed stunned, but went along with it, obeying her command.

Bridge started at the sleeves of his shirt, feeling his arms and the muscles beneath. She stepped near to touch his shoulders, their breaths colliding—his smelled like chocolate. The stubble on his skin drew her attention to his lips. A buzz formed in her chest, and she quickly swallowed it down. This was not the time for attraction.

With two fingers she traced his armpits. Once, she'd concealed a razor blade wrapped in tissues in her own, leaving her assailant with a gash that needed at least twenty stitches. She shuddered from the memory.

"Sorry, I'm probably sweaty," he said, his voice still thick with pain.

Hadn't she gotten enough proof that he was hurting? Her mom's warnings blared in her head. No, she had to be certain with zero room for doubt. But her eyes drifted to his, finding the sadness he was claiming. Her heart stilled, letting herself experience what he felt. Loss. Guilt. They were the heaviest, hardest words she knew, and they came at her unrelenting.

Weight built in her chest, in her throat, tugging at her. This man and Bridge were experiencing the same grief—his fresh and raw, hers almost a decade old—and that connection, that shared knowledge made her need for human interaction, for acceptance, for healing all descend on her at once.

Her hands fumbled as she returned her focus to his body. "It's me, not you." Did that even make sense?

Bridge moved down his toned torso and along his waist. She needed to speed this up and have separation, but also somehow needed him—someone else who understood all the things she constantly tried to bury.

"I'm Cowen," he said, his voice startling her. "Cowen Amaratti. You can search for me on Google next."

"I will." Anything for a distraction. She was *not* connecting with him. She couldn't. "Amaretti? Like the biscuit?" Bridge focused on stilling her breathing as she crouched, patting the outside of each leg. But her breaths had a mind of their own, coming out fast and irregular like his. "Is that why you smell like cookies?"

"I smell like cookies?" His lips shifted with the slightest hint of a smile, and she imagined what a real one would look like. A zing of energy pulsed between them—she was sure of it from the bob of his Adam's apple. "The name is similar," he said, "but mine is all A's. The biscuits have an—"

"E. Yes, I know how to spell." She got to his bare feet, chiding herself for the pull he had on her, and started on the inside of his legs. She needed to find some fault, something to dispel the heat rising in her chest. Whenever she flirted with men, it was always a grift. An act. But these actions, words, and reactions were *her*, and he wasn't running. "What kind of person lets a stranger frisk them?"

His voice was heavy, full of pain. "One who's miserable enough to entertain any sort of distraction."

She stopped, resting her hands a few inches above his knees. "I'm sorry about your partner." All signs pointed to him telling the truth, and when she checked her gut, it agreed. Cowen was truly grieving and not out to get her. For once in her life, the person in front of her was real. And that felt more dangerous than any attacker she'd ever faced.

"His name was Noah," he said, and Jasper barked with awareness, wagging his tail. Cowen's shoulders crumpled as he looked at the dog. "We were partners for five years."

Bridge stood without physically inspecting the rest of him, searching the hollowness etched across his face. "That's a long time to work with someone."

He let out a shuddering breath. "Is the pat down over? I'm not suggesting I want you to check the rest of my pants, but I want to be prepared if—"

"If you have a weapon concealed down there, I could knock you out before you could retrieve it."

Cowen tilted his head, considering her. "Somehow, I don't doubt that now. Should I be concerned about my safety?" he asked, his voice sprinkled with playfulness. Even through his pain, he was bantering with her like they were old friends. Could they become friends?

"I won't hurt you unless you try to hurt me," she said, trying to understand what was going on. He was so comfortable to talk to, and that never happened in her world. People were complicated and difficult to be around, but Cowen was simple and easy. None of this made sense in her head. For years, life had revolved around work, eat, sleep, train, and if she was lucky, a little baking. Never did she imagine she would connect with someone over shared pain.

Cowen stepped in front of the swing and sat. "Good to know. I won't hurt you, either."

Bridge held her finger up and with her phone and searched for him on a database she shouldn't have access to, mostly just as a distraction, but also for tangible proof. Sure enough, he came up as an agent for the Portland Federal Bureau of Investigation. But anyone with decent skills could fake that. Her hard-wired suspicions led her to search his name with "smoochie." It was one of those terms that if you know, you know. The closest match to Cowen's name was a hitman out of Salt Lake City. Cristoff Arnita was at least sixty years old and selective about which clients he took.

She snapped a picture of Cowen next, running it through the same database. While it was processing, she sat on the opposite end of the swing, nearest the knife. That's what her instincts told her to do, even though she'd already decided his intentions were good.

Cowen met her gaze, his expression slightly hopeful amid his pain. "If I'm strange for letting a stranger frisk me, what does that make you for sitting next to me?"

She couldn't help the laugh that came out. This really was the oddest interaction she'd ever had. "Someone who likes watching storms." Her phone buzzed with the results, confirming with hard, tangible proof that Cowen wasn't sent to watch, kidnap, or hurt her, but he'd entertained her quirky behavior *and* wanted her to stay. Tingles crept up her back, making her vulnerable in a way she hadn't been before. The last ten years since her mom's death, she'd been a drone, doing anything and everything to take care of her brother and help her dad while ignoring her own needs. Her own emotions. But in a few short minutes, Cowen Amaratti had unlocked her gates.

"I watched my mom die when I was sixteen," she said, her voice quiet. Her dad often said that every dam eventually breaks. Maybe it was her turn to let some things out, and maybe it was best with a stranger she'd never see again.

"I'm sorry." Cowen leaned forward, both elbows on his thighs, his hands fiddling. "I was nineteen when my dad died, but he was at work. He was an agent too." He swallowed, and the next words came out patchy and cracked. "My partner was shot beside me. And I killed one of his attackers."

Bridge angled toward him, wanting to take away his pain, wanting to spare him from the hurt that never seemed to fully disappear. If only she could do that for everyone, she would work until her ledger was clean. "That must have been awful."

He looked at her and their shared sadness seemed to pull them closer in a horrible, common bond. Lightning struck over the ocean and the boom hit three seconds later. Jasper whined and curled against Cowen's feet.

"What was your mom like?" he asked, repositioning with his back against the swing.

"Chuck Norris mixed with Martha Stewart." Bridge hadn't meant to share—this conversation and encounter was becoming too personal for someone with her past—but the truth was harder to hide when her heart was in her throat.

"Chuck Norris, huh?"

Bridge twisted her lips. "I bet you won't guess that I'm just like her."

"I wasn't going to comment." The change of topic had a calming effect, and he placed his hands behind his head. Did he know how much that showcased his muscles?

A few raindrops fell in the sand nearby before the clouds opened overhead, dumping on the roof. Gusts of wind sprayed the rain, and Bridge shivered. The West Coast really was cooler.

"Want a blanket?" Cowen asked. "You can grab it off the couch near the gun. Or you can come with me, watching my every move so you don't have to frisk me again. Unless you want to—"

"I'll get it." There had been a hint of teasing in his tone, she was sure of it. She hurried inside, her cheeks warming. Truthfully, she would enjoy performing another search, but like she would admit that. She grabbed the throw blanket and passed the gun on the coffee table. He'd trusted her far more than she deserved since she could easily grab it and do her worst. How did he already know she wasn't like that?

Bridge returned to the same scene—knife in the sand, handsome guy on the swing, and Jasper at his feet. The last time she'd attempted anything social, her date had left the table for the bathroom and never came back. Most people didn't have patience for the real Bridge. And that made her conversation with Cowen cosmically huge. It had her wondering what could come next…if she didn't have to leave tomorrow to get back to her regular, boring life.

"Here," she said, sitting close to him and covering them both with the blanket.

"Oh." He cleared his throat and straightened.

Bridge left the blanket on him and scooted away, her face falling. "Ryan Gosling," she swore under her breath. Somehow, she'd misinterpreted the way he'd looked at her. "You're right, I don't get out much. You're probably married or in a relationship, and I don't know what I'm still doing here." Except she did know. She needed human connection too. "I'm struggling to read this situation. You're in pain, and I dislike the idea of leaving you alone. But I'll go if you want."

Cowen lifted the blanket and motioned her over as the wind picked up. "No wife. No relationship. Please." His eyes pleaded with hers. "Stay."

His invitation stirred something foreign in her chest. Hope? She wouldn't know how to define it. Slowly, she moved next to him, their shoulders touching. Heat from his body mixed with hers, zinging currents along her skin. The change in his breaths told her he was feeling their chemistry too. Bridge wasn't imagining this.

He spoke first. "I hate to ask, but what did you do with the cookies?"

Bridge laughed. Maybe it wasn't the right reaction, but he had to be the nicest guy to entertain all of her crazy. "I searched them. They're in a crumpled heap on the counter."

"I have more," he said. "But you probably wouldn't…"

She shook her head. "I trust you now." At least when it came to cookies. And snuggling on the porch.

"Just like that?" He shifted, placing his hand on the swing's back behind her. Was it just to see her better? Or was it a romantic gesture? She didn't have enough experience to know. But in the movies…

Bridge bit her lip, heat swelling in her chest. "It wasn't that easy. There were several steps in my deduction." She searched his eyes. What was this energy between them?

"Have people hurt you to make you suspicious?"

She looked out over the water, the lightning arcing across the sky. Cowen was suffering, and the conversation should stay on him, but she didn't know how to shift it back. "Many have tried, only one was successful."

Cowen tilted his head toward her. "I happen to know this FBI agent that could make their life miserable."

The offer and slightly flirty tone he used would have made her smile if she didn't know the truth. "He's dead." Bridge hadn't intended to share that part of her past, her story, her trauma—but it came out anyway, slipping past her safeguards, snaking through her barricades. Her fingers shook first, followed by her legs, and then her core.

Cowen slipped his arm around her, pulling her close. He had no idea how Mason Rossi had died and why it hurt her so much, but Cowen was willing to offer her comfort for something that was all her fault when his wounds were fresh. If only she'd met him in a different life, or a different time when her sins were all atoned for. She might even consider settling down if she could just find Harley, Mason's sister.

More than anything, she wanted to find the girl and make things right. As far as she knew, Mason had been her only family. Even though he'd killed Bridge's mom to secure his own escape, she still worried about the girl. Harley had no one.

More lighting struck and Jasper stirred, but Cowen continued to hold her, his own breaths turning ragged. She remembered the gunshot, her scream, and Mason's lifeless body collapsing to the ground. Her mom's death had ripped her own heart out, shattering it into a thousand tiny shards and only returning a few with time. But Mason's death was revenge. Murder. She hadn't pulled the trigger, but his death had sucked out her soul, blackening it with a stain that might never come out. Her hands dripped red with his blood for not preventing it.

She'd never cried over that day. Couldn't. There'd been no time. Sirens had blared with police closing in, and her family needed to escape. And after they outran the danger of being apprehended, she'd spent weeks working with her dad and brother, covering every one of their tracks so Mason's death wouldn't be tied to them. Every minute, every hour, every day, she'd buried the truth and her guilt into the tiny cracks left open with her mom's passing. But in the safety of Cowen's arms, fat tears fell down her cheeks. His own wet the top of her head. She gripped his free hand with both of hers, and together, they grieved as the storm surged.

When their breaths quieted, Bridge pulled away and used her fingers to wipe his face. He returned the gesture, and her heart pounded as she leaned into his touch.

"How long are you staying?" he asked, his voice hoarse.

Hers was barely a whisper. "I leave tomorrow." Lightning flashed across the sky, the boom sounding almost immediately.

His face fell. "Do I get to know your name? And where to find you?"

Bridge already knew his, and after her search, she could easily contact him. But there was no future for them. She lived across the country, *and* she was an ex-thief. With his role in the FBI, they were oil and water. "I've got a lot of wrongs to repair. I'm not the type that someone like you should be concerned about."

Cowen swallowed. "No contact. I got it." The mood crumbled with the dejection in his voice. He was probably like her and wishing this could turn into something more. "But what do I call you in my head when I think about you? This moment will be impossible to forget."

Bridge searched his eyes. His closeness and her attraction were real, and he wasn't out to get her. And hadn't she already given up enough of her life, living every moment in pretend or working to help someone else? For once, she wanted to let her guard down. She wanted to be herself. And they'd bonded more in an hour than she ever had with Mason.

"Telling you my name isn't easy. It's…complicated." Her family always had a rule to steal or grift only with aliases so their true identities were never exposed. Even though Cowen wouldn't find anything compromising if he looked Bridge up, her name was the only thing she truly owned. Her identity and connection to family was everything. "This might not seem much to you, but it is to me." She took a slow breath, debating the entire time if she should follow through, but eventually, "Bridge" slipped out as a whisper.

Cowen took a moment to dip his head, mulling her gift over. "Is that short for something, or a metaphorical word I'm supposed to decipher?"

She shrugged and nestled her head against his shoulder so she wouldn't do something stupid like tell him more. Or kiss him. Both crossed her mind. "You decide."

Another flash of lightning lit the sky. "Thanks for helping me through my grief," he said, his tone indicating gratitude but also that he wanted more than just this moment. Except they were two strangers, only crossing paths. Sharing pain wasn't a foundation for a relationship. Especially as complicated as theirs would be. She could never tell him her whole story—some things always had to stay hidden.

"Thanks for helping me through mine." Bridge snuggled closer to him, savored each of his breaths, the rise and fall shifting her head on his shoulder. "As soon as the rain quits, I'm gonna go. No goodbyes." That wasn't what she wanted, but it was the reality of her life. She didn't belong here. Her responsibilities to her brother's education and the payback of her crimes had to come first.

Slowly, as if asking permission, Cowen slid his arm around Bridge's shoulder again, holding her close. "Then I hope it never ends."

chapter five

Burned

True to her word, Bridge stood up seventy-six minutes later, traced her fingers along Cowen's hand, picked up the knife, and returned to her rental, her chest heaving, her spine tingling. She watched him from her window as she ate a dry dinner of crackers and sausage from the gift basket. He stayed on the porch for a half-hour more before disappearing inside. And when he did, she shifted her attention to fixing things with a tool set she found in the linen closet: the leak under the kitchen sink that was causing the moldy smell, the fridge compressor that hummed too loud, and the alarm clock with a broken button.

Had she been wrong to go? Her business was in New Jersey, not here, and if she wasn't working, she wasn't eating. The cost of Liam's tuition and books stole everything non-essential. So that left no room for visiting Oregon. It was better to walk away than to give either of them false hope.

At least that's what she told herself as she reset her traps and settled in bed to sleep. Before she could close her eyes, her phone buzzed with a text from her "doctor," asking to confirm an appointment for Tuesday at 4:19 p.m.

The "T" in Tuesday was her dad's clue to use the Tokyo website to find his message. Liam had built the system when he used to help with operations.

He was a flat-out brilliant hacker, giving Leverage's Alec Hardison's character steep competition. But Liam went too far. So she forced a close to their family profession and allowed him one final trick to fake his way into college. They'd all lived legit lives since—except for her dad's stunt a year before. And now this—whatever it was.

After seventeen backdoors, Bridge reached their decryption platform. Google gave her a quick copy and paste of Genesis 4:19—thanks to the listed appointment time, which she put into the decoding box. The letters in the scriptures were the key to deciphering the message. She'd gotten the idea to use sacred text from Mission Impossible's Job 3:14 scene.

"Jeremy Renner," she swore as she read.

Meet in Milwaukee. Tomorrow. 3:00 p.m. Italian restaurant near gate thirteen.

An impromptu meeting was never a good thing, especially so far from their home. What had her dad gotten himself into? Possibly gotten her into?

Bridge booked an early flight, tucked a knife under her pillow, and snuggled under the covers. Her bed swallowed her with a loneliness she was used to, but now, after time with Cowen, it was more intense than ever.

A gunshot sounded in the far distance, and she spent the next hour worrying about where it came from and what the meeting in Milwaukee meant. But when she closed her eyes, all she could think about was Cowen's arm around her and how she wished she could see him again.

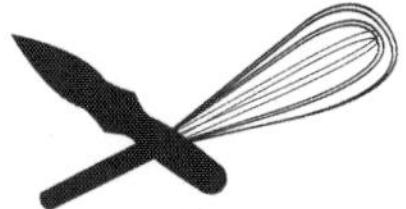

The sky was still dark as Bridge put all the dishes in the dishwasher and started the load. She wrapped the leftover chocolate meringues in tin foil and shoved them into her bag, licking the gooey remnants off her fingers. Normally, she'd leave without looking back, but she found herself spinning around the room, memorizing the details. This weekend was one she wouldn't forget.

A salty breeze blew in as she opened the door and found an empty bullet casing and rock on top of a slip of paper. She scanned the area before shoving the rock aside and picking up the note. Cowen's name was written on the bottom, and her heart skipped as she started from the top.

I'd love to be wrong, but I'm guessing you won't see me before you leave.

How did he understand her so well?

I wanted you to have something to remember me by, but I packed light without many options. I could have left cookies, but we both know how you decimated the last ones, and they obviously won't last. My remaining options are a bullet and my fingernail clippings. With anyone else, I'd only consider the bullet, but with you, I have a feeling I might have made the wrong choice. I get the vibe you might have your own collection?

Bridge lifted her hand to muffle a snort and kept reading.

I wasn't sure if you'd be flying, and I know bullets aren't allowed on carry-ons, so I fired one to give you this casing.

That's why she'd heard a shot.

Guns can be used for dangerous things, but they can also signify the start of a race. And maybe in our case, it's the start of something. If you ever want to test your theory that someone like you isn't right for someone like me, keep this as a reminder that I'm ready to begin whenever you are.

I might not return to the FBI. It's something I've been thinking about. I'll leave my number in case I find a different career and you can't look me up with whatever you were using.

If I never hear from you, I'll try to understand. I'll always be grateful you helped me cope.

"Will Ferrell," Bridge cursed, pressing the letter to her heart and committing his phone number to memory. That was the most beautiful gift she'd ever received. And if she wasn't careful, she'd march right over and do something stupid like give Cowen her number. Or a kiss.

Regrets swarmed Bridge as she gave the dark bungalow beside hers one last glance before pocketing the note and casing in her leggings. Then she drove away, feeling like she was leaving something—everything—behind.

Her connecting flight was delayed, and she arrived in Milwaukee at 2:37 p.m., her heart sore from missing what could have been. But she didn't have room in her life to hope for the impossible. She had too many things to take care of. Too many guilts to right.

Like her mom had taught her, Bridge watched the restaurant instead of going in, just in case their messages had been infiltrated and she was walking into a trap. The scent of garlic and tomato pasta made her think of Cowen's Italian last name, which led to thinking about him. More than likely, things wouldn't work out, so why bother tempting the fates to align them again? She'd tried every tactic to forget about him since last night, but still, she dreamed.

At 2:56, Rory O'Niall passed by as Bridge pretended to watch reels on her phone. Her dad's red hair was cut short like usual, but the sides were beginning to fade. He still looked as muscular as ever, his biceps expanding his shirt sleeves, but he had the tiniest hint of flab on his stomach—that was new. Bridge watched him take a seat inside the wall-less restaurant, but she didn't budge.

Three o'clock, their meeting time, came and went. At 3:02, another player entered the game, and Bridge dropped her phone in her lap. Liam O'Niall had inherited their mom's Italian genes with his dark hair and always-tanned skin while Bridge was a carbon copy of their dad. They couldn't look more different. His swagger had started when he was eleven, and it had gotten worse with time. She loved her little brother—she was putting off her life to ensure he made the most of his—but she wouldn't mind punching the smug grin off his handsome face every once in a while.

What was he doing here? This whole weekend, Bridge had assumed her dad wanted her out of town since she'd run heists with him in the past, and her face could be recognized. She'd never considered Liam was in danger.

Her brother entered the restaurant, and their dad stood to meet him, his expression tense. A few words were exchanged before a hug, but Bridge couldn't decipher them—her mom had been the lip reader. She let two more minutes pass before joining them, her dad grinning as he pulled her in for a tight embrace.

"My bonnie lass." He kissed her forehead. "You didn't need to watch so long. We're safe here."

She wanted to believe him, but in their line of work, the number of enemies they'd acquired always made her uneasy. If something needed stealing, there were often several individuals or teams vying for the chance. Competition created dangerous adversaries.

"It's good to see you, Dad." She breathed him in, a mix of aftershave and black licorice.

Liam took a turn and gave her a quick squeeze. "Hey, little sis." She was four years older and only two inches shorter, but he always rubbed her slightly smaller size in.

"Who's hungry?" Rory motioned for Bridge to sit beside her brother and picked up his menu.

"Shouldn't we discuss why we're here, first? Or maybe why we had to leave town?" She sat, fixing her dad with a hard stare.

Rory flinched ever so slightly, but he covered it with a laugh and gave his son a knowing look. "She's always down to business."

"Annoyingly so." Liam glanced at her, but turned his focus to his menu, his fingers nervously tapping the vinyl edge. He probably had a test to get back to.

"Someone has to be responsible." She gave them each a glare, but neither paid her any attention. Their waiter brought bread and water, glancing her up and down, and took her order of lasagna and a salad, heavy on the ranch. Her dad asked for a gnocchi soup, which wasn't his usual, and her brother ordered a steak, medium rare.

"So?" she asked once the waiter left and she finished a bite of the bread. "Why are we here? I thought we were in danger, so this better not be about a job. Liam has a promising future as long as he steers clear of your bad choices."

Rory dropped his head. "I deserve that. And I'm not asking you for help. But I had to set something right. And now we're all burned."

Bridge dropped the bread. "What do you mean, burned?" Maybe the word's definition had changed in the last few years, because he couldn't suggest that—

"Our identities are compromised." He met her gaze, his expression meaning he was deadly serious. "O'Niall is blown."

"No." Bridge's fingers shook as her stomach's contents worked their way to her throat. "No. Liam is in dental school, he can't just—"

"I hate putting my fingers in other people's mouths," Liam said unapologetically. "Do you know how disgusting breath is? And don't even get me started on tongues, unless I'm kissing—"

"Do not finish that sentence." Bridge rubbed her face, trying to put emotions aside so she could focus on facts. "How far does it go?"

Rory glanced at his son. "Our family name is in the open, and the crest was flagged again, but Liam managed to scrub the image off, plus he switched out our pictures. As long as you don't dye your hair black and grow your nose, you should be fine."

Bridge slapped her brother's chest. "You are not supposed to know how to do that anymore."

"I can't unlearn what's already in my head," he said, his jaw tight.

She slapped him again. "And you knew about this before me?"

Liam picked up a piece of bread and shoved half in his mouth, clearly not wanting to talk.

"So," she said, turning back to her dad. "What else are you hiding? How long have you been working?"

"I haven't done a job since I promised you." He fixed her with a stare. "I don't break my promises."

"Except you did." She crossed her arms over her chest, willing her lungs to keep breathing, even though they were ready to cave. Her questioning, functioning exterior was just a facade. Inside, she was crumbling. She'd never imagined giving up her real name.

"Like I said, I had to right a wrong. And when things went south, I had to do a little more to make sure you're both okay." He passed each of them a bulky white envelope. "The plane tickets will take you in different directions. The address is for an apartment with rent covered for a month. The key is for a safe deposit box. You'll both be able to start a new life. Cover your tracks, and move somewhere new with whatever identity you want. Just send me a card at the cabin each month."

The food came, the waiter glancing Bridge over again before he left. She refused to eat. "How did you burn our real identities? We've never stolen with them."

Rory dropped his head. "Sometimes, people make mistakes. Let's eat, and then you both need to get going."

Bridge pushed the food around her plate and managed to get a few bites in, her envelope still unopened.

When Liam finished, Rory placed a couple of fifty dollar bills on the table.

"Your plane boards in five," Rory said to his son. They all stood and gave a round of hugs.

Liam turned to his sister. "I'm sorry," he whispered. "I hope you enjoy your new life."

Bridge searched his face. He'd never been one to express sympathy. "I'm sorry, too. Maybe you could be a doctor instead of a dentist?"

He backed away, the distaste on his face clearly rejecting her suggestion. "See ya around, little sis." He gave her a two-finger salute and sauntered away.

Rory waited for him to disappear from view before folding his daughter into his arms. "Don't think of this as a setback. Think of this as an opportunity. You've been living in squalor to take care of him. I could have—"

"Your money is tainted. And so is whatever you have waiting for me."

He shook his head. "I knew you'd protest. So I sold something else."

Her heart sank. "Not our land." They still had two-thousand acres on Ireland's northern shore. At least, they used to.

"Aye. And I know that little head of yours will understand the money will take a while to transfer, so yes, I fenced a few impressionist pieces to cover for now, but the money is legit. It's your inheritance, and your ancestors would want you to use it. Out of everyone, I think they'd be the most proud of you. You're the one with the purest heart."

"Dad." She blinked back her tears. "Without our land and our name, what do we have left?"

He held her tighter. "You have my love—always. And your future. You can do anything you want with it." He had a way of making her feel safe in his arms.

"But I don't know what to do," she said, pulling away. Bridge found herself reverting to her dependence on his wisdom and judgment.

He gave her a pointed look. "Yes, you do. You've dreamed of one thing since you were little."

Bridge nodded, but her mind drifted to the cookies Cowen had made for her, not her own creations. "Owning a bakery."

"Dreams disappear, you know. If you don't give them any thought, any attention—eventually they die."

His words hit hard, and Bridge had to stuff her emotions down so they didn't emerge. "When will I see you again?" She wasn't ready to say goodbye. Or to move on with her life. Not with her ledger still full. Not with Harley Rossi out there, all alone.

Rory squeezed her hand. "I'm not sure." He glanced down at her pocket, where the book full of their mistakes always resided. "You're still carrying that around?" The creases on his forehead deepened. "You don't have to make up for all of the wrongs before you start living."

That was easy for him to say. Their profession had never pricked his conscience.

"Your plane is leaving soon." He gave her one last kiss on the cheek and directed her away. "Remember to send me a card each month. I'll come to you."

Bridge opened the envelope and searched for the flight details, not even caring where she went, focusing instead on the gate number. She walked toward her terminal with her head spinning. Everything was so much to take in. She was mourning the loss of her identity, upset at her father's actions, and still processing her interactions with Cowen.

What did this change mean for the going-nowhere narrative she'd written for him?

chapter six

Decisions

Cowen stood on the porch of his childhood home, a midcentury modern split that he'd poured his sweat and blood into, keeping the maintenance manageable for his mama. The late afternoon heat made it finally feel like summer, the sky unusually clear. But the beating sun had him missing a certain rainstorm with a certain someone who had yet to message or call in the forty-eight hours since she'd left.

Bridge. How had he let her go with only that portion of her name? He'd been an idiot, trusting fate to bring them together again. It was so unlike him. The world revolved around laws and order. But whenever he thought about Bridge, everything concrete and absolute flew out the window as if rules didn't belong. He'd fallen for a woman while grieving. That didn't make sense.

The door opened and his five-foot-two mama stood in the entry wearing sympathy on her lips.

"Are you sure it's okay to come over?" he asked again. He'd already texted her twice about it.

Jill Amaratti Gasnet gave him a fierce hug, her short gray bob bouncing.

"Honeymoons in your sixties are not the same as they are in your twenties. We've mostly been watching movies and taking walks."

And going to dialysis, but he knew she never liked to point that out.

"Okay, but I won't stay long." He followed her into the family room decorated in cottage core and family pictures.

His new stepdad, Ed Gasnet, stood from the recliner he'd brought over after the wedding. "Stay as long as you want," Ed said, extending his hand for Cowen to shake. He was the best man Cowen could ask for his mama, but it was still unnatural to see her with someone other than his dad, even if it had been nine years.

"How was Pilpil Bay?" Jill sat on a tan sofa across from a matching one that Cowen had settled on.

"Better than expected." His grief still stabbed with every mention of Noah or when he looked at Jasper. It had lessened after his time with Bridge, but the guilt over killing Antoine Benoit remained steady.

"Do they still have that cute little bakery? I remember getting these ginormous raspberry croissants with your dad." She kept the conversation light, but she was searching his expression and his tired eyes.

He doubted anything on his face could convey what he was feeling. He hardly knew. One minute, the pain and guilt about failing Noah and taking a life were indescribable, and the next, he'd remember Bridge. Just the thought of her lightened his mood—unless he rationalized how he'd probably never see her again. And then he'd start the whole cycle again.

His fingers fidgeted as the memory of Bridge's head on his shoulder replayed. "The bakery is gone."

"You're…smiling?" Jill blinked hard until she seemed to gain clarity, her expression shifting. She scooted to the edge of her seat. "What's her name?"

Cowen straightened the pile of books on the coffee table. He should have known he couldn't keep anything from his mama. "I'm not exactly sure."

"Do I need to teach you how to talk to women?" Ed asked, his voice teasing. "One of the first things you ask is her name."

"I did. Well, not first. There was kind of a lot going on. She um…she's a bit different."

Jill settled back into the couch cushions. "Different, how?"

Cowen couldn't help the smile breaking through as he shifted the books, misaligning the spines. "She means what she says, and I think she could probably take me down in a fight."

Ed coughed. "*That* there is a unicorn. Or a man disguised as a woman."

Jill threw a pillow at him. "Don't mind Ed." She focused on her son. "So…she's on the beefy side?"

Cowen covered his eyes. "That's not what people say." How could he explain Bridge? "She's perfectly balanced. And gorgeous. But there's so much more. We…connected."

Ed sat forward. "But you don't know her name."

"I've got a partial, I think." She'd been so reticent about it that he wasn't sure what it meant. "Or a nickname." But he wasn't about to use government resources to track her down. That was a misappropriation of resources.

"When are you seeing her next?" Jill asked, her hands on her knees.

Cowen's shoulders fell. "I don't know. I left her a note with my number and a bullet casing."

Jill dumped her forehead into her hands. "What would possess you to give a bullet casing to a woman?"

"It's a long story." He should have asked Bridge for a way to contact her. He should have made it clear how he felt. She'd piqued his interest when it felt impossible for anyone to do so. Maybe she *was* a unicorn. "I might not ever see her again. I don't even know where she lives."

"We can canvas Pilpil Bay within an hour," Jill said, drumming her fingers on the edge of the sofa. "I'm guessing they have what, two or three hundred residents?"

Cowen frowned. "She was visiting, and I have no idea where she's from." He needed to change the subject before his heart rate spiked. The thought of never seeing her again had already caused multiple, minor panic attacks since she'd left. And whenever his breathing became too shallow, his mind would take over, shoving him back into the gunfire he wanted to forget. "Do either of you want me to bake something?"

Jill watched her son. She'd taught him to cope by baking and that gooey chocolate or cinnamon spice could lift any mood. "Always."

An empty plate, previously towering with raspberry scones, sat on the dining table between Cowen and his mom. Ed had left to get some dinner, but more than likely, he'd gone to give them some time.

"So?" Jill asked. "What are you going to do about the director's offer to hire you as a consultant in Pilpil Bay? My two cents is he's asking a lot from you too soon."

"I don't know." Cowen leaned back in his chair. He still had unfinished business at work, something he should have taken care of weeks ago, but he wasn't eager to be a snitch. And maybe what he'd seen wasn't real. If he was going to report his boss, he needed more information first. "Technically, I'm still on paid leave until they clear my firearm and finalize the investigation."

"But he wants you to stay in Pilpil Bay and watch?" Jill clucked her tongue. "That doesn't seem right."

Unfortunately, when things came to Director Spandy, a lot of areas were morally gray. "I agree. And I don't know if I can handle the pressure of being responsible for other people's lives." He had to keep his eyes open so his mind didn't recreate the images of Noah bleeding out beside him. He had no idea how to get through the funeral tomorrow.

"Then don't accept. Do something without pressure."

Cowen shrugged, not believing a life like that existed for him. "Like what?"

"Bake."

He shook his head. Without protecting others, he didn't know what purpose he could possibly serve. Baking seemed trivial in comparison. "That's your answer to everything."

"Because it makes you happy. And it makes others happy too. Remember that time you made that lemon meringue pie for Mrs. Barker?"

How could he forget? His neighbor became teary eyed every time she saw him, thanking him for helping her remember her late husband's pie he'd made every year on their anniversary.

"Sweets aren't just amazing to eat. They can lift a weary soul or diffuse anger," his mama said. "Sometimes, they can even heal hearts."

Cowen wasn't so sure of that, but he knew better than to disrespect his mama's opinions.

"You love to bake, so find a way to use it to support yourself." Jill spun her empty milk glass. "You said the bakery is gone in Pilpil Bay?"

His next breath felt different as he nodded. "There are two kitchens for sale."

"That sounds like an opportunity," Jill said, giving him a pointed look.

If only he could. "I don't have that kind of money to start—"

"I can give you your inheritance early."

Cowen shook his head. "I can't, not with the uncertainty of your health. And plus, I don't want to let you down if I fail."

"My health is fine," she said. "And how could you disappoint me when it's your money?"

He grasped for more excuses. Dreams were sometimes scarier than nightmares. "But you have so much life left—"

"Ed and I have simple needs. We'll be fine. And I'd rather watch you enjoy the money than wait until I'm dead."

"Don't talk like that." The idea of her dying was more than he could handle.

"I'm making the transfer tomorrow." She placed her hands over his. "My mind is made up."

"Mama, I don't—"

"Know how to thank me?" She gave him a mischievous smile as if knowing that was not what he was about to say. "Please do this for me. I want to see you enjoy your life before I go. Plus, I know you. The guilt is eating you up inside. You need something different so you can heal."

Heal? He wasn't sure that was possible. "What if I fail?"

She shook her head. "What if you succeed?"

chapter seven
The Neighbor

Dry heat seeped through the dingy, furnished apartment Rory had arranged for Bridge. She sat at the tiny table, barely big enough to hold a meal, and stared at her throwing knives and a bag full of a hundred and fifty thousand dollars she'd found in the safety deposit box of the Phoenix Sun Bank. It was all she could carry in one trip without drawing attention. Another hundred and fifty waited for her to pick it up.

Sweat dripped from her forehead and she wiped it off. It was only ten in the morning, and the thermometer already read a hundred and nine degrees. She couldn't help imagining that the universe was telling her she didn't belong. That she needed to be somewhere cooler. Somewhere like Oregon.

"Don't go there," she warned herself as thoughts of Cowen circled her head again. What woman ugly-cries in front of someone and then wants to see him again? Obviously not one with all her screws and bolts in place. The whole thing with him had been bizarre, and she'd already been through all the *what-ifs*.

What if they had nothing in common, other than both knowing grief and how to shoot a gun?

What if he was appalled by her past?

What if he didn't like her once he got to know her?

That last one hit the hardest. The only guy who'd ever stuck around was Mason, and he'd used her for her family's skills. No one else had ever gotten close. So did that make her unlovable? She constantly worried she was fatally flawed. That her life without a normal education made her bizarre. Her learning had centered around repairing equipment, cracking safes, picking locks, throwing knives, and preparing to take down guards. Practice. Practice. Practice. That's what she'd done in and out every day, honing every skill possible. And when her mom died, she'd taken over the roles of watching her brother and performing heists. She felt incapable of understanding other humans—other than what she'd gleaned from the movies.

Over and over she told herself that what she'd felt with Cowen was probably a lie, born from her exhaustion and hyper focus on staying safe. She'd dropped her guard for a moment, letting crazy thoughts swarm in. And anyway, she'd told Cowen her name. Being burned meant cutting off all ties.

"What do you want?" she asked herself, disappointed that she would never get a chance to explore if Cowen could care for her once he got to know her.

What do you want? Those words were the last message she'd received from the New Jersey Family Food Coalition before she'd ditched her phone in Milwaukee. *What do you want out of your volunteer experience?* The organization had suggested long lasting friendships, a sense of community, and peace for helping others. She'd wanted all of that. She still wanted that.

But how could she have that with her past? Her dad's words broke through her thoughts. *Dreams disappear, you know. If you don't give them any thought, any attention—eventually they die.* Why would someone like her get what she wanted? Bridge had so much to make up for. So many wrongs to right.

And what about her responsibilities? Liam wasn't just her brother—he felt like a son. Even though he probably had a similar pile of cash, she still worried. He was skilled enough to fake diplomas to anything he wanted, and his sponge-like brain could learn a new profession almost as fast—they were very similar that way. He was twenty-two and capable of taking care of his own life. But she'd been his stand-in mother for so long, basing all of her decisions on how it would affect him, skimping and saving to make sure he had an education paid for with honestly earned money. It felt wrong to want something for herself.

Bridge lifted her hair off her sweaty neck and stared at the number on the screen of her new phone. One call would give her information, probably enough to prove her idea was insane. But what if it wasn't? The possibilities terrified her.

She'd once tiptoed through a security guard shack full of Rottweilers, not waking a soul. The hardest safe she'd cracked took an hour and forty-seven minutes—en route on a train while a competing thief held a gun to her head. And she'd fought a Russian hitter just days after the knife fight that had left scars on her arms, walking away while he lay in a breathing but bloody heap on the floor.

Making a single phone call scared her more than all of that. It would bring her closer in proximity to Portland and Cowen. Bridge knew she shouldn't attempt to contact him since he knew her name.

But still...

She wanted to see him.

With shaking hands, she hit the green button on her burner phone and waited.

A perky female answered two rings later. "Sydney Friggins, Pilpil Bay Realty. How can I help you?"

"Uh," Bridge swallowed. "I'm calling about the shops for sale. The ones with kitchens."

"This is yours and my lucky day. I just sold one this morning, but the larger one is available. Want to come take a look?"

"How much?" Bridge asked.

"The shop is in incredible shape with seven hundred and fifty square feet of cooking space, and four hundred and fifty for retail…"

Bridge rolled her eyes. She understood the lady's sales pitch: shine a light on the positives so the person gets hooked and doesn't notice the negatives. It was a standard grifter move, though this one was legal.

"Your monthly payment would depend on the interest rate and how much you're able to invest, but I can help you get a competitive—"

"How much if I pay in cash?"

"Oh, um…two hundred and eighty thousand dollars."

"Tom Cruise," Bridge cursed. She'd expected her dream to be impossible. But was it feasible with her three hundred thousand? She still needed to buy a used car. And she wanted to donate to the Family Food Coalition since she had to back out of volunteering. That would leave zero room for mistakes and nothing to fall back on.

"Can I take an hour to think about it?"

"Of course." The woman's voice lost enthusiasm. "I hope to hear from you."

Bridge tossed the phone and fell to her knees. "Mom? Virgin Mary? Anyone who will listen?" She waited, not knowing what to expect—asking for advice usually wasn't her thing. "I don't know what to do. All the signs…" She swallowed. "All of my dreams are pointing me toward opening a shop in this tiny town." It probably didn't help that her heart was still pining for an illogical chance with Cowen. "I know I don't deserve much yet, but I'm trying. I'm also terrified. What if I invest and fail?"

With every heist, they'd always succeeded. Sure, a mark would get suspicious and throw a wrench into the plan, or guards would change up their shifts, or codes would unexpectedly get changed, but her family had always come out on top. When businesses went under though, they usually lost everything. She didn't know if she could honestly build herself back up.

"If I start a bakery, I might be setting up a situation where I'll lose it all. I don't want to ever resort to stealing, but it's in my blood." She shook her head repeatedly. "What do I do?"

Her phone rang from the same number she'd just dialed. "Hey, this is Sydney again. I just talked with the owner. They said if you pay cash, they'll drop the price to two hundred and seventy thousand dollars."

With an extra ten grand, Bridge would have enough to get the business up and running and cover a few months of rent for an apartment. This had to be a sign.

She glanced up at the ceiling and mouthed a thanks. "Send me a contract, and I'll wire the money. I'll need a place to live too."

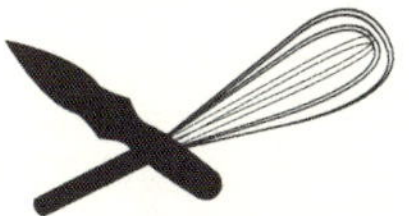

Bridge spent the next seventy-two hours working out the details with Sydney and analyzing the pictures the woman had sent over of the exterior and interior of the shop. She'd whipped up a tentative menu, designed and ordered a temporary vinyl sign—plus a permanent one, and shipped supplies to get there after she arrived. She couldn't wait to start, though she still had to get her food and business licenses. The thought of faking them crossed her mind, but she wanted to do everything the right way. And plus, she'd already gotten halfway through the process.

The furnished house Bridge was going to rent needed all sorts of items, but instead of shipping them from Amazon and having them arrive after she did, she figured she needed to carry in boxes. That's what normal people did when they moved, right? So she went shopping, stuffing the older, new-to-her SUV she'd bought with linens, a rug or two, new tools to fix stuff, and a few fake plants. Plus, she purchased summery dresses, more leggings and tees, replacement makeup, the eucalyptus and mint shampoo that she loved but never splurged on, and all the other toiletries a grown woman would own if she was moving to a new place. She couldn't help the smile on her face as she took everything out of bags, pulled off tags, and roughed a few things up in case Pilpil Bay had nosy, busybodies like the people in Anne of *Green Gables, The Man Called Otto,* or pretty much every Hallmark movie. She kind of hoped they were, wanting a place where she could get involved and do some good.

Her ledger needed to be wiped clean.

Cowen's bullet casing and note sat in the pocket of her jean shorts as she left the devil's inferno four days later and drove eight hours to Tonopah, Nevada to sleep in a seedy hotel. She transferred Cowen's words and gift to her leggings as she entered Oregon, stopping in Klamath Falls and taking a hike to the waterfall before driving the rest of the way to Pilpil Bay around dusk. The whole time she drove, she repeated her new name over and over—Esty Ryan.

Bridge O'Niall was gone forever.

The weight of that loss sat heavy on her heart. Sharing her name with Cowen was a mistake she'd regret for the rest of her life. She couldn't ever contact him now that he knew it, not with the chance that her identity could be leaked. If there was some other way, she would think of a solution—the problem was constantly on her mind. For now, she had to focus on his memory and the hope that someone else could be interested in her someday. Someone that only knew her as Esty Ryan, the owner of A Pinch of This Bakery.

She parked in front of Leftovers and dragged her stiff body inside. Karen looked up from the hostess stand, her eyes growing big. She approached like a freight train, gripping Bridge's hands, her feet doing a happy dance.

"Why are we celebrating?" Bridge asked, as she joined in, bouncing on her toes. This was exactly the small town vibe she'd longed for.

"I knew you'd come back." Karen slowed, panting. "And I heard you bought one of the kitchens. And you're renting the house across from me. I just knew you'd return."

A grin slid over Bridge's lips. Someone wanted her around. "Of course I came back. Where else can I get my dill weed burger fix from the best waitress in the world?"

Karen gave her hand a squeeze, her cheeks morphing to a flattering hue. "Go find a seat, and I'll bring you your usual."

Warmth spread through Bridge's chest, confirming this was the right decision to start a new life on the Oregon coast. She'd spent so much of her existence blending into shadows, limiting interactions to necessary conversations, and pretending to be someone else. But the baker in a small town was who she was meant to be. She just knew it. The fake name was a minor detail.

Karen brought the meal and promised she'd come chat, but a few cars of teens unloaded, and she was slammed. Bridge left a good tip and slipped out, her mind calculating every dollar spent. First and last month's rent had eaten up almost everything left.

The empty bakery across the street—her bakery—called her name and she floated over. She could almost smell Paris-Brest, Biscoff cupcakes, and raspberry cheesecake cookies—the three things she planned to make first. And she couldn't wait for summer to be over and for the holidays to start. The scents of pumpkin spice and cinnamon would fill the entire town.

She was tempted to pick the lock and slip in, but that was behind her. The keys would be in her hands by tomorrow morning—she could wait another twelve hours. *And* she was exhausted. Two days of driving and listening to online lessons for her food handler's permit was enough to warrant a good night's rest.

Bridge drove to the rental house, a cute turquoise-painted single-story home built in the 1940s with blooming flower beds and a mailbox by the sidewalk. She felt like Samantha, played by Nicole Kidman, in *Bewitched*. Everything she'd ever wanted was becoming a reality.

The code on the door worked—unlike her first experience in Pilpil Bay—and she carried her bags inside. The tiny home had one bedroom, a bath with a soaker tub, a dining nook attached to the kitchen, and a living room with two armchairs and a sofa shoved up against the walls. The decor had a boho vibe with neutral tones and lots of different textures. It was the perfect canvas to add her own style—which she wasn't a hundred percent sure of yet. There'd never been a point in decorating her spaces before. She'd been living someone else's life, even when she'd used her own name. Her brother's needs had always come first.

In the bedroom, Bridge felt along the walls and floorboards, looking for the perfect spot to store her cash. With a little grunting, she pried up a panel under the bed and laid the remnants of Bridge O'Niall to rest.

"You'll always be a part of me, but I've got a new life now." She probably should have destroyed the driver's license and passport, but she had so few tangible memories. And plus, someone would have to suspect her and have some serious skills to find her stash. She wasn't going to give anyone a reason and was doubtful someone like that would live in this small town.

Her eyelids drooped as she placed a thousand in cash on top. Five hundred, minus tonight's dinner, sat in her account. The throwing knives went into the hole next. Her mom had bought them for her twelfth birthday, and she'd successfully dissuaded a pursuer with them by thirteen and a half. She'd only lost two of the ten, and it meant the world that her dad had retrieved the knives from her New Jersey apartment and left them in the safety deposit box.

The ledger was the last thing in Bridge's hand. But she wasn't ready to bury it. Just because she was moving on, it didn't mean she could forgive all of her mistakes. Her family had hurt other people. For that, she still needed to pay. And it was a constant reminder to look for Harley, though the last search before she'd left Arizona came up empty, like always.

After securing the floorboard, Bridge stuffed the ledger under her pillow and set traps at each entry and along every window before falling onto the bed in her leggings and t-shirt. Thoughts of Cowen lulled her to sleep, her mind struggling to find a way around her mistake of sharing her name. Even her subconscious couldn't figure out a solution. Seeing him again was impossible, but still, she dreamed.

Bridge's phone buzzed her awake the next morning with a call from Sydney, the realtor. "You should have told me you made it in. I would have come over and helped you unpack or something."

That's exactly why Bridge hadn't said anything. Even with all that she'd bought, there wasn't enough for her *normal female* role, especially since most of the boxes were only a quarter full.

"I was so tired last night," Bridge said as she rubbed her eyes. "But I've got everything covered."

"I can help you move in the rest of the boxes right now."

Bridge pulled back a curtain and saw a brunette standing by her SUV. "Keanu Reeves."

"What was that?" Sydney asked.

"Oh, um, I was just clearing my throat. I'll be out in a minute." She brushed her teeth, threw on a bra, pulled her hair back into a messy bun, and exited, the cool humid air kissing her good morning. She was already loving Oregon. Except the part about missing Cowen.

Sydney approached, enveloping her into a hug. "Karen told me all about you. I'm so happy you're joining our Pilpil Bay community."

Bridge bit back the grin on her lips. Community—she was finally part of one. "Thanks for helping me get here." She pulled away and unlocked her car. "I'm sorry I've taken so much of your time the last few days."

"Are you kidding me? I've already got my commissions. That, plus the finder fee on these rentals has put me on cloud nine, even though my husband is already planning what to spend it on."

"I'm happy you're happy." Bridge opened the back door of the SUV and barred the way in front of her boxes. "I've um…I've had a hard life, so I don't have many things." It was the most honest way she could word it.

Sydney tilted her head, her lips squishing to the side in a sympathetic gesture. "You don't need to say more. I could sense the urgency in your need to relocate. You'll be safe here. Especially with your new neighbor. He's ex-FBI."

A screen door slammed.

"Speak of the devil." Sydney grinned as she waved.

Bridge turned, her gaze locking with familiar eyes that had sugared every recent dream. Her heart thrummed in her chest so hard she wondered if it had even beaten for days. "Cowen." Everything inside her collided—one half doing a happy dance, the other preparing to bolt. How was he here? He shouldn't be. He couldn't be.

His eyes widened, his lips curved into a grin. "Bridge?"

chapter eight
Breakfast Gone Wrong

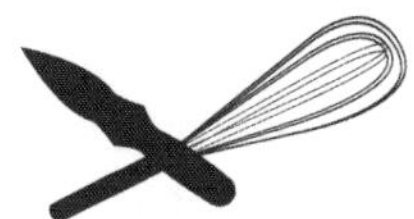

Jasper ran to Bridge, his ears flopping, his tongue hanging out. Her lungs collapsed as she scratched his ears. Cowen. Here. How? This wasn't good. *So not good.*

Cowen approached barefoot, wearing jeans, a fitted tee, and a grin the size of two shotgun casings. It fell when he noticed the panic on her face.

"Bridge Over Troubled Water," she said with the sternest look she could muster. No one else could know her name. "That's what was playing that night, right?"

"You know each other?" Sydney asked, a delicious smile crossing her lips.

Cowen searched Bridge's eyes one more time before giving a nonchalant shrug. "We crossed paths once." He motioned to Jasper, and the dog returned to his house, flopping down on the porch. "And you're right, that was the song we danced to."

Bridge allowed herself to breathe, grateful he'd picked up on her cues. But her stomach was fluttering at a thousand beats per second, the air around them building a static charge.

"Well, you know what people say about crossing paths twice?" Sydney picked up a box and carried it toward the door. "Destiny."

Kismet, serendipity, or any of those froofy definitions did not pertain to this situation. Not with Cowen knowing her name. "Destiny is a farce made up by Hollywood in movies like *Only You* with Robert Downey Jr. and Marisa Tomei. Or *The Adjustment Bureau* with Matt Damon and Emily Blunt."

Sydney blinked at Bridge's robotic response. "Believe whatever you want." She gave a look that said she didn't buy it, and took the box into the house.

"What are you doing here?" Bridge asked, charging toward Cowen until their breaths collided. Thank goodness she'd brushed her teeth. By the smell of things, he already had too.

"I could ask that of you." He kept his voice hushed. "What's going on? Why are you covering the name Bridge?"

She crossed her arms over her chest. She didn't want to lie to him, but she definitely couldn't answer.

His eyes widened as if he'd figured something out. "Witness protection program?"

That explanation would probably make sense to him. And he'd supplied the suggestion, so it wasn't technically lying when she let her shoulders relax.

"I wish I'd known." He ran his hand through his hair. "And that explains everything." He stepped closer, the gap between them narrowing. "I can't believe we're both here."

Time stilled. Bridge's chest rose and fell in sync with Cowen's fast breaths. His gravity seemed to pull her in. Warnings blared in her mind, but she didn't want to heed them. What if this *was* destiny? What if they could have a chance to see if there was more than just this electricity between them? Something that could last? She was getting a second chance at life with the bakery. Why not hope for something more?

The screen door of her house closed. "I'm just gonna go and let you two do whatever it is you're going to do," Sydney said, happy notes carrying her tone. "I left the keys to your shop on the counter." She got into the car and zipped away.

Bridge crossed her arms over her chest. "What if I'm not as excited to see you as you're assuming?" She was never one to make things easy. And she was still so unsure. He knew her name…but he seemed to understand it had to be kept secret.

Cowen smirked. "My shell casing is in your pocket."

She patted the bulge on the side of her leggings. "How dare you look that close at me."

His grin widened. "I think it's fair after you frisked me."

"Chris Pratt," she swore, and stormed to the car, grabbing a box. Her mind kept warring between fears and dreams, making her head spin.

"Do I remind you of Christ Pratt?" Cowen asked as he followed, picking up two boxes and tagging along as she entered the house.

"No. Just…you…I can't." She set her box on the floor.

Cowen placed his load on top. "Your secret is safe with me."

She crossed her arms. "You know I don't trust people."

"There's always time to learn something new," he said with a delicious smile.

Even though that was a good answer, she scowled at him and turned away again. "No one else can know anything. No mention ever of Bridge, or that I threatened you with a knife, or anything. I'm starting a new life here."

"What about the pat down?" He stepped closer. "Or cuddling on the swing? Can I share those?"

Her cheeks flushed as she glared at him. Being around Cowen was like roller-blading through a sea of angry Rottweilers—exhilarating and terrifying. "That was not cuddling. We were strangers…sitting on the same—"

"You were in my arms. And I'm pretty sure you liked it."

Heat coursed through her body, but Bridge pushed past him, hurried out the door, and grabbed another box. "My feelings are irrelevant," she said as he followed, picking up two. "You can't know anything about my past." She returned inside and set hers down.

"I don't." He placed his on top. "You gave me one *word*. For all I know, it's part of the title of a song like you said."

Her head swam with the consequences of both possible decisions. Leave and miss him or stay and put everything at risk. She shook her head. "I can't."

"You can't what? Is there another guy?" He raked his hand through his hair. "You're not married, are you? Did I *cuddle* with another man's wife?"

"No." She glared at him for teasing her with that word again, but he was whittling away her excuses. "I can't stay and pretend to have a normal life when you know I'm not normal."

He stepped closer and slowly touched her fingers. Zings ran up and down her arms. "I know normal people, and they're…okay. But I like your version better."

Everything in Bridge's head told her to run. To never trust. But all he knew was one word. That was it. And wasn't she supposed to live her dreams like her dad had suggested? Wasn't Cowen all she thought about when she wasn't making plans for the bakery? Or even when she was?

Like she often had to do in a heist, Bridge made a split-second decision. "I'm hungry," she said as she pulled her hand away and grabbed her keys. As long as Cowen didn't ask any questions, she could give him a chance.

She walked out the door, waited for him to follow, and pressed the lock button on the keypad of her rental house. He stayed on the porch while she got into her car and started it. "Aren't you coming?" she asked, sticking her head out the window.

He quirked an eyebrow, took Jasper into his house, and got in beside her. "I didn't know that telling me you're hungry was an invitation to join you."

In a quick move, she reached across him, their bodies close, and snagged his seatbelt, locking it into place. "I only eat food with people I trust." Or if she was on the grift, but he didn't need to know that. Though, if things ever progressed beyond friendship, she would tell him what she used to do—without specifics. She'd seen far too many movies where a single, omitted piece of information was enough to break two people up. That trope was far overdone. Even though he was ex-FBI, she had a feeling he would hold her secrets.

She threw the car into reverse and backed onto the empty street full of potholes. The sirens in her head still screamed danger. How could she trust someone with secrets that had to stay buried forever? The rest of her countered with how could she keep living without a fully functioning heart? It definitely beat differently around Cowen.

"You do know I'm not wearing shoes?" he asked.

"Same as it ever was." Bridge flashed him a grin and drove to Leftovers with a comfortable silence that made the corners of her lips soar. Was this real? Was he really here? "Any allergies?"

"At this point, I'm only allergic to being away from you." His lips twitched as he tried to keep a straight face.

"You're a dork." She parked and shoved his shoulder, opened the car door, and paused, her mouth drying. This wasn't like her. Her training had always made her calculate all the risks. But she wasn't making a plan for five steps ahead. So many things could go wrong. Except all the signs were pointing to Cowen. She'd prayed to anyone who'd listen for help. Maybe it was time for her to learn to trust like he'd said.

"Stay here." Bridge left him and ordered a couple of breakfast plates to go, her stomach doing flips as she waited. If he was crazy enough to still be in the car when she got back, wasn't that worth giving their relationship— whatever it was—a chance? She could do this. It could all work out. Kismet, destiny, fate—they were all real.

"So," Cowen asked as she got back in. "What do I call you?"

"Esty Ryan." She held out her hand, and he took his time shaking it, his skin warm against hers. Silence filled the air, full of possibilities as she let go and threw the car into reverse. "So, what are you doing in Pilpil Bay? Did you leave the FBI?"

"I resigned," he said with so much heaviness that Bridge could almost taste it. "It's too much pressure right now, so I'm starting a bakery on Main Street."

Bridge choked, slamming on the brakes. She should have seen the signs. She should have been calculating to see that everything was too good to be true. The universe wasn't going to dish out serendipity to someone like her. With all the wrongs in her ledger, she didn't deserve a happily ever after. And to rub in more misery, it had brought Cowen here so she could see and witness everything she couldn't have.

"Are you okay?" He gripped the center console so tight, the veins in his hands plumped.

"What kind of a bakery?" she asked with gritted teeth, ignoring his question and putting the car back into motion.

He watched her, his words measured. "Um, some of everything sweet. I don't really do—"

"Bread." She didn't either. This made sense—another sign that no matter where she went or what she did, she'd be tortured for her past until she made up for it.

"How did you know?" he asked, his lips puckered with worry.

She slammed the car to a stop in front of his house. "Get out."

Cowen turned his body toward her, confusion baked into his face. "What?"

Bridge grabbed one of the containers for herself and unbuckled his belt. "Get out."

"What did I do wrong?" He eyed her like he was waiting for some joke or punch line.

"Don't make me push you, 'cause it'll hurt." Why did he have to get dragged into this? Couldn't the universe attack her and only her?

"I'm not leaving until you tell—"

Bridge pulled a switchblade from the back of her leggings and flipped the knife toward him. "I won't ask you again."

"Okay, okay," he said, stepping out and crouching down to see her. "Will you please tell me what's wrong? I'm sorry for whatever I did."

"I'm sorry too." She set her food on his vacated seat, wishing there were other options. "Whatever this was, it's over." She had to focus on her breaths. Everything she had, minus the money under her bed and in her account, was tied up in her bakery. She couldn't afford to start over again. She couldn't afford competition. "You and I are enemies."

Cowen shook his head, not understanding. "Why?"

Her patience with the situation was fading. "I bought the shop next to yours."

His head tilted as if confused why that was a bad thing. Then his eyes rounded. "You're a baker too."

She nodded. "Now get out of my way." Bridge waited for him to back up then stoked the gas, the door between them slamming shut.

chapter nine

Ice Cream with One Spoon

The sun was fading toward the horizon when Cowen knocked on Esty's door with a plate of fresh baked s'mores cinnamon rolls. His legs shook, not wanting to mess things up more than they already were. Her reactions to everything were over the top, but there were reasons behind them. The witness protection program was no joke, and he could only imagine how difficult her life had been. The luggage car for all of Esty's emotional baggage was probably at least a mile long, and she played by completely different rules, but Cowen couldn't wait for whatever came up next with her…assuming she'd let him have a chance.

He was still floored that she was in Pilpil Bay. He'd imagined never seeing her again, living the rest of his life wondering what could have been.

A pair of birds played chase above as he sensed her watching him through the peephole. He knocked again.

She opened and pointed to the pastry, her mouth twisted to the side, her eyes narrowed. "What's that?"

"It's an apology. And an invitation to talk things out. What if we sold different sweets—"

Esty left, returning a moment later with a red-swirled cinnamon roll on a plate, her similarly colored lips angled down. "I'm not budging on these."

His cinnamon roll recipe was his mama's favorite, but if this was what it took, he'd give them up. Gladly. Anything to get her to talk to him. "Fine." He feigned being put out. "I'm sure we can work something—"

"Hello," a brunette interrupted as she sauntered up the sidewalk in a blouse and a mid-thigh skirt. Her hands were swallowed in oven mitts, and they gripped a covered casserole dish. "I'm guessing you're Cowen Amaratti, the new baker?" She gave him a ridiculously long once-over.

"Uh. One of them." He winced, not wanting to deal with anyone else right now. He'd waited hours to let Esty cool down—hours that had felt like years. There had to be a solution to their problem. No one had ever created sparks the way she had, had never pulled out his emotions, or created such a safe pocket for him to be himself. He was determined to work things out. This intruder could take a hike.

"I'm Alex Madderton. What's that supposed to mean about being *one* of the bakers? Is this your partner?" She gave Esty a quick, disapproving glance and turned her spotlight of attention back to him.

"No." Esty joined them on the porch. "We're nothing." Her words had bite, sinking into Cowen. "Apparently we're both opening a bakery."

"Oh," Alex's expression softened into a sadistic grin. "That's really too bad. Our town isn't big enough to support two."

Based on her attitude so far, he could guess who she'd buy from, regardless of taste.

"That's what I figured." Esty gave Cowen a pointed glance.

"That's why we might team up?" he asked, his voice hopeful. For hours, he'd thought out different scenarios. Maybe they could knock out a wall and combine shops.

Alex shifted, pushing her hip out. "You wouldn't want to do that with a *neighbor*." She made the word sound like a bad thing. "Business is such a messy process." She showed him the dish. "Are you hungry? I came over to welcome you into town. We could take this back to your place?"

Not a chance. Cowen opened his mouth to refute, but Esty nodded.

"That's a great idea," she said. "You two should get to know each other while I finish icing my cinnamon rolls."

Cowen ground his teeth. The only person he wanted to get to know was Esty. Thoughts of her had gotten him through Noah's funeral. And he'd pictured her during the brutal dark of each night when his memories howled. Working things out was his only agenda. "I'm not—"

"You don't want to burn *bridges*," Esty said, her hand finding her hip.

He lowered his shoulders in defeat, knowing her well enough already that she wouldn't back down. For now, he'd give her what she wanted, if only to show her he was a team player. That they could work things out. "I guess we're going." He handed Esty his frosting covered peace offering.

Alex looked at both plates of cinnamon rolls. "I think we need a town meeting to decide what to do about two bakeries." She started down the sidewalk then paused, waiting for Cowen to follow.

"We're not done talking," he whispered to Esty, his gaze falling to her lips before trudging after Alex.

This was not how he'd envisioned his night. Alex let herself into his house and Jasper met them, growling. The woman flinched, backing away.

"He's friendly." Cowen told Jasper to go to his bed, and the old boy trudged to his pillow.

"This is cozy," Alex said as she slipped out of her heels.

All he'd done was unpack his kitchen boxes and some clothes. Everything else belonged to the house, but he didn't want to explain. "Thanks." He placed a trivet on the table, and Alex put the dish on top.

"I haven't eaten yet," she said. "Mind if I join you?"

Yes, he did. But he was smart enough not to burn any *bridges* in a small town. He'd thank Esty later tonight for the unwanted guest. After seeing that knife she'd pulled, maybe *she* needed a pat down. "I'll get some plates." He opened several cupboards and drawers, trying to remember where he'd placed everything.

"What's an attractive man like you doing in a small town like this?"

Cowen wasn't about to entertain the seductive notes in her conversation. "I'm running away from my problems." Hopefully that would turn her off. "What do you do?"

"I own The Essential Oil Bizarre across the street from your bakery." She helped herself to the glasses, filling them both up from the tap.

"That's not far." He set down two plates. Everything was practically within a few steps in Pilpil Bay. Maybe a little too close.

She sat, and he swore she crossed her legs in a way that showed the most amount of skin. Her efforts were pointless—his mind was on someone else.

"I heard you used to be an FBI agent." She said, waiting for him to nod before continuing. "What made you give it up?"

"Personal reasons." He found silverware and a serving dish and joined her at the table. If he wasn't interested in pursuing Esty, he'd probably find Alex gorgeous. But she was currently an obstacle in his way, nothing more. Plus, she was a bit pushy for his taste.

"Why baking?" She lifted the lid of some sort of chicken and rice casserole and dumped three helpings on his plate.

He shrugged and started in. In all honesty, the dish was delicious. And the sooner he finished, the sooner she'd leave. "It was my mama's answer to everything. If I got hurt playing outside, we'd bake cookies together. If kids were mean at school, we'd make a pie. Somewhere along the way it became ingrained that baking makes things better." As much as he loved making treats, maybe he should find something else to do with his shop. That way Esty could keep her bakery and not think of him as an enemy.

"That's beautiful. If I were a journalist, I'd quote you." She took a small bite from the single scoop on her plate.

This was going to take forever. He faked a yawn. "This is really good, but I'm pretty exhausted. Maybe we can—"

"Take this to the couch?" she asked, her eyelashes batting.

"Not a chance," he said before he had time to think through his words. "Sorry, I'm not sure where this conversation is going, but you should know I'm interested in someone else."

Alex shrugged like that wasn't a problem. "I'm interested in lots of people too."

Great. She was one of those types. He wished she'd take her things and leave. "How about you tell me about you," he said when he couldn't think of another way to get her to go.

As Alex talked, Cowen took the opportunity to shove his mouth full. She came from a single-mom home, built herself up from nothing, and was on the city council. Multiple times she mentioned she was constantly improving herself while she waited for Mr. Right.

Cowen finally finished the last bite, his stomach overfull and aching.

"We could go for a walk," she said, and Jasper perked up from his bed in the corner.

"Alex, it was nice meeting you, but I have to pass." He stood, waiting for her to follow suit. "It's been a long day." He tried to hand her the dish, but she shook her head.

"You can bring it by when it's empty. I live at number two sixty-six on the street behind you."

"Uh, thanks." When it came time to return the dish, he'd leave it on the porch and run. Cowen opened the front door. "I'll see you later." Hopefully, much later.

"Tomorrow," she said, gripping his bicep to balance herself as she put her shoes on. "I'll get the town together, and we can discuss what to do with both bakeries." She slid her hand down his chest and slipped out.

A whoosh of air escaped Cowen's lips while he waited for her to disappear from view. That had been a waste of time. "Let's go see our friend," he said to Jasper, and the dog hurried as fast as his old bones could. They walked next door and found a sign taped to the screen, written in dots and dashes. "Morse code? Seriously?"

It took him a minute to decipher the message: *I'm exhausted and going to bed. Please don't bother me.*

Of course he was going to respect Esty's wishes, but he didn't have to like them. The longer there was a wedge between them, the longer it could fester. He didn't believe in coincidence. They were brought together twice for a reason.

Cowen took Jasper for a walk, letting him mark his new territory, and returned to the house, digging through twelve boxes until he found a paper and pen. Jasper curled up beside him on the bed as he wrote.

Estee? Esty? Estie? I'm sorry for not knowing how to spell your name and for opening up a bakery next to yours. I'm determined to find something that will work for both of us.

I know you're mad. If I knew what would make you happy, I'd do it. There's so little I know about you.

He tapped his pen on his lips. How personal should he get in the letter? He knew better than to push too hard and flip Esty over the edge, though he wanted to tell her how he'd felt when he saw her that morning. He'd known the odds of finding her were so slim that getting another chance felt like winning a galactic lottery. He had no idea what was going to happen next, only that he had every hope. A little banter seemed to be the best option.

When do you want to talk? I'm open to frisking. Or not. Cuddling could also be arranged.

Jasper nudged him.

And Jasper says hi.

He folded the letter and thought twice. If she spoke in a code, shouldn't he do the same? Cowen spent the next hour drawing out twenty-six geometric images that corresponded to each letter and rewrote the message for her to decipher.

A light was still on in her house as he opened the screen and set the note next to the door.

It took all of his willpower to walk away instead of bugging her and demanding they work things out right then. He'd rather spend the night getting to know her instead of finishing the paperwork for his food handler's permit. And he'd rather hold her than slip into the nightmares that would come when he had nothing left to focus on.

Esty's light was still on when he turned his off, tossing and turning for hours until he drifted.

The next morning was warmer than the day before, and he showered and dressed in shorts as he waited for her to knock. Or show her face. He itched to go over to her house, but he gave her time.

Alex showed up at 9:00 a.m., inviting him to lunch, which he passed on. "Meet at the town hall at seven," she said, running her hand down his bicep.

He flinched at her touch. "I'll let Esty know."

"I already told her," Alex said, one hip jutting toward him while she twirled her hair.

Cowen glanced away, intentionally showing his disinterest. "When?"

Alex scowled, seeming to not like all this talk about another woman. "She's working on fixing the ovens in her bakery. If you ask me, it's a man's job."

The comment was no doubt intended to taint Cowen's opinion, but instead, it reaffirmed the fact that Esty kept surprising him. "I'll be there tonight," he said and closed the door.

As soon as Alex left, he jogged to town and walked into his own bakery. Dust sparkled in the morning light, the air smelling of possibilities. But he didn't want them at Esty's expense. They needed to talk.

He knocked on the back door of her shop, and she opened a moment later with grease smudged on her forehead.

"You've got a little something…" he motioned to her hairline.

She stared at him with a blank expression and dragged her fingers down her cheek, leaving a greasy trail.

He had to fight to keep from laughing. Her childish antics wouldn't push him away. "I've missed you too." Cowen waited for her to say something, but she turned and walked into her bakery where a handful of metal pieces littered the floor. "Do you need some help?" he asked.

"No." She sat and fiddled with the heating element. Like the day before, she wore leggings and a plain t-shirt, this one olive green. Something large and rectangular was in one of her pants pockets, and the casing showed through the other.

"Look, I get that you're mad, but I had no way of knowing anyone— including you—was turning this into a bakery. So you don't have to push me away. I can help."

"I don't need your help." Esty worked something a little more and a click sounded through the empty space. "See?"

He shrugged. There wasn't anything to see other than a pile of parts.

"Give me a minute." She pushed her curly red hair out of the way and walked the pieces to one of the wall ovens. Within seconds, she was going back for more parts, her deft fingers flying.

"I have no idea why I doubted you," he said as she returned every piece in place and all screws were accounted for.

"That's a mistake you should never repeat." She closed the oven door, cranked the heat to four hundred, and set a timer for five minutes.

He placed a hand on the side of the appliance, leaning toward her. "Can we talk about the elephant in the room?"

"I don't think we should until the meeting tonight." Esty walked away. She crouched next to the walk-in freezer and began unscrewing the cover panel. It would seem that their conversation was going nowhere, but she hadn't threatened him yet. This was progress.

He knelt next to her like he would a scared cat that needed to warm up to him. "How about I ask you something else? How do you spell your name?"

She yanked off the cover panel with one hand and pulled out her license from her back pocket with the other, handing it to him.

"Is this the part where I comment about your weight or that you handed this to me because you don't know how to spell your fake name?"

"The only important thing about a person's weight is how they use it." She tugged on the wires inside the panel. "And questioning the name I was given at birth is something else you should never do again." She gave him a pointed stare, making him understand that anything about her witness protection details was off limits. She selected a wire and stripped it.

"We're talking about a lot of *can'ts*. What *can* I do?" He held up her license, undeterred. "Should I put it back in your butt pocket or—"

Esty smacked his chest, feigning a glare.

He grinned, leaning closer. She had a way of pulling him in. "You said something about Chris Pratt yesterday. Do you like him? Or Hollywood stars? Or movies?"

"You could say that," she said, not actually answering his question. "Hand me the electrical tape."

He let their fingers touch as he passed it over. "Is your arm okay?" He pointed to the large bandage on her wrist.

"It's fine." Her voice said she didn't want to talk about it. "How's the grief?" she asked, softening.

"Still looming." He hardly felt it around her. And the fact she was asking about him spoke volumes. He didn't buy her gruff act. "How's yours?"

"Manageable." She continued to work, inspecting every wire in the unit. "If this is a free question zone, did you cuddle with Alex last night? She was over there for a long time."

A twinge of jealousy? That was another good sign. Cowen chose his words carefully to convey the meaning he wanted her to hear. "I only cuddle with people who interest me, and she's not one of them."

"Long lashes and longer legs don't entice you?" Esty asked as she twisted two wires together. She stood and flipped a switch on the electrical panel near the back door. The walk-in freezer hummed to life.

He joined her. "It depends on who they're on." His eyes met hers, and their rapid breaths competed. "Are you done being mad at me yet?"

"I'm not mad." The timer dinged and she left him to check the oven.

Cowen followed, standing close while heat spilled out of the appliance. "Your jaw is tense."

"That's because I'm focused." She slammed the door and moved to the stove top, searching as if hoping to find something else broken.

"Why are you so focused?" He would keep talking, keep asking her questions until she pushed him away.

"Because the way I grew up, you had to be the best at what you did, or you could die." She let that weight settle, though he didn't know what it meant. "Now I'm a baker, and if I'm not the best, my business will die. It's all I have left. So if you don't mind leaving…"

"What about working on a solution?" He placed one hand on the counter, angling his body toward her. "We could find a way to compromise."

She glanced him over, her lips and eyes conveying different messages. "I compromised once and learned my lesson. You. Door. Out."

He moved closer to her, his hand hovering close, wanting to eliminate the gap. She was torn between her business and him, he knew it, but there had to be something to fix this. "That was a single event—in the past. You're not even giving me a chance to—"

Esty pointed her screwdriver at the exit. "This is the last time I ask."

Cowen shook his head as he walked toward the door. If she hadn't flirted back, he would be worried he'd blown his chance. Still, he had to be careful not to push her. The last thing he wanted was for Esty to feel the way he did around Alex. That woman needed to keep her hands to herself.

"I'll respect your wishes. But I want to talk tonight after the meeting. Is that okay?" he asked.

Esty shrugged, and that was enough.

"I'll come over. What ice cream do you want me to bring?" he asked.

She considered him for several moments, to the point that Cowen thought she would never respond. "Anything with chocolate."

He opened the door and turned back, pointing to her thigh where the casing showed through the fabric. "I'm glad you've still got my present."

Esty's cheeks glowed as he gave her one last glance before leaving her shop.

Cowen spent the rest of the day listening to classic rock while running through the checklist he'd made before Esty arrived in town. Now, his business felt pointless. They both wanted to run a bakery, and she seemed unwilling to compromise. How would the town hall meeting change that? He stopped by to offer her lunch and dinner, but both times, she was gone. At least she'd agreed to meet that night. He bought a carton of Tillamook Mudslide and put it in his freezer at home.

At fifteen to seven, he walked to the city office, which was basically a double wide surrounded by beds of flowers and vines. About a dozen people milled around inside, none of whom Cowen recognized. A woman with tall, gray hair stood near the back of the room and waved him over with her free hand, the other was wrapped around a plush, stuffed cat.

"The name is Gertie." She shook his hand, her python grip stronger than he'd expected. Small towns always had one of those weird types. Maybe Gertie was it.

"Cowen. Do you know how long these meetings last?" He couldn't wait to talk to Esty.

She glanced him over and used the cat to hiss at him. "It depends on you. As soon as one of you backs down, I'll get to eat the refreshments. Does that make—" Gertie paused, her mouth twisting into a smile. "Is that your competition?"

Cowen turned to see Esty enter in a flowing floral dress, her eyes darting around the entire room as if scanning for threats. What he wouldn't do to put her at ease. He'd even be willing to keep talking to this lady. The hissing was beyond unusual. "Yeah. Do you know her?"

The smile stayed on Gertie's lips, her gaze following Esty's every move as she petted the cat. "She fixed some things when she stayed in my rental."

Fixing things seemed to be a consistent theme. "That was nice of her." He couldn't think of more to say to the lady without questioning her sanity. "I'll see you around." Cowen made his way toward Esty, but Alex entered, intercepting him and snaking her arm through his. He managed to hold in his groans.

"This way," she pointed him to the right side of the room and led him to the front where two chairs sat opposite of each other.

"I have to sit up here?" He was more of a middle of the room kind of guy. And he was the type to like only one woman at a time. His gaze met Esty's, and she quickly covered a smile, looking away.

"Don't worry, you'll do fine," Alex said.

A man in a Hawaiian shirt, shorts, and socks under his sandals pounded a gavel on the podium. "Let's get started."

Cowen glanced at the clock—there were still three minutes until seven. Clearly, the man didn't understand island time like his outfit suggested. Alex gave his hand a squeeze and sat directly opposite him in the audience. He expected Esty to plop down onto the chair, but she gracefully lowered herself onto the seat.

"I'm Mayor Dinwiddie. Thank you all for meeting today." The numbers in the room had risen to about thirty. "As some of you may be aware, the storefronts where Micky's Pizzeria and Coastal Bakery were located have been purchased separately by Ms. Esty Ryan and Mr. Cowen Amaratti. Both owners intend to open a bakery. Our town simply can't sustain two, so we're meeting to come up with a solution. Let's let our new neighbors introduce themselves. Ladies first."

Esty stood, and the scared, timid woman who'd entered the room was gone, replaced with poise and confidence. "I'm Esty Ryan. I grew up in North Dakota where I was homeschooled and learned to bake from the fresh ingredients on our farm. And yes, I can milk a cow and churn butter. You can feel my muscles later." She waited politely for laughs to die down. "My mom taught me everything she knew in the kitchen, but she's no longer with me." Esty hung her head. "I feel her near whenever I bake. Thank you for your help."

Cowen blinked repeatedly as he watched her. How much of that story was true? She wouldn't give her home state away if she was in the witness protection program. What did he really know about her? Warnings flashed in his head, but he pushed them away. His gut had never been wrong about someone's character, and it constantly drew him toward her.

He stood and gave the crowd an awkward wave. "I'm Cowen Amaratti, like the cookie but with all A's." Blank stares met him, and it took a moment to find something else to say. He didn't want to make things worse between him and Esty, but he figured she wouldn't appreciate him conceding. So he settled for the simple truth. "When I was young, my mama would suggest baking any time I was sad or hurt. It's become synonymous with healing. I recently lost someone close to me, and I came here to repair myself and start a new life. Thank you."

"What do I always say?" Mayor Dinwiddie asked, beaming. "Mothers are the most important force in the world." He let that marinate for a moment, his body swaying as he shifted from foot to foot. "I'll turn the time over to the town for suggestions to fix our problem."

A fifty-something, plum-shaped woman stood. "I say we keep the guy. He looks tasty."

Cowen swallowed as laughter and groans sounded through the room. Maybe there were multiple crazies in this small town.

Mayor Dinwiddie banged his gavel. "Denise, you are censured again. Any more comments will result in an hour of community service. The next need is to clear out debris around the dock, and I know for certain you don't swim." He scanned the audience. "Are there any other suggestions that are actually helpful?"

"What if one of them makes something else? Like pizza?" A man said from the back.

Mayor Dinwiddie looked to Esty. "What do you say to that?"

"When it comes to salt, I only make salty comments." She smiled at the laughs that came her way. "Sweets is all I've got."

Everyone turned to Cowen.

"I'm only good at baking, but I'd be willing to try something else." If it meant a chance with Esty, he'd do almost anything.

"I have a suggestion." Alex stood, glancing around at everyone. "What if the bakeries have a competition? The winner stays." She looked at Esty. "The loser can leave town."

Mayor Dinwiddie banged his gavel again. "Now let's not pronounce edicts. We would never force anyone away. We're grateful that you've both chosen Pilpil Bay as your new home, especially since Ms. Ryan has already fixed the copier at town hall when no one else could." He looked between the bakers. "I'm willing to entertain the idea of a competition, but I hope you'll both stay. Who has something to say about it?"

Gertie stood. "I second the idea and propose they make five treats over five days. We'll vote, and the winner gets to open shop. The loser can sell their real estate or keep it and do something else."

"That seems as fair as it can get in this situation." Mayor Dinwiddie turned to Esty. "What do you say?"

She glanced at Cowen. "I'm always up for a challenge. If my bakery isn't the best though, I'd rather leave. What about you Mr. Amaratti?"

He would have preferred working something out with her. But if this is what she wanted, he'd compete. He could always lose and figure something else to make. Cooking and baking couldn't be that different. Except there wasn't much room to have tables and chairs in his shop. Whatever he made, it would have to be portable. "Sounds good to me."

Mayor Dinwiddie grinned. "As soon as you can get your appliances working and supplies ordered…"

"Mine are running great." Esty turned to Cowen, her eyebrow lifted in a challenge.

"Mine are too." Though he hadn't practiced to check how reliable the thermometers were yet. But that didn't matter if he was fixing to lose.

"Let's start on Monday with chocolate chip cookies," Mayor Dinwiddie said. "That gives you the weekend to prepare. The town can cast votes for the other challenges. Ms. Madderton," he pointed to Alex. "Will you coordinate that?"

"I'd love to." She flashed Cowen a winning smile.

"Meeting adjourned."

Twilight hovered overhead as Cowen stood at Esty's door with the carton of ice cream in one hand and a nervous twitch in the other. In the hour since the meeting, all he'd worried about was Esty. His mama's money was tied to his success, and that should have taken precedence, but it hadn't. Esty had hinted at leaving if her bakery wasn't the best. It wasn't right to force her out. He wouldn't do it.

Techno sounded from inside her house, the steady pulse matching his heartbeat. Nervous about the unknown, he lifted his hand and knocked.

She answered in a tank top and tight shorts, her hair pulled back. Sweat glistened on her exposed skin as she failed to hide her smile. "You're early."

Jasper nudged his head toward her, and she bent to scratch his ears.

"We never set a time." He still couldn't believe she was really here. And even with all her threats and the competition looming between them, she was still happy to see him.

"Yeah, well I'm not ready to process the mess we're in." She left the door open and picked up an exercise mat off the floor.

"You don't have to stop. I'll watch."

She glared at him, the reaction he'd hoped for.

He entered, noticing their furniture and layout were practically identical. "Is it okay if Jasper comes too?"

She motioned the dog over, and he ran to her for another scratch.

Cowen set the ice cream on the coffee table, his feet shifting but his mind was made up. "I don't want to compete against you."

She rolled the mat and stowed it beside the sofa, her expression hidden. "Because you're afraid of losing."

"No." He stepped closer. "Because I'm afraid it will push us apart."

She wouldn't meet his gaze as she wiped her skin with a towel. "How can it when we're not together?"

He took another hopeful step toward her. "We can fix that."

Esty shook her head. "If I lose, I'm leaving. The only other marketable skills I have are repairing things, and that's what I *used* to do." She gave him a look that meant he needed to read between the lines.

He understood it was part of her former life, and her new character shouldn't do the same things. "Are you really from North Dakota?"

"You're not supposed to question the facts I present." She grabbed the ice cream and entered the kitchen, pulling a spoon from a stack of others on a board next to the window. The wood was angled in such a way that if anyone opened a panel, it would dip and utensils would clatter to the counter.

"I'm trying to get to know you." He glanced back at the door he'd entered. A series of pulleys hung above it, attached to buckets of who knew what. Maybe she was paranoid to set traps, or maybe she had reasons to be. Neither scared him. "I want to help."

She took a bite of ice cream, then handed him the carton and the spoon. "I know you do." Slowly, she crouched and settled on the floor, leaning against the cupboards.

Cowen joined her, taking a bite and passing it back. The bandage on her wrist lifted as she took it. "Want me to look at your wound?" he asked.

She pulled her hand away quickly and pressed the bandage on her leg, resealing the edges. Clearly it was another thing she didn't want him to know about. "You're dangerous for me to be around."

He leaned closer, glancing at her lips. "How so?"

"You know too much." She passed the ice cream back. "And it's probably best that I leave town."

Cowen stuck the spoon in the ice cream and set it on the floor. "Then I'd come searching for you."

She shook her head. "I'd change my name."

"You know that isn't how the witness protection program works. It costs a lot of money to relocate someone." He paused, the look in her eye saying that it wasn't a problem. "*Are* you in the witness protection program?"

Esty blinked, but otherwise her face was a stone. "I need to get to bed. Thanks for the ice cream. I'll see you on Monday." She stood, trying to end their conversation.

His training told him that her refusal to confirm her involvement in the program meant she wasn't in it, but what else would make her change her name? And he'd seen her driver's license. It was legit.

"Why Monday and not all the days in between?" he asked, settling on a safer subject.

She put the ice cream in the fridge, not the freezer, and started on washing the spoon. "Because all the custom things I ordered for my bakery are arriving tomorrow, and I'll be busy installing them so if I win, I can open shop."

Cowen put the ice cream in the freezer where it belonged. "What if I *lose?*"

She wouldn't meet his gaze. "I don't have answers for you. Goodnight, Cowen."

He didn't want to leave her on this note, but he respected that she was done. "Night, Mystery." He passed a pad of paper on the table and wrote his number down. "In case you're ever scared, here's my—"

"I don't get scared. And I already have it memorized." Color rose up her cheeks as she endlessly washed the same spoon.

If he was reading her correctly, she didn't actually want him to go. "You can call if you ever feel…unsafe." He stepped close, his lips near the nape of her neck. "Or if you want to help me process my grief. The thought of you gets me through each night."

The spoon clattered in the sink and Esty turned toward him. Her lips were pursed, her chest heaved. She grabbed his arm and led him to the couch, sitting snugly against him. "I'm a horrible friend. I completely forgot about your partner and your pain in all of this."

The ache was so much less with her near, and Cowen itched to put his arm around her. "I thought we were enemies."

Her walls seemed to come down as she looked up at him. "We are when it comes to business…"

"So outside of work, we're…something more?" He placed his upturned hand on his leg, fingers spread. It was there if she wanted to take it.

"We're neighbors." She slid her hand under his, flipping it over so he was holding his own knee, nothing more. "One of us will have to leave. There's no sense in making things complicated."

Cowen didn't buy her logic, but he let it slide. At least she was sitting next to him, not threatening him with a screwdriver or knife. "What are acceptable actions between neighbors? Do they ever hug? Or...kiss?"

She swatted his chest and settled her head on his shoulder. "Don't push your luck."

"I can settle for this. For now." He slid his arm around her and closed his eyes. Esty seemed to have a completely different playbook than every other woman, yet he was determined to study it from cover to cover so he didn't lose her.

Jasper curled up on the other end of the couch, and she turned on nineties hits on her phone before snuggling back into his arm. At ten, her phone buzzed with an alarm, and she sat up, shifting and cracking her neck.

"Is that how you prepare for a kiss?" he asked, fully expecting the glare she sent his way. "What about a hug?"

She pointed to the door.

"Okay, okay." He stood, stretching. His side felt colder without her next to him. "Will I see you tomorrow?" The hours until he saw her again already felt like too many.

"It depends on if you respect my wishes and leave."

"Understood." Cowen rushed to the door to show he'd obey, startling Jasper. The dog yowled as he waddled over. "I'll see you tomorrow. And I still think things are going to work out." He fixed her with what he hoped was a smoldering stare and left with Jasper following.

As soon as he got to his place, his phone rang with a call from Director Spandy. Cowen had already silenced four calls from him today.

"Look," his former boss said, "I know you don't want to work the case, and I respect you're taking a break—"

"Mark, I resigned." Cowen shut and locked his door. It was futile to point out how late it was. His old boss was always working.

"I know, but I was hoping if you see something, you'll report it. It'll be months before I can send someone out. Just take two minutes to look over the email I sent. If you see the tattoo on anyone, let me know."

"I'll think about it." Cowen hung up and raked his hand through his hair. Spying on his neighbors was not in his moral code—he was a civilian now. But wasn't he breaking that same code by not reporting his boss? He shrugged off the thought and pulled up Google. There were more pressing matters. He typed *pizza dough recipes* and hit enter. How hard could it be?

chapter ten

War

The air smelled of caramelized sugar and browned butter as Bridge sat on a stool in her pristine bakery, folding boxes with the logo she'd designed. She had nothing better to do. Her hips couldn't handle any more baked goods without customers to buy them. Plus, she'd already fixed every hinge and tightened every screw in the whole shop—anything with moving parts worked far better than it probably ever had. And every inch was clean enough to pass a white glove test.

Fold. Double fold. She put together another box, stacking it on the others. Her heart sat heavy. A future with Cowen wasn't possible if they both wanted to bake. As much as she wanted to stick to her plan and her business, he'd mixed himself into her life. He seemed willing to give up his dreams for a chance with her, but she couldn't let him. But what if she lost on purpose? Then Cowen could be happy, and that would make *her* happy.

And maybe the universe would give her a break.

Sacrificing her wants was the best idea she'd had all day.

Bridge's phone buzzed with a local number.

"Esty? It's me, Karen," the waitress panted, her words hurried. "Do you know anything about dogs?"

"Like how to take them for a walk? Or scratch their head?" Bridge wasn't about to admit she could name every breed and their strengths and weaknesses. It was just another thing she was an expert at—anything worth stealing was usually protected by guard dogs.

"I should have said puppies. Both of my goldendoodles had babies last week and all sixteen survived. I swear it was the full moon. My husband, Virg, is watching them while I work, but his schedule changed and his nightshift in Tillamook starts an hour before I get home, and I've already called everyone I know. Would you be available to help?"

Bridge traced the edge of her ledger, though she wouldn't cross anything off for assisting a neighbor. "Of course. You're right across the street?"

"Yes, number two-seventy-seven. Five p.m. I owe you."

"Forget about it." Bridge coughed, her New Jersey accent more legit than she'd intended. "I'll be there."

As soon as she hung up, her thoughts drifted back to the baking competition. What if she lost but stayed in Pilpil Bay? She was a quick learner and could start a different business. It was really the only way she could explore anything with Cowen since the other option was to leave town. But how could she go? She already had friends, already had people asking her for help. The mayor had called her earlier to fix something at his house. She was useful here, and that made her happy—as long as people didn't demand or finagle the use of her skills. Like that would happen here.

Her mind kept running through *what-ifs* as she continued to fold boxes. What if she relocated and no one talked to her there? Or she didn't fit in? Pilpil Bay was already more of a home and community than anywhere else she'd ever lived. Her family had never had a home. Sure, they'd lived in several houses, but there was never one place to return to that held all of her memories. Or where she'd felt safe. There had never been a place to leave the ledger, knowing it would always be there when she returned.

The ledger. If she were focusing on that, this decision would already be made. Clearly, baking made Cowen happy, and he needed it to heal. If she lost, he could open his shop and that would justify marking off several lines in the book. That had been her focus for so long—to clear the slate. Losing on purpose was the best choice. But if she couldn't create a different, successful business, she would have to leave. Would he really be happy then? He seemed determined to get to know her.

A groan pushed through her clenched jaw. Why did everything have to be so hard?

Bridge stood to march over to Cowen's and sat back down, her decisions and resolves ping-ponging back and forth between the different courts. Maybe leaving and living forever with the unknowns was better than trying and failing miserably at a new business and a relationship. She could slip away tonight. Leave a note that the town could sell the building and donate the money to charity. She could move to a different country. Somewhere in Europe would be good so she could easily travel and brush up on her German, Italian, and French. Spanish too if her skin could tolerate Spain's heat. Fifteen hundred dollars wouldn't go very far, so she'd either have to work her way over or steal a little.

The pit in her stomach wouldn't let her consider this plan further. Bridge knew Cowen would try and find her, though he'd be hard pressed to track her, even with his FBI connections. And that would mean he'd be too busy to bake and therefore unhappy.

Why did the universe hate her when she was trying to fix things?

Bridge pulled out the ledger from her pocket. Cowen had commented about the casing she was still toting around, but he hadn't mentioned the book that had to be far more noticeable. About half of the pages were full of all the people she'd hurt. There was the security guard who was in the wrong place at the wrong time. She'd inflicted a concussion that put him in the hospital for four days when he wouldn't stay down. At least she hadn't killed him like many other thieves would.

There were enough out there that didn't care what they did to people who got in their way.

For months after his concussion, she stole enough to cover the man's medical expenses and paid off his house. And she'd secretly covered the cost of items "borrowed" during other heists like cars and bikes. But there were some things she couldn't restore to the people she'd hurt. No amount of money could make up for the heritage of a stolen painting that was already sold so many times she could no longer track it. She was still working on making amends.

Her heart was torn the most when it came to Harley. She couldn't understand how the girl had become a ghost after Mason's death. If only she knew Bridge wanted to help.

She fingered the ledger again. If she told Cowen about it, he'd probably think twice about his interest in her. And he might turn her over to the authorities, though the only proof would be her word. His reaction would make any decisions she had to make easier. With a brave breath, she stood and marched over to his bakery, but as soon as she pushed the door open a crack, a female laugh echoed back. Quietly, she snuck through the dining room and peered into the kitchen. Cowen stood on one side of the island, a burger in his hand, and Alex stood on the other, eating sweet potato fries.

Doubts weaved through her chest. Had he invited Alex over? Maybe he was playing Bridge, making sure he won. There was so much she didn't know about Cowen Amaratti that every suspicion bouncing through her head seemed plausible. Like a mouse, she tiptoed backward, pushed her way out, and stepped onto the sidewalk.

A throat cleared behind her. "Come with me."

Bridge turned to find Gertie, her lips flat and unreadable. "Uh, where are we going?"

"You need a haircut." Gertie was dressed in a polyester, lime green jumpsuit, straight from the seventies, as she held and stroked the fur of one of her fake cat figurines.

"I um…I like the length."

Gertie grabbed a fistful of Bridge's split ends. "It's supposed to be pretty, not a mangy tail. Come." She walked off toward her salon and Bridge followed. It *had* been a long time since she got a decent hair cut. Most often, she trimmed it herself. *And* Gertie probably needed some business. Most tourists probably ran after one glance at her stroking a fake cat.

They walked into the salon and Bridge scanned the creepy wall, focusing again on the jade feline in the corner. It still looked familiar, but she had a crazy notion that the cat in her memory had a chip on its ear. This one was perfectly intact.

"You've noticed my favorite." She motioned Bridge to the sink and once situated, began washing her hair. "It's a replica. The real one is worth over four million and was stolen from The British Museum in 1998." Gertie turned the temperature up, massaging Bridge's head. "Have you seen anything like it before?"

Bridge relaxed. "I think I might have seen the real thing."

Gertie shut the water off, watching her.

"I went to that museum in the nineties." Her parents had often mixed business with family vacations, pulling a few jobs in Europe. What were the chances her parents had stolen the statue when visiting England? There were many jobs she didn't know about, being too young to understand what was going on.

Gertie plopped some shampoo on Bridge's head. "Actually, my memory has failed me. That particular piece was stolen from a private collection back east. My mistake."

"You know your art."

"I know a lot of things," Gertie said as she ran her nails along Bridge's scalp.

At 4:45 p.m., Bridge knocked on Karen's sage green door with a plate of assorted treats she'd made in her bakery, her hair two inches shorter, now reaching the middle of her back. Cracks lined the crumbling cement porch, but there were vibrant colored pots of flowers that would keep some people from noticing.

"Come in," shouted a voice from inside.

Bridge let herself in, her eyes widening. The living room was covered in wood paneling from the seventies. Knick knacks lined shelves, shag carpet decayed on the floor, and two kiddie pools sat in the middle, each with a momma goldendoodle and a sea of babies. A man with a bald top and long hair sat in a worn recliner, bottle feeding several puppies.

"The name's Virgil. And you're an angel. Virgil. Angel. Look, they rhyme." He pointed to a spot of sofa. "Make yourself at home. Both mommas are worn out, and there's not enough milk to go around." He shifted and held up a bottle. "The vet done told us to give them this mixture. I've got plenty made, but in case you need more, the powder is in a bag in the kitchen. Mind if I go get ready?"

"Not at all." Bridge worked with him to scoop the puppies up and resettle them on her lap, their adorable whines tugging on her heartstrings. "How can you walk away from them each day?"

Virgil shook his head. "It's mighty hard." He left to change and came back five minutes later in a blue, security guard uniform. "Watch for the ones who are rooting but not nursing. They're the hungry ones. Those two," he said, pointing to the puppies in her lap, "belong to this mother." He showed her where they went and she returned them, picking up two more.

Bridge struggled to look at him in his outfit. She had too many memories of hurting or sabotaging guards. "I'll take good care of them."

He gave her a nod and left through the back door, hollering a goodbye. The sound of an old V8 pickup roared. That was another skill Bridge had. Knowing the different sounds of engines had saved her more than once.

She didn't want to have anything to do with that life anymore. More than anything, she wanted to set down roots here, in Pilpil Bay. Being a part of a community seemed like a fairy tale, and the fact she was living in one now made her foolish to question leaving. But weren't those stories too good to be true? Was her story destined to fail?

By the time Karen returned, Bridge had fed any puppy who was hungry and gave both moms a good scratch. She'd also hashed and rehashed the arguments on every side without finding a solution.

"You're a lifesaver," Karen said as she collapsed onto the sofa beside Bridge, her dress smelling of charbroiled burgers. She picked up one of the caramel-drizzled chocolate croissants Bridge had brought and took a bite. Her eyes widened. "You made this?"

Bridge nodded. "Is it okay?"

"Okay? I don't think I've ever eaten anything better. This is amazing." She ate more, savoring bites until only gooey residue remained on her fingers. Instead of wiping it on a napkin, she licked it off, sighing. "How are things going with you-know-who? I saw him leave your place late last night."

Bridge stood, not knowing how to handle this personal conversation, especially when too many worries about the future were creeping in. "Don't read into what you saw. We're enemies." And he'd eaten lunch with Alex. He was one strike away from having too many against him.

Karen laughed. "Sure ya are. I heard all about his expression when he saw you the morning you returned. Sydney said he was so happy, he looked like he was going to cry."

"Sydney has a big mouth." Bridge bent and rubbed one of the mommas again, trying to quell the heat rising to her face. "And it's not going to go anywhere. We can't both stay. And I think he's interested in someone else."

"*Can't* is a dirty word. And I don't buy that *other woman* bit for a second. I bet something will work out."

Bridge gave her a mock glare. "You sound like Cowen."

"I like him even more." She motioned to the door. "You should get going. I noticed *someone* trying to find you earlier." Karen lifted both eyebrows repeatedly. "And don't pretend to hide your feelings. I know you like him."

Bridge paused, her hand on the doorknob. "He's easy to like. But things are complicated."

"Of course, they are. It's called *life*." Karen picked up a puppy and started another round of feeding. "Since it's all difficult, you might as well choose to include some things that bring you joy. Or rather, include some *people*."

"Does that mean you want me to stay?" Bridge smirked, challenging her friend's comment.

"Always, but you know who I'm talking about. I'll see you tomorrow."

The goodbye forced Bridge outside and into a light rain. At home, she exercised and showered quickly, dressing in leggings and a baggy green t-shirt. A knock sounded as she sat down with a bowl of popcorn, her laptop ready to watch a movie.

Cowen's face filled the peephole, making her stomach flip.

"Hey," she said as she answered and scratched behind Jasper's ears. She still had the image of Cowen and Alex burning a hole in her head.

"I missed you today." He looked past her like he wanted to come in.

She placed her hand on the doorframe, barring the way. "I'm sure you did."

"What did I do wrong this time?" His face was relaxed instead of angry as he tilted his head. "If you're looking for an easy way to get rid of me, stonewalling isn't it."

"I saw you having lunch with Alex."

He winced, but not like he seemed guilty, more like annoyed. "She stopped by while I was eating and stole some fries. I've told her multiple times I'm interested in someone else, but she's struggling to take the hint." His eyebrow lifted as if he realized something. "How did you see us?"

"I see and know everything."

He got two points for telling the truth. Mason Rossi had repeatedly lied to her when they were together. She'd been too young, too naive to point out his faults because she was happy to have someone give her attention. But he'd betrayed her, using her and her family. And he'd killed her mom to escape. There were so many differences between the way he treated her versus Cowen's actions.

Bridge dropped her arm and walked into her house, leaving the door open. Jasper and Cowen followed. The dog sprawled out next to Bridge on the couch, leaving only a small space beside her.

"Do you mind?" Cowen asked, pointing at the tiny spot. When she shrugged, he pulled his gun from behind his back and placed it on the coffee table before sitting beside her. Slowly, as if asking for permission, he draped his arm along the back of the couch.

She pulled up Netflix on her laptop.

"What are we watching?" he asked.

She passed him the popcorn she'd made. "*Love at First Sight.*" It was the next movie on her romance list. Tonight, she was willing to entertain options with Cowen to help her make a decision about staying or leaving. Winning or losing.

He leaned closer. "Perfect."

By the time the end credits rolled, her head was on his shoulder and his arm was wrapped around her. Jasper snored in her lap. "What did you think?" she asked.

Cowen traced the hem of her sleeve with his finger. "I'm thinking we have a similar story. We met and had a moment, and now we're here, getting a second chance."

Bridge sat forward and put her head in her hands. She wanted that, wanted an opportunity to explore options with him, but she also wanted what was best for Cowen. "There's so much you don't know about me."

He touched her back. "That's usually how it goes."

"My stuff is big," she said, shaking her head. "Dangerously big."

"I'm sure I can handle it."

Without shifting her gaze from him, Bridge grabbed the gun off the coffee table, pulled out the clip, took the whole thing apart, and reassembled it without a single glance. "You should be asking yourself why I can do something like this. If it doesn't scare you, you can come back tomorrow." She stood and opened the door, her heart pounding. This was the part where he could make his own decision and forget about her.

Cowen looked Bridge over, and she could tell the cogs were spinning in his head. At any moment, he could run out that door and never come back. He retrieved his gun and met her with Jasper at his side. "That doesn't scare me," he whispered in her ear as he passed, sending her stomach into fandangos. "I'll see you tomorrow."

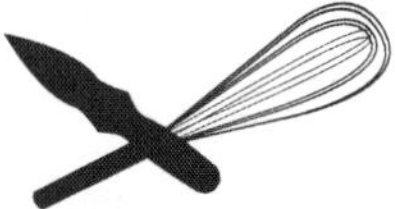

It took Bridge four tries to make the perfect batch of chocolate chip cookies in her bakery the next day, learning each time how the ovens fluctuated and how the flour and eggs rose on this part of the continent. She didn't want to win or lose. She just wanted to bake and sell browned butter ginger oatmeal cookies, dulce de leche scones, blueberry muffins with lemon glaze, and chocolate cobbler with Mexican vanilla whipped cream. Plus a million more sweets. Couldn't the universe give her that? She was trying to make amends. She was trying to do right. Couldn't she get a break?

Cowen tugged at her thoughts as she cleaned up. It seemed that anything she did could hurt him. Leaving and staying both had consequences. What should she do?

Karen invited her over to play with the puppies after her shift at the restaurant and Bridge said yes, helping her friend bottle feed the tiniest ones while watching Cowen stop by her vacant house three times.

"I'm not going to say anything about it," Karen said, nibbling one of the cookies Bridge had brought, "other than I hope you notice what lengths he's going to. And maybe you should pay attention to the scents coming from his kitchen."

"You mean the burned garlic? How is that even possible to miss?"

Karen laughed. "That man is willing to give up his passion for you. That says a lot."

Bridge didn't want him to give up anything for her, someone he hardly knew. He deserved better with a life that gave him everything. She wasn't worth ruining his dreams. "But that's not fair," she said, flinging her arm. The bottle in her hand slipped from her grasp and flew, turning over and over in the air. It thudded against a large urn on the top shelf of one of Karen's bookcases. The jar teetered, rocking back and forth. Bridge jolted to grab it, but she was too late. The urn tumbled, the lid flying and ash spreading through the air. It landed on the floor, the vessel splintering into dozens of pieces. Dust filled the room so thick, the light turned ten shades darker.

"Whose ashes are they?" Bridge struggled to ask as she searched Karen's despondent eyes.

"My…" she strained to speak. "My mother's."

Bridge's body caved. She put herself in Karen's shoes, her heart heavy, weighed down with the constant guilt that had consumed her life. Her own mother's death had been her fault for trusting Mason, for dropping her guard because she'd wanted him. No matter what she did, she could never atone for that. Her grief swirled with the dust in the air, pressing in on her weaknesses. Why was she always ruining everything?

"Don't worry, I'll fix it." Frantically, Bridge returned the puppies to their mother, her fingers fumbling with every motion. She couldn't imagine how much Karen must hate her. "Do you have an air filter?" If she could pull the remains from the air, theoretically she could blow them out and into a bag. Bridge bent and picked up the jar's shards. It would take days to reassemble, but she could get it to function again, and with some supplies, she could make the jar look like new from a distance.

A hand touched her shoulder. "Esty, it's okay."

"No." Bridge shook her head as she collected the pieces, wrapping them in her shirt.

"Put them down, it's okay."

Bridge sniffed. She hated herself for what she'd done. "I'm so sorry. I'll do whatever it takes to make this right."

Karen kneeled beside her. "You need to stop. My mother wanted me to release her ashes. She didn't say where, only that she wanted to be free. I've tried multiple times, but I could never get myself to do it. You did it for me."

It was a nice gesture to placate Bridge's feelings, but she didn't deserve it. "She probably didn't mean for you to spread her remains in your house."

It took a moment for Karen to respond, and when she did, she laughed. "I don't know. You never met my mother." She placed her hands over Bridge's. "Please stop beating yourself up. This is a blessing for me. And even if it wasn't, it was an accident. I would never get mad over a mistake."

"But this is her remains. Your way to remember her. I have to fix this. I—"

Karen picked up the biggest shard, stood, and placed it on the shelf. "The pot was a little ostentatious for my taste. This suits me better. And now I have a funny memory to tie with it when my friend and I laughed over an accident." She waited for Bridge to look at her. "I'm happy. You should be too. But if it makes you feel better, I'll let you vacuum."

Bridge wobbled to her feet. "I...I don't know what to say."

"Where do you keep the cleaning supplies is probably the most fitting right about now," Karen said, giving her a warm smile and pointing down the hall. "First door on your left. The vacuum is one of those R2D2 shaped ones from the eighties. You're gonna love it."

Bridge sat on the couch in her rental, her hair wet from a shower. She still couldn't help thinking the whole urn-breaking incident was a catastrophe and Karen wouldn't talk to her again. Her friend had called and texted twice and even Virg had visited to reinforce that his wife really was okay. That things were better this way. Bridge struggled to believe it.

A knock sounded, and she opened the door to Cowen and Jasper.

"What's wrong?" he asked, instantly folding her into his arms.

She wasn't used to all the hugs she'd received in this small town, but somehow, with Cowen, it felt normal to be tucked inside his embrace.

"Karen didn't say?" She'd half expected the entire town to know—that's how it was in the movies.

"No, what happened?"

Bridge rested her head against his neck. "I accidentally broke her mother's urn."

He held her tighter. "How did she react?"

"That's the weird part." Bridge let go and sat on the couch. "She said it's okay and even better this way because her mom didn't want to be trapped in a jar. But I feel horrible."

Cowen sat beside her, and with his hand, softly turned her face toward him. "Did you know that your constant caring for people makes you prettier?"

It didn't feel pretty on the inside. If she ate a whole pound of butter cake—or even straight butter—it would probably make her feel lighter than the weight of everything she wanted to amend in the ledger.

"Can we watch a movie?" she asked, her voice higher than normal.

He watched her like he was concerned about something, but he kept his mouth shut. Like the night before, Jasper curled up next to her, Cowen snuggled beside her, and they watched The Proposal.

"She kind of reminds me of you," he said after the movie finished, referring to Sandra Bullock.

Bridge got up without responding and left the room, returning with a lock and her picking kit. Her thoughts were still swallowed up in spilled ashes—she still couldn't believe that Karen was okay with it. And how could Cowen be okay with her? He deserved to know who and what she was.

"Another show and tell?" he asked.

"Hold please." Bridge kept her lips in a flat line as she placed the lock in his hands. He'd come back for another movie, so until she scared him off, she'd continue to show him what she could do. Their fingers touched as she worked. Four, three, two, one. She yanked and the lock came undone.

Cowen's jaw dropped. "Will you do that again?" He secured the lock and held it as she repeated the process. "I've never seen anyone do that so fast."

She stood and walked to her door, holding it open. "If you're not afraid, you can come back tomorrow for more." At any time, he might get scared and leave. But then it was his choice, not hers to end this, whatever it was. Then it wouldn't be her fault and another thing to feel guilty about.

His lips shifted as if deep in thought. He met her with Jasper at his side. "Is this hard for you to show me what you can do?" Cowen had to know that anyone with her skill set was either a government agent or someone completely opposite. The fact she wasn't telling him outright had to give the vibes that she was on the wrong side of the law. But he hadn't run. Not yet.

Bridge looked away and gave an almost imperceptible nod. "I've seen enough movies to know that lies always come out. I want to be honest with you. I *will* be honest with you if you're patient. This is a lot for me, but you should know what you're getting into. I'm not worth throwing away your dreams for. This whole pizza thing has to stop. Tomorrow, you need to play to win."

"Funny thing about dreams," he said, moving closer as if ignoring her comment. "They can shift and change and still be just as good." His lips grazed her cheek, dancing shivers along every nerve in her body. "Thanks for sharing this side of you." He stepped back, searching her eyes. "I'm still not scared." The wind played with the flowers near the foundation as he left her standing breathless in the doorway.

Cowen stood at his kitchen sink, sipping a glass of water while thinking about Esty. Who was she? What was she?

He wasn't naive enough to believe she had an innocent past. Shouldn't that bother him? It might if he knew nothing else about her. Karen and Mayor Dinwiddie kept telling him about the ways she'd gladly assisted them with various problems. People who were willing to help others deserved second chances in his book.

His phone dinged with another text from Director Spandy. *Have you found anything yet?*

Not yet, Cowen responded.

Like the incriminating papers on Director Spandy's desk, there were some things that he couldn't unsee. He still hadn't opened the director's email for that very reason. If it had anything to do with Esty, he didn't want to know yet, especially without understanding the specifics of her past. And with regards to the information he had about the director, he still wasn't sure of the best approach to address it.

He tucked that responsibility away, focusing on his plan to lose the competition without Esty knowing it was rigged.

The morning of the first battle arrived, the late June sun rising. Bridge opened her door to a note. Her smile widened, expecting it to be from Cowen, but the message was from the town council.

Every business has to deal with the unexpected. We've invited the neighboring towns to join in the tasting, so you'll be required to make four hundred cookies by 12:30 p.m. If you don't, you'll be disqualified for the day.

Bridge's nose wrinkled. Who thought they were God and could make pronouncements like this? She hadn't signed up to be a slave to the city council's wishes. But if they were questioning her skills, she would show them. She planned to win the first competition, so Cowen didn't suspect she was playing the martyr, and then lose the others. Cowen would become the resident baker, and then…well, after that, she didn't know. He was seeing bits and pieces of her and not turning away. She couldn't just leave without knowing what could happen next.

She hurried to the bakery to calculate if it was even possible to make that many cookies with her ingredients, but the back door refused to budge. That didn't make sense. She double-checked that the key had worked. There was a little play when she turned the knob, but it stayed stuck. The idea of kicking it down crossed her mind. She'd done it twice before to different doors, though both had been worn wood, and this was heavy metal. Plus, it might cause a scene.

The timer in her head ticked as she booked it around the back of all the buildings and stepped onto Main Street, finding a crowd assembled in front of her bakery.

"What's going on?" she asked as she joined them, following their focus to the windows. She scanned the drippy brown words—*I give up*—painted on the biggest pane. "Mark Wahlberg," she cursed under her breath. "I did *not* write that," she said loud enough for everyone to hear. She pulled off her jacket and wiped the window, but nothing happened. The words were on the inside.

"Who would do something like this?" A woman with poufy, graying hair asked.

"Maybe it's the other baker," someone else suggested.

Why would Cowen do this? He'd been such a gentleman. So… perfect. Too good to be true? She shook her head, unable to picture him betraying her.

"I'm going to skin alive whoever did this." Bridge unlocked the front door and stepped inside, her foot slipping. Her hand shot out and she gripped the doorframe, preventing a fall. A glance down showed the entire dining room was covered in wet, slimy mud.

The crowd gasped and someone supported Bridge from behind.

"We'll help," a woman said.

"Just wait here," said another.

Bridge sensed them leave, and she carefully stepped her way to the window, smearing the message with her jacket. The beat of her heart pounded in her head. Her brain whirred with calculations. There wasn't enough time to clean up *and* make four hundred cookies.

Was she so blind to have painted the wrong picture in her head about Cowen? She didn't want to believe it. She'd been thwarted before—that was the name of the thief game. Art and money were constantly in motion, being stolen here for revenge, there for greed, and most often for a payout. But this? She'd never had anyone betray her, other than Mason.

Some of the mud had dried at the edges of the room so Bridge walked along it to the back where the disgusting brown sludge covered every surface.

The broken handle of her previously perfect mop was jammed against the back door. Pain rushed to her face as she clenched her jaw so tight that she could hear her teeth grind.

Whoever did this was going to regret meeting her. And if it was Cowen—though she highly doubted it—he wouldn't get away with toying with her heart.

Bridge opened a drawer near the sink and sighed. The stack of towels she'd bought were still clean and dry. She turned on the water and started on the island. The front door opened, and she heard the muffled voices of the members of her town. A peek showed her they were working their way in with a mop brigade. Clean water went in. Dirty went out.

By the time she had all the counters cleared and sanitized, her community reached the kitchen, led by Sydney.

"I heard what happened and came running. You don't believe Cowen did this, do you?"

Bridge shrugged, her shoulders jerky. "I don't know what to believe right now."

"I saw the chemistry between you," Sydney said. "This wasn't him."

Chemistry. She'd had that with Mason—at least that's what strangers had said. But it had been all one-sided with her pining after him.

"What's the best spot to clean first so you can get baking?" Sydney asked.

Doubts about Cowen slithered through Bridge's thoughts as she surveyed the remaining muddy mess. "You all don't have to help, this is my problem."

"Esty, this is our community." Sydney placed her hand on Bridge's shoulder. "We look out for each other. Well, except for whoever did this."

Bridge dipped her head. This is what she'd wanted her whole life— well, not the betrayal part, though she was still holding out for some sort of explanation. Maybe someone got a little high and had some fun. This *was* Oregon. "Thanks." She sighed, shifting her anger into productivity, and got to work gathering ingredients on the counters while her neighbors worked around her. She had her first batch mixing as they finished.

"Do you have enough time to bake everything?" Sydney asked as she washed her hands.

Bridge wiped her brow with the back of her arm. "It'll be close."

Sydney took an apron off a hook and pulled it over her head. "I can stay and help."

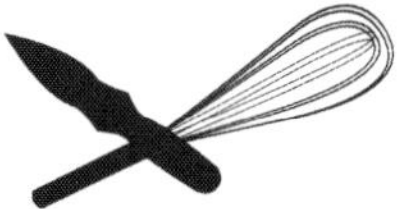

A warm mist fell as a crowd assembled in front of A Pinch of This and Cowen's unnamed bakery. The street was blocked off, creating pedestrian-only traffic near rows of wet flowers drooping in their beds. Even though the note said to make four hundred cookies, Bridge only counted ninety-nine teens and adults surrounding the plastic canopy in the middle of Main Street. Kids moved too fast to count, but there were probably only a couple dozen.

Cowen placed his last tray of cookies on the table. Their desserts were hidden from the crowd's view with a temporary blockade made of sheets tied to the canopy's poles. It had been the mayor's idea to make the voting fair.

"I feel like everyone is glaring at me," Cowen said as he moved next to her.

"That's an odd perception." Bridge tried and failed to keep her frustrations out of her words. The doubts about him had grown while she'd baked, imagining he was playing her like Mason had. "Maybe you should discuss your observations with a therapist."

"You're using that tone of voice with me again. Are you mad?"

She crossed her arms over her chest. "Maybe I am, maybe I'm not. It all depends."

Cowen got in her face, his puzzled expression not consistent with someone who'd sabotaged her. But some people were excellent actors—Bridge had learned that the hard way. "On what?" he asked.

Before she could answer, Karen rushed up beside them, bouncing on her toes. "What did I miss?" She glanced at Cowen and pulled Bridge out of his hearing distance. "What did he leave you?" A bigger than normal grin lit her face.

"What do you mean?" Bridge asked, glancing back at Cowen as he watched them. But unless he could read lips, there was no chance he could hear what they said over the crowd's chatter.

Karen glanced from side to side. Her forehead glistened, and the thrumming in her veins was visible on her neck. If she hadn't just run over, Bridge would suspect she was about to lie. "I uh…I saw him taking something into your uh…your bakery."

"Russell Crowe," Bridge swore, the pain of his betrayal stabbing as she swallowed it down. She'd cuddled with him, even shared a spoon, and he'd swarmed her thoughts since the day they met. But none of it was real. It was all pretend to him so he could get what he wanted. That's how Mason had been, and Bridge was stupid to fall for someone like him again.

She put on her nonchalant face and steadied her voice. Since Cowen hadn't let on about the sabotage, she didn't want him to suspect she was aware of his deception. She'd use it to her advantage. "That is very good to know."

"Is everything okay?" Karen asked.

"Yeah." Bridge assured her friend with a practiced smile.

"I have to get back. I just came to wish you luck. Tell me later how it goes?" Karen gave Bridge a quick side hug and returned to the restaurant.

Karen's testimony was everything Bridge needed to put the blame on Cowen, and the pain sunk deep through her veins and into her bones. Acid reached her throat, but she swallowed it down. He wouldn't get the best of her. And she would make sure he'd regret ever meeting her.

The mayor tapped the mic. "Thank you everyone for coming out," he said. Today's outfit was a grass sun hat, a floral button-up shirt, cargo shorts, and flip-flops with toe socks. "As you know, we have a dilemma, and in typical Pilpil Bay fashion, we're solving it together. Leave a donation for the bakers and take one of the large cookies and two or three of the small ones. There must have been some sort of miscommunication there."

The tips of Bridge's ears burned. Was the letter from "the city" part of the sabotage too? Cowen was so going to pay.

"When you've made your choice on which you like better overall, check the appropriate box on the provided papers and cast your ballot. We'll announce the winner as soon as everyone has voted and the tallies are in. And in case you're wondering, tomorrow's treat will be cupcakes." He pointed to the setup next to the cookie table. "Unveil the desserts now." The mayor pointed to Alex, and she pulled the covering away, revealing the treats.

Kids rushed up first, followed by a couple men with distinct signs of hygiene issues. The rest of the town took their turn, most slipping money into the donation jar. Cowen opened his mouth to say something to her, but Bridge darted into the crowd. How dare he try to talk to her? He didn't deserve to be in her presence.

When Bridge reached the table and bit into one of Cowen's cookies, she knew he had her beat. It was probably the best chocolate chip cookie she'd eaten in her whole life. His were ginormous, crispy on the outside, soft on the inside, and overly sweet. But the flecks of salt on top did more than balance the sugar out. They were like tiny, happy explosions in her mouth—made by her sucker-punching enemy.

Accepting defeat was an important skill required to regroup and focus on a different attack. And that's exactly what Bridge did as the mayor announced Cowen the winner amongst jeers and taunts.

He should have known what he was starting when he attacked her bakery.

Because now, this was war.

A Bake War.

chapter eleven

Revenge

As soon as the winner was announced, Alex snaked her hand through Cowen's arm. "I knew you'd win."

He glanced out at the sea of angry faces and politely pulled away from her. "Why is everyone so upset?"

Esty was nowhere to be seen, and his mind spun with one thought. How was she handling the results of the competition?

Alex grabbed his hand and tugged him into his bakery. "Oh, you know. Women want women to succeed."

Cowen yanked his hand free and entered his dirty kitchen. She wasn't getting the message that he disliked her touch. "But some men were upset too."

Alex hoisted herself onto a clean spot of counter, her bare legs dangling in front of him. "They reflect the interest of their wives. Don't worry. I'm sure it will all smooth over soon. Your cookies were amazing. This town needs them."

He turned his back toward her, placing anything that could be washed into the sink. "Esty's were incredible too." He'd figured she would catch on fast if he was losing intentionally, so he went for the kill today. "I should go check on her."

"You need to focus on getting ready for tomorrow. I'll check on Esty." Alex hopped down and sidled up close, pressing her body against his side. "I'm so proud of you." She squeezed his arm and left him to clean up the mess.

Cowen shook his head. She was a problem he needed to deal with. Every day he'd repeated that he was interested in someone else and turned down every one of her offers. Apparently that wasn't enough to dissuade her. The next time she came around, he'd make his refusal unmistakable, even if it hurt her feelings.

As soon as he got the big items washed, he dried his hands and called Esty. No answer. He tried a text. *Hey, I hope you're doing okay with today's results. I liked your cookies. Want to get dinner before our movie tonight?*

Twenty minutes passed without a reply, so he stepped outside and tried her back door, giving it a knock. No answer. He tested the handle. Locked. Cowen went around to the front. Also locked.

A woman in a pale purple dress approached, giving him a sneer. It was a good thing he'd only won a contest. If he'd done something wrong, he imagined he'd see pitchforks.

He spent the next two hours listening to The Eagles and Third Dog Night while cleaning and placing his ingredients order for the morning. He wouldn't have to do much to lose the cupcake competition. He was used to making things taste good—not look good.

After locking up, he called Esty again and went by her house, but her car was gone. And it didn't return at dinner or when the sun went to bed.

"Hey," he said, leaving a voicemail. "I haven't seen or heard from you. Are you okay? I'll wait up." By ten, his gut was telling him something was wrong. She'd acted mad at the cookie tasting, and he wasn't sure what her emotions would tell her to do.

Jasper hopped into the back of the Jeep, and they drove along the coast, looking for signs of her car. But she wasn't anywhere. He called again.

"I'm sorry for winning today. This competition is dumb, and I say we stop. I'll set up shop in a different town, or I'll figure this pizza thing out. It's stupid that business could come between us. Call me."

He made another loop on the highway that surrounded the town when his phone rang. Cowen pulled over to the side of the road and rested his head against the steering wheel. "You had me worried."

"Sorry, I've been busy preparing for tomorrow," Esty said, her voice perfectly even. "My cupcakes take extra time."

"Where are you? Have you eaten? I can come—"

"I'm fine. I'll see you tomorrow," she said and hung up.

Fine? He knew that was the female code word for pissed off. Of course she was still mad that he'd won. He shoved the Jeep into drive and headed toward the rental he'd stayed at along the ocean. The hill nearby was the perfect place to shoot. He double-checked that the area was clear, that his bullets couldn't somehow hurt anyone, and fired off the entire magazine. Jasper helped him find all the casings, and he shoved them in his pocket. When he returned to town, Esty's car wasn't on Main Street or in the alley behind the bakeries, but it was parked in front of her house where all the lights were off.

He got Jasper settled and placed the casings in the shape of a heart on her doorstep. The wind came up, knocking them over. His eyes drooped as he returned to his house and made a paste with flour and water then glued them to her porch, waiting until each had dried and wouldn't move before going back to his place. He reloaded his gun and slipped it under his pillow, hoping she'd appreciate his simple message.

But in the morning, the casings were strewn around the yard, and her car was already gone. She might not have even noticed a single one.

Cowen rubbed at his face and walked into town, unlocking the back door of his bakery and entering with his thoughts focused on Esty. She was the first thing he saw in his kitchen, but his gaze was quickly diverted to the oven parts strewn all over the counters. Even the doors were off.

His shoes slapped the slippery floor. "What—"

Esty put her finger to her lips and pointed to a handwritten sign on the wall, *There's a bug. Play along and trust me.* "Did you think you'd get away with sabotaging my bakery?" She wore an apron with pockets full of eggs and held a broom with the sludge of dozens of them broken at her feet. Hundreds more littered the floor.

Cowen had no idea how to respond. Sure, he understood from the beginning that life around Esty was never going to be normal, that she was highly suspicious and full of twists and turns. But this mess? And a bug in his bakery? That was a little far-fetched.

As if understanding he was struggling to believe, she pointed to the shelves above her head. "Are you seriously going to deny smearing my floors with mud?"

He took a step closer to inspect the small black dot that almost blended in with his bottles of spices. When he lifted a hand to be sure, she pulled an egg out of her apron and threw it at his feet.

"The broken eggs are my response to the mud," she said, shaking her head as if warning him not to get closer.

He shrugged his shoulders *and* eyebrows. What did she want from him? He had no idea what she was talking about, so he had no way of responding. And who would bug his bakery? Nothing made sense.

Esty pulled out her phone and typed, her eyes trained on him. "The ovens are my payback for the note telling me to make over four hundred cookies."

His phone buzzed with a message. *Deny it.*

He wanted to think this was a game, but she *had* made way too many cookies. "I don't know what you're talking about, but I didn't—"

"Like I'm going to believe anything you say." She gave him a thumbs up, though her voice was dark and cold. "Good luck on today's competition. I'd get started on fixing those ovens soon if I were you." She held her finger up like she was going to do or say something else, but she turned and huffed out of the kitchen. The front door slammed a moment later.

Cowen hurried toward the black dot on the shelves. He'd placed enough bugs to recognize the tech immediately, a Saint Petersburg 1080HD. Anyone could buy them on Amazon, probably even at Walmart. His heart raced. Why was there surveillance in his shop? Was someone watching him to get to Esty?

He pulled out his phone, ready to send her a text to get answers when a hand slipped along his shoulder blade. Fight or flight kicked in and he flipped around, throwing a punch. Esty expertly dodged his fist. His stomach plummeted with the thought of the damage he could have done. She stepped close and touched his cheek, her breaths colliding with his. Her other hand lifted, showing him her phone as her fingers pressed the screen, her eyes on him. A moment later, his device buzzed with a text.

I'll explain everything later. Clean up while I put your ovens back together. You should act mad. Maybe mutter and make noise. Pretend I'm not here.

Cowen put his arm around her waist and pulled her close. "Are you safe?" he whispered.

Shrugging, she leaned into him and accepted his hug. Her touch sparked a flame in his chest, spreading throughout his whole body. If he became a diabetic, he would grudgingly give up sweets, but her hugs…he wasn't sure if he could live without them now that he'd had a taste.

"Act mad," she whispered before picking up a screwdriver and slamming it on the island.

"Esty!" Yeah, he could act upset because he had no flipping idea what was going on. What if the bug was there specifically for him? What if the director was aware of what he knew? "I'll get you back," he said, playing into the charade.

She gave him another thumbs up before getting to work, her hands flying. He was supposed to be cleaning, but he struggled to take his gaze off her. She slammed the first oven door in place and motioned with her hand for him to say something else.

"Doesn't trust me..." he muttered. "Like I'm the untrustworthy type. I've done nothing wrong. Who is she to mess up my place?" What if someone *was* after him—someone he'd arrested? Or maybe Antoine Benoit's family was watching him, waiting for a chance to retaliate. He hoped he wasn't putting Esty in harm's way.

She held her hand up, signaling that was enough, and pointed to the broom. Right. Cleaning. By the time she'd finished reassembling both ovens, he'd managed to corral most of the sludge into one spot. It was hard for him to focus as dangerous scenarios played through his head. Each one ended with their deaths because he was too scared to pull another trigger. And that made him gag. At first it was silent, but his stomach rose along with the panic in his chest, and he leaned over the garbage can and heaved. Esty was instantly at his side, her face concerned as she rubbed his back.

Weak stomach, he tapped out in morse code on her shin, though that wasn't really him. The vomiting had started after the shootout, never before.

Worry etched her face as they resumed, working together to scoop the broken eggs into the dustpan before tossing them into the garbage. Cowen grabbed a mop, but she pointed to her wrist like there wasn't enough time for that. She grabbed a fistful of his shirt and pulled him toward the back door, leaning against it.

"I'm sorry. For whatever this is," she whispered and pulled away.

"Me too," he mouthed. He had to believe he'd protect her in an emergency, but he wasn't sure. In his nightmares, he'd been cowering in fear when the shootout began. It was his mind's way of preventing him from reliving the moment when he'd pulled the trigger.

She texted while she watched him, and his phone dinged a moment later. *At the competition, I need you to hate on me. Dagger glares. Icy stares. Give me everything.*

He would love to give her everything. A hug. A kiss. A piece of his heart. It took him twice as long to text back. *Fine. I'll dish the hate. But when do I get to love on you?*

Her lips twisted, fighting a smile. *You might not want to when you hear everything. But it's too much to explain now. We both need to bake. And I'm sorry for the mess in the walk-in. At least my creation has been disabled.* She released his shirt, her lips tugging down as if already missing him.

Cowen had no idea what she meant by *creation.* He caught her hand, lifting it above his head to kiss the inside of her wrist. He hoped his eyes conveyed the message that he would protect her. But could he? Out of habit, he constantly carried his own personal gun, but could he ever use it again?

With one awkward thumb, he clumsily texted her. *I'll see you tonight?*

She nodded and left out the back door so quietly he almost didn't believe she'd been there. But when he turned and took two steps, slipping on the leftover mess of eggs, straining his hamstring to stay upright, he knew all too well this was reality, not a dream.

Despite Esty's insistence at paying attention to the time, he mopped a path around the island and to the walk-in while Styx and Foreigner played, drowning out his fears. Hopefully, whoever listened hated classic rock. Cautiously, he opened the door to the freezer and found the back half stacked full of all sorts of household items that hadn't been there before. Vacuum hoses. Cookbooks. Hinges. Glass bottles. Bent metal hangers. Ropes and pulleys. None of it made sense. He couldn't wait to hold Esty again and have her explain. But hopefully not by text. That took way too long. If she was in his arms, there were other things he'd rather do, assuming they were safe.

He didn't have enough time to measure out ingredients his usual way—adding this and that until the consistency looked right, so he Googled a cake recipe and got to work quadrupling the batch. Within thirty minutes, he had his cupcakes cooking, and he moved on to frosting. He could make his desserts taste good—that wasn't in question—but making them look presentable wasn't his forte.

While the cupcakes cooled and his mixer beat the frosting, he did another mop pass on the floor. Eggs? Really? And what was the talk about mud? He couldn't wait for Esty to explain. And after that, he was ready to track down whoever had bugged his bakery.

One p.m. rolled around, and a crowd assembled outside. Cowen took his trays to the table in the pop-up canopy, and Esty bristled past with a glare that made the hair raise on the back of his neck. Right…he was supposed to be mad at her. "Remind me to never get on your bad side," he whispered.

It took a lot of willpower for him to narrow his eyes at her each time they passed to bring all of their cupcakes out. He'd rather fix her with a smolder.

As soon as they had all the desserts ready, Mayor Dinwiddie instructed Alex to unveil the cupcakes and pointed to the donation box. "Please remember to give generously to sustain our bakers. We don't want them to give up on us and leave town." He turned and looked at both Cowen and Esty. "We don't want to lose either of you." He faced the crowd again. "Drop some money, try each cupcake, and pick which one you like best on the ballot. Tomorrow's dessert is cinnamon rolls. Let the competition begin."

Esty approached Cowen, glowering. "If the competition were based on appearances, one of us would easily lose." Without waiting for a response, she slipped into the crowd and took her place in line.

Mayor Dinwiddie sidled up to him. "That woman is a spitfire. You should have seen her in the diner this morning, cursing your name."

"Me? Why?" Cowen asked.

Dinwiddie tilted his head to the side. "Don't deny it. Everyone in town knows what you did to her. I'm surprised she didn't retaliate."

What did he know that Cowen didn't? Is that why people kept glaring? "How do you know she didn't?"

He walked off, joining the line, and when he ate both cupcakes, Esty's was superior to his in every way—perfectly moist, yet fluffy. Frosting that was sweet, but not too much. And the decorative swirls made his knifed on plops look like Pinterest fails. He wasn't surprised when her cupcakes won.

The crowd lingered while he grabbed his empty trays. He paused when his phone buzzed with a text from Esty. *Long legs approaching. Make Alex think you like her. Until we know what's going on, suspect everyone, but keep them close.*

Alex's hair bounced as she hurried to him, throwing her arms around his shoulders. "I'm so sorry. You'll beat her tomorrow."

Cowen wanted to push Alex off, but he followed Esty's commands and pulled her tight against him. "Yeah, we'll see." He let go, and it took Alex a moment to get the hint that her impromptu hug was over.

"Do you want to get a late lunch? Or an early dinner so there's time for dessert?" Alex wet her lips, glancing him over.

He wasn't sure if anyone was supposed to know about the ovens or the eggs, so he chose his words carefully. "My kitchen is a mess, and I honestly didn't sleep well last night. Can I take a raincheck?"

Alex dropped her bottom lip in a pout, but a grin still poked through. "I'll cook for you at my house tomorrow." She ran her hand down his arm, starting at his bicep and ended at the tips of his fingers.

He faked a smile. Esty better have a good reason for all of this.

"It's a date," he said, drawing on the deception classes he'd taken as an agent. Sometimes, lies were necessary to keep people safe. That's what he'd been taught. Was this one of those times?

He watched the back of Alex's head as she left, though Alex would probably prefer him to drool over her swinging hips.

"Better luck next time," Esty said as she bumped into him, secretly slipping a small metal tube into his hand. Without looking, he was pretty sure it was a bullet casing. She walked to her door and opened it as several townsfolk watched them. "I'm surprised you didn't tell anyone about the mess I left for you this morning. Too proud to let a girl one-up you?" She gave him a challenging stare. "If you think we're even, we're not. This is war."

She let the door slam behind her, and a crowd approached Cowen.

"How did she get you back?" a sixty-something woman asked, her voice eager for some gossip.

"Let's just say there's more than one way to egg someone. Speaking of which, I have plenty to clean up. Excuse me, ladies."

He returned to his bakery, locked the door behind him, and opened his hand. Sure enough, he held a bullet casing, and for a moment he worried it was the original one he'd given Esty, but the bottom still had a bit of the dried floury paste. And tucked inside was a scroll with five words.

I'll come to you tonight.

chapter twelve

Stalker

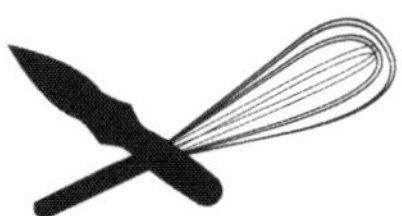

When the sun completely disappeared and Bridge had finished a round of helping Karen with the puppies, she pulled her hair back and dressed in black. Whoever was watching them had installed two solar-powered cameras—one on the telephone pole in front of her house and another one in the back. But that one had a run in with a rock and was currently pointed at the ground with minimum visibility.

Her instincts had told her to run when she discovered the first camera that morning. But if someone wanted her dead, they would have already made a move. This game was being played with rules she didn't understand yet. If she quit, she'd lose all hope of figuring out the who and the why. She needed to know what she was up against before moving on so they didn't follow her or do anything to Cowen or Karen.

As silently as possible, Bridge left her house and stuck to the shadows, creeping along the perimeter of her backyard so the camera in the front couldn't pick her up while she dodged the visibility of the one in the back. Her hop over the fence felt effortless, landing without a thud. As much as she didn't approve of the morals of being a thief, she'd missed the thrills of behaving like one. Scaling walls, breaking into safes, and leaping from buildings were adrenaline rushes. Those excitements weren't found in the kitchen.

Bridge texted Cowen as she approached his house. *Open the back door in five seconds, step onto the porch, and watch the sky for a minute before returning inside. Don't scare if you see me.*

He opened the door as instructed, his eyes searching before looking at the sky as directed. Quietly, she slipped past and sat at his dining table, scratching Jasper's ears with one hand and sampling the crusts on his table with the other. He'd labeled them as Brooklyn. Chicago. Thin crust. "What's with the pizza?" she asked as he entered. "I thought we were over this."

He glanced at her tight outfit, his cheeks reddening when she caught him. "Sorry, you're um…usually dressed differently." He pointed to the pizza. "I needed a distraction while I searched for answers about the bug. If we can make things safe, I want us to both stay here. The town could use a pizza place."

Bridge's throat turned dry. He shouldn't do anything for her, not with her past. Not with the threat of whoever was spying on them. "The Brooklyn is too yeasty. The Chicago is too dry. The thin crust is perfect. And I think we should cut ties."

He sat across from her, shaking his head. "Whatever this is, we can get through it together."

It was a nice sentiment, but she'd ticked off enough dangerous people in her past to know she couldn't include Cowen. Even though he was ex-FBI, she couldn't imagine anyone being after him. He was too kind. Still, he deserved to know what she was up against. "Yesterday, I woke up to a note on my doorstep from the city council saying the neighboring towns were invited, and I needed to make four hundred cookies."

"I didn't get any—"

"There's a lot to cover. It will be easier without interruptions."

He zippered his lips.

"When I got to my bakery, someone had written '*I give up*' on the front windows, and when I opened the door, I found the entire floor and countertops covered in mud. There was a crowd, mostly older ladies, and they suggested it was you. Without proof, I didn't want to believe them, but when—"

"You trusted me?" he asked, reaching out his hand and touching her fingertips.

Her lips struggled to stay flat as she let his skin connect with hers. "That's not important, because at the competition, Karen told me she saw you go into my bakery that morning. I immediately—"

"I didn't go—"

"I know that now." She glanced away. "I immediately made plans to return the sabotage. That night, I drove to Tillamook for supplies to build the contraption that you probably found in your walk-in."

"What *was* that?"

"I said no interruptions." She pulled out her phone and played a video. "As soon as you walked in, you would have been met with this." A series of domino-like effects took place ending with the release of a jug over the door.

"What was supposed to drop?" he asked.

"Molasses. And I had feathers that would have blown once the fan kicked on. Pretty brilliant, right?"

Cowen watched her, open jawed. "You built all of that?"

"It was a rush job."

"How are you amazing at so many things? You can text without looking. And seem to be able to fix anything. Your lock-picking skills are unreal, and you're insanely quiet on your feet. And this domino attack? I can't even piece my mind around it. What are you?"

They were veering off course. Cowen needed to be scared enough to back away. "I've been a lot of things that I don't want to be anymore. And there's more to the story." She wiped a stray red curl out of her face. "I was so mad that I also took apart the ovens and dropped the eggs. When I went to the diner for breakfast, everyone was asking me about what you did, but Karen was acting weird, like she was hiding something. I pulled her aside and pressed her to tell me more about what she saw."

"Did you threaten her with a knife?" he asked, his expression souring.

"Of course not, but she sang like a choir boy when I used my threatening voice."

"I'm guessing now isn't the time to ask if I get a taste of what that sounds like?"

Heat crept up her neck from his flirty response. "No interruptions. Apparently Alex asked Karen to lie about seeing you in my bakery, promising that she had a surprise that would push us together. I thought Alex was behind my sabotage, but when I checked around, she had a solid alibi that morning, so she couldn't have spread the mud, and she doesn't seem like the type to get her hands dirty. I went back to our bakeries confused, and I don't know, looking to the heavens for help. That's when I found the camera in the alley behind our bakeries. It was hiding in a creepy fake bird on the tree in the alley. I tapped into it, and it's now on a continual loop."

Plus, she'd called in a favor to trace where the signal was going—if her brother still knew how to do it. Hopefully he'd respond soon. "And then there was the bug in your bakery, and there's one in mine. And someone put a tracker on my car, but not yours. I already searched our houses. They're clear."

"I know, I already checked mine." He blinked as if realizing something. "You've been inside my house?"

She shrugged like it was no big deal. "Does that bother you?"

"Not as much as it probably should." Cowen rubbed his face. "I want to ask how you know how to tap into a camera feed, but I guess what I want to know most is who is watching us if they're after you, not me? I was thinking it's my boss or someone out for revenge against me." He shook his head. "I don't get what's going on."

"I have zero answers. If it was someone from *my* past, I'd assume they would have already tried to kill me."

Kill. The word seemed to send Cowen down a nightmare hole. His face scrunched, his lips twisted, and his breathing turned ragged. Bridge slid her hands around his, pulling him out.

He swallowed, gripping her fingers back. "I won't let anyone hurt you."

His words were sweet, but he really had no idea who he was up against. Her family had outsmarted some of the world's best thieves, had stolen from drug lords, the Italian Marconi mob, and the Bratva. If any of those groups were after her, even the two of them combined probably didn't have a chance. "I've known a lot of dangerous people."

Cowen didn't seem to hear her as he concentrated. "The fact that Alex asked Karen to lie points to someone in town being involved. Maybe this is an odd form of initiation. Maybe our neighbors like to weed people out."

Bridge tapped her fingers along the table. She hadn't considered that, and the more she thought it through, the more his idea made sense. Her enemies wouldn't enlist local citizens to help them with anything. And they really would have made an attempt to hurt her by now.

"Do you think Alex is trying to force me out of town?"

Cowen stroked her hand with his thumb. "That makes more sense than anything. Her moral compass is left of center."

A pent-up sigh escaped Bridge's lips. "I can't believe I let an amateur freak me out." She pulled three throwing knives from her pants and set them on the table.

Cowen's eyes widened. "I shouldn't be surprised to see those, but I am. Do I need to frisk you for more weapons?"

Bridge's stomach fluttered at the thought. "These were all I brought." They were plenty enough to thwart an attack. "I say we pretend like we're really fighting. If Alex sabotaged my bakery, she obviously wants us to, so let's give her what she wants."

He shook his head. "Why not confront her right now?"

Bridge lifted her lips in a mischievous grin. "I want to see how this plays out. Let her put all her cards on the table, and she'll have nothing left. Then we'll use it to our advantage, showing her and everyone else that we fell for each other in a perfect enemies-to-lovers plot."

His gaze traveled to her lips. "I really like that last part about lovers."

She stood, her hand still holding his, each of her nerves tingling with his touch. Apparently with a risk of a threat, she'd made her decision that Cowen was important enough to stay and work things out. "Do you want to see a movie or not?"

"I do." He laughed at her change of subject and pulled her into the living room where his laptop was already waiting on the couch. They sat hip to hip, his weight on the cushions making her slide into him. He took advantage of that, lacing his arm around her. Jasper jumped up, nuzzling his head against her legs.

"If we watch *Mr. And Mrs. Smith*," she said, resting her head on his shoulder, "will the shooting scenes bring up painful memories?" After the day she'd had, an action movie with romance was the perfect way for her to unwind.

Cowen turned, searching her eyes.

"What?" She wasn't used to the attention of someone so close.

"Most girls I've dated are more concerned with making sure their Stanley fits into my car's cup holder than anything I care about. It means a lot that you're constantly thinking of my needs."

Bridge dropped her head, hating her lack of relational experience. "I wish I was better at it."

He grabbed her chin and gently pulled her toward him. "I like you the way you are." He let his fingers linger, the heat penetrating her skin as he glanced at her lips. And then he let go, opening the laptop and pulling up the movie.

Bridge nestled against him, afraid that if she looked him in the eyes again, she'd fall. Even if it was just Alex spying on them, she was still on high alert. If her enemies weren't after her now, what was to say they wouldn't be in the future? The thought of constantly watching her back made a wave of exhaustion roll through her. Would she ever get to settle down and live a normal life like this one with movies and cuddles? And Cowen?

"Tap out if it gets too tough," she said, and they watched the beginning credits roll. But as soon as the first action scene started, his heart rate sped up, his breaths turned ragged. She pushed the pause button. "I'm sorry. I shouldn't have suggested this." She typed in a new option and pulled up *The Wedding Singer.* "Is this okay?"

Again, he searched her expression, and the appreciation on his face turned into a heat and electricity that spread between them, drawing them closer. "Thanks," he said.

Bridge knew that he'd kiss her if she gave him the chance, so she burrowed her head against his shoulder. She wasn't ready for that next step. The movie finished, and the end credits played. Neither of them moved, the air thick with possibilities. She wished she had a different past, one that would allow her to easily welcome him into her life.

But hadn't Karen hinted that everything was difficult, so why not make the best of it?

Cowen traced the edge of her bandage with one finger. "Is this something you'll ever show me?"

Bridge wanted more than anything to open up to him. To let him into her world. "If we can make it through this bake war and Alex's meddling…maybe."

"I feel honored you'd even consider it." How was he so incredibly patient? "So tomorrow is my turn to retaliate?"

"Technically, yes." Bridge dared a look in his eyes. She never wanted to lose the way he accepted her. "But if we were really fighting, shouldn't we both attack?"

"What do you have in mind?" he asked, a sly grin shifting his lips.

"If it were me, I'd change your food order. Or put laxatives in your drink."

Cowen's face greened. "That's low. Maybe we skip the skitters?" He waited for her to nod. "What should I do to you?"

"I could rig a simple molasses pour to dump on my head."

"That would definitely get people's attention. But maybe we should switch it. Dump the molasses on me in case anyone sees you installing it."

Bridge nodded. That made sense. "Sounds like a plan." She pulled her hand out of his. "I should probably get going."

He stood and helped her up, their breaths inches apart. "How do you want to say goodnight?"

"I um…I don't have much experience with real relationships…" Bridge circumnavigated the coffee table and started toward the back door.

Cowen followed. "Real?"

He had to understand by now that Bridge had lived her life outside of the law. But in case he didn't, she wanted him to know.

She paused in the kitchen, turning toward him. "Grifting is all pretend."

His mouth twitched like he was mulling that over. "But this," he pointed between them, "isn't a con. Right?"

"Not a con." Bridge fingered the ledger in her pocket. "I have something to show you. But maybe tomorrow. It's getting late, and you'll have questions. I want to give you all the answers." For better or worse, he deserved the truth. "You should know exactly what you're getting into."

"Whenever you're ready." He leaned toward her, as if saying he wasn't scared, but he pulled away, his expression falling. "Crap. I just remembered you told me to play the Alex card. She's making me dinner tomorrow."

Bridge laughed at the torture on his face. "That will keep up the ruse."

He stepped closer. "You're not jealous?"

She ran her hand along his arm the way Alex had this afternoon, and his eyes dilated, his breaths quickened. "If she made you react like this, then I'd slip her some laxatives." She turned to go, but he caught her fingers.

"Do you uh, want to test my reaction again, just to be sure?"

She bit her lip, holding in another laugh. "We'll try again tomorrow, after your date."

"It's not a date." He gave her a hard stare. "Text me when you get home?"

Bridge paused, soaking in his concern for her. No one had ever cared enough, got close enough to say that to her. She could no longer just disappear. If she left, it would crush him. It would crush her too. So for now, she'd stay. "I will."

chapter thirteen

Visitor

As planned, Cowen stepped into a molasses trap the next morning, complete with a feather drop. It was engineered differently than the video Esty had shown him, catching him off guard even though he knew to expect it.

"Esty!" he yelled through the sticky mess for the bug's benefit. He still couldn't imagine Alex would listen to them. And for what purpose? He would never be interested in her. Cameras and bugs were a complete violation of privacy and punishable by law, and he wasn't quite sure why they were letting this continue. Esty seemed positive this was the best approach, letting Alex try every angle so she'd know when she was defeated. But would she ever understand? Clearly, she was mentally unstable if she'd stooped to such lengths to crush her competition.

He trudged out the front door, the dark sugar dripping, sticking to everything with each step. Outside, he flagged down the two fifty-something women walking toward him on the street. One screamed and got out her phone. The other rushed over, wearing a purple dress.

"It's not tar," he said, licking his lips but getting a feather in his mouth. He bent and spit it out.

"Let's get you cleaned up. Did that other baker do this to you?"

Cowen forced his lips into a scowl, playing the part. "That's my guess."

"You poor thing." She found the bottom of his shirt and helped him lift it off. "I'm Joyce," she said, her gaze roving over his naked chest.

He used the shirt to wipe molasses from his hair and face.

"I'm Denise," the shorter woman said as she approached. "I'll help you get your pants off."

Cowen recognized her as the woman who'd been censured at the meeting. He gripped the button of his jeans. The cloth had some sticky splatters, but not enough to warrant removing them. "I think I've got it from here."

Joyce's hopeful expression fell. "We'll help clean up. Denise, why don't you run and get him a new shirt."

"Like heck I won't," Denise said, sticking both hands on her hips. "You want me to leave so you can ogle him by yourself."

"Ladies." Cowen had to press his lips together to keep from laughing. Or wincing. "You can both help. I'll ask Alex to bring me a new one." A small weight built in his chest. He really didn't want to lead her on, but he also didn't want to be half-naked in front of these piranhas.

Denise gave Joyce a triumphant grin. "Show us your cleaning supplies."

Cowen led the way, and the women watched him as he showered his head off in the sink.

"We uh, we had to wait for the water," Joyce said as their excuse for standing there, gawking at him.

"Of course. Thanks for your help. Mind if I get baking?" The sound of a delivery truck parked out back. Hopefully Esty wouldn't be too upset with the ingredients he'd ordered for her. He started prepping for his cinnamon rolls when he got a text from her.

Gluten-free flour? Really? You are so going to pay.

He laughed, wanting the day to be over so she could dish out her punishment. He had no idea what she would do, and that made him wish the time away even more.

"What's so funny?" Denise asked.

Cowen turned his back to them. "I probably shouldn't say." He struggled to contain his smile. These ladies made his performance easy. "But I will if you can keep a secret."

Denise and Joyce repeated over and over that they could, so much that anyone would guess that they were probably the worst at keeping their mouths shut.

He turned back. "I hope this doesn't change how you think of me, but I switched out Esty's order. She's got to make cinnamon rolls out of gluten-free flour."

Joyce stuck out her tongue. "If she doesn't know what she's doing, that's going to taste awful."

Cowen nodded as he texted Alex about a shirt. "I know."

The ballot for the cinnamon roll competition came in ninety-eight to one. Apparently a single soul liked Esty's dessert better. Or maybe it was a sympathy vote. Cowen had struggled to finish a single bite.

The crowd milled around, soaking in the breeze and sun. At least a dozen people patted him on the back of his Essential Oils Lover t-shirt, thanks to Alex. Each told him how much they'd enjoyed his s'mores cinnamon rolls. Esty stood by her door, watching everyone. Mayor Dinwiddie had his island attire, Gertie had her seventies jumpsuit and a stuffed calico cat, and Denise smoked a pipe in the back of the crowd.

Alex stood next to him, gripping his arm like a trophy. "Two wins. One more and you're staying, and little miss frizzy hair is going bye-bye."

He had plenty of retorts, but he settled on one. This ended now. He couldn't stand her touch any longer. "I actually love Esty's—"

"Help!" Joyce came running toward the lingering crowd, her purple dress flowing. "Help."

Mayor Dinwiddie rushed to her, his sandals flapping. "What's the matter?"

"Leroy's boat is sinking. He hit something as he docked."

Cowen turned to Alex, barely able to look at her anymore. "Who's Leroy?"

"He's—" Alex paused as Esty rushed past them. "He's a local fisherman. A little crazy if you ask me." What was *her* definition of crazy? She was monitoring him and sabotaging his relationship.

"Where's the boat?" Esty asked, tying her hair into a ponytail.

"By the docks." Joyce panted. "If we can save his haul—"

"I'm on it." Esty took off in a run, leaving the crowd glancing between each other.

"What are we standing around for?" Dinwiddie hollered. "That girl just moved here, and she's already showing more community spirit than the rest of us."

Cowen broke away from Alex.

"Where are you going?" she asked him. "There's enough people to take care of it."

Seriously? Someone needed help, and Alex was going to pawn it off on others? "That's not how I operate." Cowen couldn't hide the disgust on his face. "Don't expect me for dinner. Or ever. We are never getting together." He took off in a run down the street, the dock and Esty in view. Her pace hadn't changed, and when she reached the boat, she grabbed a box from a white haired man that had to be Leroy.

Cowen descended the hill, and his feet hit the dock hard, running a few paces past her. The vintage cabin cruiser had at least a foot of water on the main deck. The living space below was already full and tipping the back of the boat up. It wouldn't take long to submerge the entire thing. "What's essential?" he asked.

Leroy pointed to the crates of fish, but his eyes focused on the cabin.

"What do you want in there?" Esty asked him, grabbing another carton and hefting it onto the dock.

"It's probably long gone." Leroy handed Cowen a crate as some of the town arrived, the dock groaning under the weight.

Esty jumped onto the boat. "Tell me what it is. I'll get it."

Cowen followed and gripped her wrist, the painful memories of Noah's death instantly surfacing in the presence of danger, making him gag. But he swallowed it down—he needed to protect her. "No, I will."

She shrugged him off, her bandage ruffling. "I've clocked four minutes on a single breath. If you can beat that, the glory is all yours."

Cowen had minimal experience. He shook his head as he accepted another crate from Leroy. The town formed two assembly lines. Another man jumped on board to help.

"What do you want in the cabin?" Esty shouted as the crowd grew louder, barking out commands to each other. She tore off her dress, revealing a crop top and leggings.

Leroy's lips twitched as if debating whether or not to answer. "A photo of my late wife. I kept it above my bed."

Esty pulled out a few pieces of paper from her pocket and slipped them into Cowen's hand. "Keep these safe. I'll be right back."

There was no time to stop her. She dove into the cabin, taking a piece of him with her. Reluctantly, Cowen accepted another crate, handing it to Dinwiddie behind him.

One. Two. Ten seconds. Twenty. Cowen kept time as everyone worked to move Leroy's cargo. He went through the motions of hauling crates, but he struggled to move. Forty. Sixty. A minute and twenty. His heart thudded in his chest. He hadn't understood how much he cared about Esty until her life was threatened. A minute forty. The boat's nose tipped, causing the crates and barrels to shift.

"That's it." Cowen wasn't about to wait any longer. Anything could happen underwater. Esty could be stuck. She could have—

The boat groaned and tilted, the nose sinking another five feet. Cowen dove in, searching for her red hair. It didn't take long to find her as she frantically moved tins, boxes, and blankets. He swam close, tugging her arm and pointing up.

She shook her head, holding up a determined finger as if to say—wait. He was already struggling for breath.

One. Two. Ten seconds. He searched along beside her, moving items. Feeling. Looking at everything. Twenty. At sixty, he would tug her out. But Cowen didn't have to get that far—she grabbed something, pulled his arm, and swam up with him at her heels. Once they reached the surface, the back of the boat shifted, lifting into the sky. Leroy and the other man abandoned deck into the frigid water, and they all breast stroked to the dock. The ship's nose sank another four feet before hitting the bottom, leaving the butt of the boat hanging anticlimactically in the air.

"You came after me," Esty said as she clung to a pylon, waiting for someone to drop them a rope.

The waves hit hard, and Cowen reached up and gripped the edge of the dock. "Of…course…how are…you not…out of breath?"

A slight smile crossed her lips as she shifted, grabbing the planks, staying close to him. "I trained for everything."

"Does that make you a spy?" Something tugged at his attention, and as he glanced past her face, he saw a tattoo on her wrist where she always kept the bandage. A spider eating another spider, pierced through with a sword.

What were the odds the director wanted him to look for a tattoo, and she kept one hidden? He wouldn't look at the email now. Even if Esty had gotten herself into some trouble before, he didn't believe she could be dangerous. He was all for prosecuting people so they could be rehabilitated, but when they already were, what point was convicting them? Whatever she'd done, it was water under the bridge.

She shook her head as another wave surged.

Hands reached down, pulling them both up and onto their feet on the dock. Someone tried to cover Esty with a jacket, but she threw her arms around Cowen, pulling him close. Whistles and *ahhs* rippled through the crowd, and every bit of him wanted to kiss her.

"Does this mean you're not fighting anymore?" Mayor Dinwiddie asked.

Esty lifted the picture, waiting for someone to take it. She pulled away enough to stare long and hard at Cowen. Instead of the kiss he felt they needed, she pecked his cheek and let go, crossing her arms over her chest and tucking her wrist out of sight. Did she know it was uncovered? "I'll call a truce if you do," she said.

Expectant faces watched him, and he hoped Alex would finally understand she had no chance. "Fine. But we need to make it official over dinner. My place. Eight o'clock."

Esty tilted her head to the side, and he could tell she was hiding a smile. "Deal," she said. "No more pranks. No more bake war. Just a fair competition. Your goods against mine. Winner takes all."

"Do we clap at that?" Mayor Dinwiddie asked. He nodded and brought his hands together. "I think we do."

The assembled crowd cheered as they made room for Cowen and Esty to walk past. Cowen didn't care about their attention, only hers.

Leroy stopped her, pulling her into a side hug. "Thank you."

"Of course," she said, quickly tapping out before sloshing back to town with Cowen at her heels. She stopped at her bakery and entered the pantry, her back to him.

"Everything okay?" Cowen asked, still out of breath. Maybe it was from the underwater swim, or maybe because he was still mentally stuck on the dock, worrying he might lose her.

"Yeah." She came out with a new bandage on her wrist, and he dropped his glance. She didn't seem to notice as she walked to the shelves above her stove, grabbed the bug, and set it in the walk-in, closing the door tight.

Cowen pulled the wet papers out of his pocket. "I'm sorry. You gave me these for safe keeping, and I wasn't thinking about them."

Esty stepped inside his bubble, taking the papers and putting them on the island. "What *were* you thinking about?" She slid one hand down his arm and grinned as his heart raced.

"I don't want to lose you." He tested the waters, slipping his fingers along her waist and back before pulling her closer. No matter her past, he wanted her in his future.

"I feel the same about you." Her eyes drifted to his mouth, lingering there before she pulled away. "But there's more you should know." She tugged a small black book from her pocket.

Cowen glanced at the wet papers on the counter, then the book.

As if understanding his confusion about her choices at the dock, she opened up the papers and his handwriting stared back. "Call me sentimental for keeping your notes. I already knew my ledger was waterproof."

He swallowed. "Ledger?"

Esty hoisted herself onto the island, her head down. "It details all of my wrongs. And those of some people I worked with. I'm not proud of my past, but it was all I ever knew." She flipped the pages, not showing him specifics, but letting him see how many lines held writings, how few were crossed out. "For every good deed I do, I strike through a wrong." She reached across the island and picked up a pencil. "Saving the picture seems worthy of Rembrandt's Landscape with Cottages."

Cowen swallowed again. "You...*stole* that?" She had to know the implications of telling him. He was no longer an agent and technically didn't have to turn her in. But if he was ever questioned, he had to tell the truth. He'd sworn an oath that didn't just disappear because he'd switched jobs.

"I was part of the assist," she said with a sigh. "It's bounced around a dozen times since the public last saw it in the seventies. I was twelve when we nabbed it from some billionaire in the Hamptons."

"Twelve?" He ran his hand through his hair. "Who is we?"

Esty looked away. "That is information I will never give." She looked up, searching his eyes. "But this is me. All of me. Each of my cards are on the table. All of my secrets are out. I was a thief, but I will never steal again. If you can live with that, knowing that I'm trying to pay back my wrongs, then we can move forward. And if not, I can walk out that door, and you'll never see me again."

Cowen rubbed at his face, covering the expressions that probably didn't make sense. She was telling him everything. Revealing all the dark parts of herself. And the thing she'd worried about before diving in was keeping his notes to her safe.

Every bit of his heart tugged toward Esty. But his gut wavered. "You know I was hired to protect the law. To protect citizens. There is no gray area in *my* book."

She pursed her lips, nodding. "I know. So you get to decide the color of my heart. If you think it's black, I get it. If you think it's gray…I understand. You should know that as soon as I fully understood the ramifications of what we were doing, I quit. I made us all quit."

"When was that?" His firm grasp on justice and honor were slipping.

"Five years ago. I was twenty-one." She lowered her head. "I wish it was earlier."

"So your reason for changing your name, for starting a new life now…"

"One of my…team members made a mistake. He burned our real identities."

"So…Bridge?"

She closed her eyes, breathing deep, and when she opened them, they were wet. "That was me, what my parents named me at birth."

"You gave me your real name?" Cowen ran his hand through his hair, pulling at the ends. Part of him was flattered that she'd shared her truths with him. But her name—he didn't want the liability of knowing it. "If I'm ever questioned—"

She leaned closer. "Don't ever be questioned."

He pulled her into a hug, hoping he'd never be cornered into betraying her for some greater good. He'd sworn to tell the truth, but hadn't he avoided that when it came to what he'd seen on the director's desk? He still had incriminating information on his boss. If he was willing to put that on hold, maybe he was capable of safeguarding all of Bridge's secrets.

"What does your hug mean? Is this goodbye?" she asked, resting her arms above the gun at his back.

"It means I'm crazy." He pulled away, his lips a breath apart from hers. "And I'm diving off the deep end with you."

Bridge—not Esty—tilted and rested her forehead against his. "It might be a wild ride. And you need time to heal from your trauma. We don't have to jump into anything."

"Says the girl who just told me everything." He cupped his hand around the back of her head and tilted her lips toward his, their wet clothes melding together. "And it's too late, I'm already falling." His mouth barely grazed hers as the bells to the front jingled.

"We're closed," she said, pulling away only enough to speak.

Cowen liked how she included him in that statement. But footsteps sounded toward them, and a man around their age strutted in with a smug look on his face. He wore a black leather jacket and a grin that deepened when he saw Esty. But she froze, all of her muscles in their embrace tightening. Cowen instinctively reached for his gun, but Esty pushed his hand away, breaking free from him.

What did that mean? Who was he? Every nerve in Cowen's body went on high alert.

The man stepped forward, pulling her into his arms and swinging her around the room. "Thanks for keeping her warm," he said to Cowen as he set her down. "I heard what you did at the docks."

Bridge clenched her jaw, glancing between them. Was she in danger? Why had she pushed him away from his gun? He definitely didn't want to fire it, just use it as leverage if needed.

"Who are you?" Cowen asked, searching the man's appearance for possible weapons. Anything could hide under the jacket.

"He's my—" Bridge started to say.

But the man finished for her, puffing his chest. "Boyfriend."

Cowen staggered back. The word boyfriend hit him like a gunshot to the chest. Bridge's face fell at the same rate as his heart. All of her cards? It was so nice of her to mention she had a boyfriend. Was that ever going to come up?

"He's your boyfriend?" Cowen asked her, his mouth stuttering. He had to be sure, had to hear it from her.

Bridge looked at the man and some sort of angry conversation passed between them, but she turned to Cowen and said, "Yes."

He knew she was capable of lying, but she wouldn't lie to him about this.

"The name is Daryl. You're Cowen?"

"Yeah." Had Bridge told her boyfriend about him? His thoughts shifted sickeningly from being willing to overlook any mistakes to doubting everything in zero to sixty. Was all of this a con? Some way to get information from him? For all he knew, she'd planted the bugs and was running the surveillance herself.

"I've got to go." He stumbled past them, his soggy shoes squishing with each step. The contents of his stomach climbed.

"Cowen," Bridge said, and he paused, staring through her lying eyes, but she didn't produce anything more. Was the pain on her face even real?

His walk out the door took an eternity. What was he supposed to think now? That Bridge liked him but wasn't monogamous or that she liked him and they were out to get him?

Neither scenario seemed likely, but what did he know? He'd fallen for someone who'd been hiding things all along, things he was willing to overlook because of...what? Attraction? Companionship? Connection? Maybe she'd pretended to like him when he'd given up everything he had to accept her. And for what? Why had she led him on?

Regardless of her answers that he had no idea how to get, Cowen couldn't handle the turmoil in his head. He trudged to the edge of the road, bent, and puked.

chapter fourteen

The Feed

The front door slammed as Cowen left and Bridge punched her brother Liam's shoulder. "Christian Bale," she swore. "Why, why, why would you tell him you were my boyfriend?" She shivered from the wet clothes, even though the heat from the ovens and the afternoon sun was still trapped in the kitchen.

Liam shrugged. "It's not like your accountant was going to show up out of nowhere. Or your mechanic."

"Cousin. Could you not have said a cousin? Or maybe a friend's boyfriend?" She groaned. "You made me lie to him."

"I didn't." He straightened his jacket. "You could have told him the truth."

"Your expression made me think something was wrong so I went with it." Bridge made a fist.

"Whoa," he held up both hands. "Calm down. What's with the guy? You like him or something?"

"Or something? He just dove after me in a sinking ship. Yeah, I like him. And he's good and honest, and you've messed up everything."

"Well, you shouldn't have asked me for help."

Bridge threw her hands into the air. "You're right. The door is there. I'm going to go repair—"

"Not so fast." Liam gripped her arm. "Someone is watching you."

"Yeah, this crazy woman in town is possessive of Cowen."

Liam shook his head. "No. This isn't some Walmart hack. I've been trying for an hour and haven't traced the signal."

Cold tendrils scurried through Bridge's veins. "You're rusty. It's nothing," she said, but the hairs on the back of her neck lifted, her senses not buying her words.

"I could do this in my sleep. Someone is going to great lengths to keep you from knowing who they are." He glanced down at her wrist. "Has anyone seen your tattoo? Or do they know about your past? Any of it?"

Cowen just found out who she was, but the surveillance was installed earlier, and there'd been no deception when he said it wasn't him.

"I swear, no one followed me. I've been careful. And only some old lady saw my tattoo. It was brief."

Liam rubbed his hands together. "Now we're getting somewhere."

Bridge glared at him. "She's certifiable. Seriously. She has a creepy cat wall in her salon."

"Define cat wall." He eyed the leftover cinnamon rolls on a pan and picked one up. "Are we talking live cats in cages or stuffed cats or—"

"Figurines. Look, she's weird, that's all, like most people here." Bridge watched as he took a bite of her dessert, chewed a couple times, and spit it out, a glob landing on her cheek. "That's rude." She wiped it off. "And actually, everything about you is rude. Why don't you leave, and let me figure this out."

"Nah," he said. "I already told a few other people I was your boyfriend and staying for the weekend. What would that say about you if I up and left?"

Bridge charged him, slamming her shoulder into his chest, barely moving him.

He grinned. "Oh, c'mon, is that the best you can do?"

She swung for his face, landing a blow to his cheek.

"Nice," Liam said, blocking her next kick, and throwing her leg away. "It's been too long since I've gotten to do this." He pulled his hands up, blocking his face from her punches when the bells above the front door rang.

"We're closed," they said in unison, but footsteps still sounded toward them. Bridge straightened, dropping her hands as Karen barged in.

"You're okay." Karen flung her arms around Bridge, holding her close despite the wet clothes. "I just heard. What were you thinking diving in there?"

Bridge shrugged, holding her friend. She needed a hug about now. If she didn't get to fix things with Cowen soon, she'd have a melt down—a full on feet thrashing, fists pounding meltdown. But what would she say to him? She'd seen the look of dismissal he'd given her. How could she tell him the truth while protecting her brother's identity? "I've had practice," Bridge said, getting a warning glare from Liam.

"And then Cowen swam in after you." Karen pulled away and glanced Liam up and down. "Who's this?"

Liam puffed his chest. "Boyfriend."

"What?" Karen took a step back, her mouth twisting. She searched Bridge's eyes. "No. You and—"

"Karen, thank you for stopping by." Bridge hated the deception. Her friend looked suspiciously at her, and she could only imagine what Karen and Cowen were feeling. "I need to get changed. I'll come help with the puppies later." Somehow, Bridge needed to fix everything. Someone with decent skills was watching her, and finding them became priority, even though she wanted to repair things with Cowen first.

"Puppies?" Liam grinned from ear to ear. "I can't wait to play with puppies."

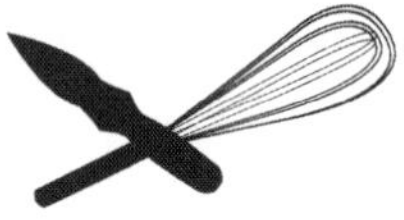

Bridge threw one of her bedroom pillows onto the floor of the living room where her annoying brother could sleep. He'd stayed by her side all evening, preventing her from slipping away to talk to Cowen. He'd been adamant that she not say anything, but she was positive Cowen could handle another secret. It was the only way she could right things between them. But her brother had kept close tabs on her. She'd failed to even sneak off a text with him always watching.

Liam was worried. When had he ever been worried? He took one step toward her bedroom.

Bridge barred the door with both hands on her hips. "Don't even think about coming in here."

His shoulders fell. "You expect me to sleep on the floor? We always shared a bed as kids. That's a king sized—"

"You were scared. That's why I slept next to you. But I'm done protecting you after this." Her worries kept circling around how Cowen must be feeling. Who knew what it would take to get him to trust her again—if he ever would.

Liam jabbed her stomach, not too hard, but enough for her to retract her arms to defend against another blow. He used the empty space to slip into the bedroom. "What are you so upset about? It's not like anything is ever going to happen with that guy. He's ex-FBI. You're a thief."

"You looked him up?" She grabbed the fuzzy throw blanket on the edge of the bed.

Liam tilted his head to the side, staring at her like she was crazy. "Of course. What are you thinking, Bridge? It's not like you to fall for someone. You're always…"

"Always what?" She dropped the blanket and placed both fists on her hips.

He flopped onto the bed. "Uptight. Busy. Making sure everything is going according to plan. How can you fall for a government guy? Really, I'm doing you a favor because we both know this can go nowhere."

She shoved his shoes until he removed his feet from the mattress. "You don't know what you're talking about."

"Just because he dove in after you…"

"It is so much more than that! He's an actual human being with feelings. Want to know how I know? He expresses them instead of locking them behind a door. And he worries about me, and checks in on me, and—"

"Look." Liam stood. "I'm here checking in on you too."

"But you've also dumped everything on me." How many of his mistakes had she covered up? Too many to count.

He backed toward the door, unable to counter as Bridge's phone buzzed with a message from Karen.

You have a boyfriend? Cowen looks about to crumble like one of his cookies.

A growl ripped through Bridge's throat, and she grabbed a blanket and threw it at him.

"You're really going to bed this early?" Liam asked.

"No, but I don't want to see you any more tonight. Do you know how it feels to sucker punch someone you care about? No, you wouldn't. Because you never think about anyone else besides yourself. Remember the Manhattan job where you had to pass a level on your game before you helped me crack the door code? Or what about the time you were hungry, so you left your post, and I got attacked by that guy with the massive front tooth?"

"Oh yeah, Beaver Guy."

Bridge threw a pillow at his head. "Goodnight," she said, pushing him out the door and slamming it closed.

"Don't you want to know who the feed is going to?" he asked, his voice muffled through the wood.

Bridge opened a crack. "You know?"

"My program just finished." He held the phone up, his hand shaking.

"Why is your face white? Liam?" Bridge opened the door wider and gripped his arm.

He struggled to answer. "The feed is going to the Marconis."

"No," She let go, staggering back until her calves rammed into the bed, her butt falling onto the mattress. "We've got to go." The Marconis were notorious for leaving no trace behind. Anyone and everyone Bridge cared about in Pilpil Bay was in danger. Especially Cowen and Karen.

Liam shook his head. "They probably expect us to leave. We've got to come up with a plan so they never follow."

chapter fifteen

The Tattoo

Morning waves thrashed the beach as Cowen aimed his gun at a golf ball in the sand. The blinding sun made it almost impossible to see, but he shot and hit the target, sending the ball ricocheting through the air. Again, he aimed and hit it. Again and again until he emptied the clip with Jasper trotting beside him.

How had he fallen so hard for Bridge when she was with someone else? She'd seemed so open with him, transparent but complex as she'd shown him layers upon layers of who she was and what she was capable of. So why not tell him she had a boyfriend? Had she been playing him all along? Was anything she'd said true?

He reloaded his gun and shot the golf ball again, tearing it apart and sending pieces scattering into the sand. What had Bridge gained from baiting him? The only thing he could think was she had to be part of Antoine Benoit's crew or family, sent to torture him. But he didn't need anyone else to inflict that pain. He inflicted it himself every day. It clawed his heart and squeezed his chest like a vice, constantly filling him with dark, menacing thoughts. The only time he'd had relief was when he baked or spent time with Bridge.

Now it would only be when he baked. Except he'd tried already this morning, mixing together the crust for the mini tarts. No matter the proportions, the dough wouldn't stick together the way it should. He'd added butter, and it became too gooey. More graham crackers and it became too dry and crumbly. Maybe this was the sign he needed that it was time to accept the director's assignment and return to work. He didn't deserve forgiveness for killing Antoine Benoit. For the rest of his life, he'd serve, honor, and protect, expecting nothing but a roof over his head in return.

The decision to return to service was the best for everyone. With bare feet, he scavenged for pieces of the broken golf ball, collected his casings, and returned to the Jeep. Jasper nuzzled the door instead of jumping in, and Cowen opened it for him.

"You doing okay, old boy?" It wasn't fair to the dog to leave anytime soon, but what other choice did he have? He'd fallen for Bridge harder and faster than he ever had for anyone else. The hurt of losing her on top of everything was too much for him to bear. He couldn't stay in Pilpil Bay longer than necessary to find the thief with the…tattoo.

Jasper settled in the backseat, and Cowen got in and pulled out his phone. He needed to know what he was up against, and he had a pretty big hunch the tattoo was his ticket for information.

Director Spandy answered on the first ring. "I was wondering when you'd come to your senses."

"You know why I'm calling?"

Director Spandy let out a breathy laugh. "No, I've been hoping you'd hate your new life. Did you look at the email I sent?"

"Not yet, but I was wondering what it would take to get my job back."

"Technically, you're still on leave while the investigation wraps up. I've done nothing to process your resignation."

Cowen's sigh initiated a nuzzle on the back of his head from Jasper. "I'm okay, boy," he whispered as he scratched behind the dog's ear. "So, what do I do now?"

"Open that email. I'll wait."

Cell coverage was horrible along the coast, and it took a few minutes for Cowen's phone to pull up the email Director Spandy had sent and even longer to load the image. Two spiders. One eating the other. Both stabbed through with a knife. Even though he'd only seen it for a second on Bridge's wrist, he'd know it anywhere. "Why are you looking for this?"

"You've seen it, haven't you?" the director asked.

As much as Bridge had hurt him, it was hard to detangle his feelings for her with the truth of her relationship with someone else. Part of him was still claiming ignorance, wanting to see her, to hold her. But the other demanded justice. She'd never been fully honest with him. Maybe everything had been a lie. "I...uh..."

"Don't tell me it's the girl."

"Girl?" Until Cowen did his own research and confirmed Bridge's ill intents, he wasn't ready to throw her under the bus.

"Don't play coy with me," the director said. "I can read you a thousand miles away. And plus, it helps that I've got tabs on social media there. Someone posted a picture of you and some woman hugging yesterday. Why were you all wet?"

Cowen's stomach surged to his throat, and he ignored the question. "I said nothing about her in relation to that tattoo." Why was he defending Bridge when she'd lied to him? What if nothing with her was real? What if she'd never liked him? The thought crossed his mind, but he couldn't believe it. Every moment with her had felt so genuine that he couldn't fully process her deception. Hearts were stupid, stupid things.

"You didn't have to say anything. Omissions speak volumes."

What did that mean in relation to Bridge? She'd told him so much. But was any of it true? Who was she really? "I'll question her. What do you want me to ask?"

"Actually, I can do it. There's been a bit of chatter about Pilpil Bay, and

I hear there's a baking competition tomorrow. I wouldn't want to miss that. I assume you'll remember which side of the line you're on if it comes to that?"

Cowen found he had to dig deep to find a response. "Of course." Even if Bridge had betrayed his trust, he wasn't eager to do the same, his heart holding out for some sort of explanation that made sense.

"Don't warn her or you'll find the paper crossing my desk will be far worse than your resignation."

"Of course, sir." Cowen dropped the phone in his cupholder and leaned his head against the steering wheel. The call had revealed nothing more than he already suspected—that Bridge was in trouble for something. This whole situation felt wrong. The wind gusted, as if confirming Cowen's thoughts, and he started the Jeep. "I don't know what I'm doing," he said to the dog and drove them home. Jasper padded to his bed, moping the way Cowen felt. Was Bridge his enemy? Or was she what she seemed—the woman who'd occupied his thoughts day and night for weeks who'd omitted one detail?

One insanely important detail.

His heart wasn't ready to betray her, even though it was crushed, barely beating. He pulled up the email on his laptop and searched the tattoo's image in government databases, but he found zero hits. It was as if someone had wiped the record clean. He tried a search on the internet, but came up with nothing. Something didn't feel right.

"Keep an eye on things while I'm gone," he said to Jasper and returned to the bakery, parking in the alley so his Jeep was close. On the back door, a series of dots and dashes were marked in the dust on the aged metal. He pretended not to notice in case cameras watched, instead, dropping his head as if he were focused on a text. Things weren't adding up.

We need to talk, is all that it said. Clearly, it was a message from Bridge, and his heart took hope in the possibility of a logical explanation. Maybe this was like *Cast Away* with Tom Hanks. Didn't the woman move on, thinking her husband had died? Maybe that was the case with Bridge, and Daryl was a boyfriend she thought was dead. But how could he approach her with the director's threats? Did she deserve a warning that he was coming to question her?

Where did the law and justice meet mercy? If Bridge was actively stealing, he'd have to agree with turning her over to authorities. But she wasn't—at least that's what he believed in his gut. She seemed willing to do anything to help someone else. Should she have to pay for past crimes when she'd already changed and sworn off that life?

Cowen wouldn't know anything definitively until they talked.

With his heart beating outside his chest, he marched to her back door, pounding loud enough to wake the dead.

Daryl answered, the smug looks from yesterday gone, replaced with bloodshot eyes and a scowl. He had one foot in front of the other, both knees bent as if expecting an attack. Bridge stood behind the island, a knife in her hand. But at the sight of Cowen, she dropped it.

"Move along." Daryl looked past him, scanning the alley. "We don't have any sugar to spare."

Bridge stepped out from behind the island and used her apron to wipe her hands. She patted her leg, drawing Cowen's attention there. The indent from his casing was evident. So if she was still toting it around, she had to have feelings for him. Right? His suspicions focused on Daryl. Who was this guy, and was he here to stay? Something was definitely not right.

"Look," Cowen said, lifting both hands in the air above his waist. "I don't want to cause problems between you two, but I need to ask one question. Are you safe?"

Daryl glanced him over as Bridge said "Yes," but Cowen waited, watching for another sign. She tapped one finger on her leg as she spelled *Yes*.

As glad as Cowen was that Bridge was okay, her answer sat like vinegar on his tongue. "Sorry for bugging you. I just wanted to be sure." But he wasn't sure of anything as he walked back to his bakery and shoved the crust into muffin tins. Why would she still carry the casing if she had a boyfriend? She'd clearly meant for him to know that it was there. So what did it mean?

The front door of his shop opened, followed by the click-clack of heels. Alex sauntered into the kitchen in a tight-fitting cream dress. "Whoa," she said, scanning the room. "Please tell me this is your last pan and you have all the other desserts ready."

Cowen shook his head, focusing on forming more crusts. At some point, he needed to confront her about the bugs and cameras—if she'd actually placed them—but not now. Bridge was all he'd thought about day and night since they met. He'd thought their feelings were mutual, so how could she have a boyfriend? How could she lie about that? Were there other secrets she was hiding? Or was something else going on? His thoughts about the situation kept sliding back and forth.

"We are so behind." Alex washed her hands, grabbed Cowen's apron off the back of the door, and shoved him out of the way. "I'll do this. Start on the next step."

With sluggish feet, he opened the door to the walk-in, instantly spotting the dots and dashes scratched into the frost. Again, it spelled out, *We need to talk.*

His phone buzzed with a text from his mama.

Just checking in on you. I hope you're having a great day.

For a moment, Cowen put himself in different shoes. If Ed had lied to his mama about a relationship, Cowen would tell her to ditch him, that he didn't deserve another chance. But something was off between Bridge and Daryl. He felt it deep in his gut.

"Earth to Cowen," Alex said, reminding him to breathe. "I know about Esty's boyfriend, and I'm sure that was a low blow. And I'm sorry for how I acted. You were right. I should have been more willing to help. That is all stuff we can talk about later. But right now, you need to finish these desserts. You're not a quitter. Let's do this."

Alex didn't know Cowen well enough to understand that about him, but she was right. He wasn't going to quit until he got to the bottom of this. Something was clearly wrong. And whatever mess Bridge was in, he'd help her out. Because if she still cared enough about him to keep leaving notes and showing that she wore his casing in her pocket, then he wasn't about to give up. Not yet.

chapter sixteen

Betrayed

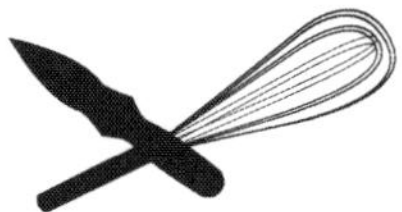

The fresh berry tarts Bridge had made paired perfectly with Cowen's key limes on the competition table. So did his look of concern—it matched hers completely—as he watched her from twelve feet away. At least he wasn't glaring. She didn't want to pull him into her problems, but she couldn't leave until he knew what he'd meant to her. If the plan she and Liam had concocted worked, they'd never return to Pilpil Bay.

Mayor Dinwiddie stood between them wearing a floral patterned shirt, hot pink shorts, and Crocs with pineapple shaped charms. "Let's get started," he said, waving to the crowd even though it was six minutes until one o'clock. "Since Mr. Amaratti has won twice, a win for him today will end the competition. If you haven't donated generously, please do so. Our bakers have worked hard to meet our demands, and it's only fair that we compensate them."

Fair. Nothing in this life had ever been fair. When other little girls were playing with Barbies, Bridge was learning how to sneak around undetected, make and diffuse simple bombs, and repair electrical circuits. Instead of going to prom, she'd been hanging forty stories up, cutting a window so they could nab a Cézanne from a cocaine dealer's penthouse in Dubai. And how had it been fair to watch her mom bleed out when she'd trusted the wrong guy?

Everything going forward was the opposite of fair. Bridge and her brother had plans and backups for the next twelve hours to fool the Marconis into believing they were dead. And after that, nothing mattered.

"Let the fourth competition begin." Mayor Dinwiddie waved his hand with a flourish.

Alex revealed the desserts, and the crowd *oohed* and *ahhed*. In their distracted state, Cowen inched closer to her, but Bridge shook her finger at him. This wasn't the time.

The community lined up, put their money into the donation bin, and took their desserts as the afternoon sun parsed the clouds. It didn't take long for grumblings to carry through the crowd. The groanings were part of the plan, and Bridge forced her mind to focus on their upcoming tasks so she didn't smile. Tarts weren't meant to be made out of salt. Her disgusting recipe would ensure a win for Cowen.

Mayor Dinwiddie hobbled through the crowd, listening and asking questions. He was laughing as he approached them in front of their stores. "Ah, you two..." he said, shaking his head before turning to the community. "Attention. Can I get your attention?" The mumblings and whispers quieted. "It looks like our bakers didn't want the other to lose, so they both tainted their desserts. Tomorrow, the winner will take all."

Liam appeared next to her, slipping his arm around Bridge's shoulders. "All set."

She couldn't help grimacing at her brother's touch, still angry he'd introduced himself as her boyfriend. "Actually," Bridge said, stepping forward and addressing the crowd. "Mayor Dinwiddie, I have to make an announcement. I've purchased a new building in Oceanside. Daryl—"

"Your boyfriend," Liam said, addressing the crowd with a charming smile.

He was so going to get it later. Maybe normal siblings wrestled, but she'd burn off his leg hairs.

"My…boyfriend—" Bridge said the words like they were crusted with salt. "We're headed over now to start working on it. So if you loved my cupcakes, or want to give me a chance at my cinnamon rolls with real flour, not gluten free, then swing on by in a month or two when we open up. I'm officially conceding the Pilpil Bay Bake War to Mr. Amaratti."

Cowen's face fell. He shook his head. "I don't want—"

Bridge patted the casing in her pocket, drawing his attention. When he looked back at her, she pleaded with her eyes for him to follow along.

"I don't feel like I deserve the honor, but I accept," he said, his tone almost even enough to convince her. But the glances he kept giving her said otherwise.

"I guess this is settled then." Mayor Dinwiddie placed his hand on her shoulder. "We're sorry to see you move your business elsewhere. But you're still staying in Pilpil Bay, right?"

Bridge swallowed and painted on a smile. "Of course. I love it here." She really did. Her heart slipped as she gently touched his shoulder and left, walking past Cowen. "Things aren't as they seem. Meet me on the porch swing," she whispered so quietly she wondered if he even heard. But twenty minutes later, he walked along the beach barefoot, carrying his shoes.

She stood up from her seat at the rental, wearing a skirt to cover the tactical gear strapped to her legs. Thankfully, the cottages weren't booked for another night, so they had the place to themselves.

"I parked a mile back," Cowen said. "I didn't know what was going on."

"Thank you for being so considerate." Her formality was intended to keep distance between them, even though she wanted to rush into his arms.

He dropped his shoes in the sand and stepped up onto the porch, his shoulders heaving with the breaths that probably did nothing to calm his heart. "What's going on?"

She heard the pain in his voice, so palpable she could feel it. "I can't tell you who Daryl is, but he's not my boyfriend. I told you the truth. I've always told you the truth."

Cowen nodded like he'd already pieced that part together. "How do I know this isn't all a lie right now?"

Bridge dipped her head. "I guess my word isn't good enough." She pulled up her phone and sat on the swing. He joined her, leaving a gap she didn't want. "If you picture me with black hair, maybe you'll see the resemblance." She showed him an image of a woman leaping between buildings in Manhattan, her braid flying in the wind. "It's pretty much the most brilliant image of all time."

Cowen looked between her and the screen so many times, she imagined he'd get motion sick. "This is you?"

She nodded, proud of her skills at nineteen but not what she'd done. "The guy who took it was a bird watcher. That year, a flock of rare warblers were rumored to be in New York, and I happened to be in his scope."

Cowen choked. "This image is famous. And if that's you, then you stole a Degas from the Marconi mob."

"Yes. I did." Bridge hung her head. "You have more than enough to turn me over to the FBI or to Interpol."

"Why are you telling me this?" he asked, moving an inch closer.

"Because I want you to believe me. I want you to know what you've meant to me."

"Meant?" Cowen shifted closer again, his fingers shaking as if itching to grab hers. "That's past tense."

Bridge managed a smile, though emotional daggers were poking her heart. "There is no happily ever after for us."

"Why?" He shook his head. "Explain to me what's going on. Why is your fake boyfriend here?"

Against her better judgment, Bridge reached out and gripped his hands. "The less you know, the better. The people chasing us are dangerous. But I wanted you to have closure so you can move on with your life."

He groaned. "You're not really the type of person I can move on from."

"You have to. I'm not safe to be around. And even meeting here is probably pushing it. Li—" Her chest fell. She'd almost said her brother's name. Cowen had a way of pulling down all of her defenses. "Leaving you is the hardest thing I've ever done. But I have to."

"Fine. Leave." He let go of her hands, only to slip them around her back, bringing his nose next to hers. "But tell me where to follow. Because I think you're right, we should go. My boss—"

"You don't know what you're asking," she said, scooting away.

Cowen took a moment, as if thinking through all the consequences. "I'm asking you to include me in whatever it is you're planning." He let his words drift. "Unless you don't feel the same way about me as I do about you. Is that what this is?"

Bridge knew Cowen couldn't come, but her whole intent with this last moment with him was so he knew how she felt, so he'd never question her feelings toward him. "Why do you have to be so difficult?" she asked before wrapping her arms around his neck and pulling his lips to hers. Instantly, his own softened, opened, and accepted everything she could give.

And she gave everything.

Cowen had understood her. He'd accepted her. And he still liked her, willing to risk his future to follow after her. Words could never express what that meant. A kiss probably couldn't either, but she tried, exploring every inch of his mouth with hers, her fingers tangled in his hair.

Nothing had ever felt more dangerous and exhilarating. Not rappelling off buildings. Not escaping a scene with bullets flying. She was certain she could do this again and again, and the feeling would be the same every time. Because Cowen Amaratti was her person.

And she had to leave him behind.

"I've got to go," she said after she broke apart, resting her forehead against his. "It's not safe here. If I could stay, I—"

A gun cocked behind Bridge. Danger warnings blared in her head, and muscle memory kicked in. She pulled a knife from her pants and Cowen's gun from behind his back in a single, seamless spin, facing her attacker. She wasn't expecting the fifty-something stranger with a potbelly.

"Hello, Ms. Ryan," the tall, balding man said. His suit looked crisp, like he sat at a desk all day. "Though I doubt that's your real name. I'm impressed how deep your deception goes."

"Who are you?" Bridge backed protectively in front of Cowen, sweeping her eyes around their perimeter as movement encroached in their space. At least six men and one woman approached, their guns drawn. Each wore unflattering suits. That made her relax a little. "Let me guess. Feds?"

"Director Spandy. FBI. How did you know?"

She shook her head, calculating their chance of escape. She'd placed her and Cowen in a kill box with the wide-open ocean on one side, the treeless street on the other. It was a mistake she never would have made if she hadn't let her guard down. There was nowhere for them to go unless she knifed and shot her way out. And what about Cowen? She could already hear his labored breaths. He couldn't handle an action movie, so how could he process a standoff in real life? "It's the shoes. I mean, the suits definitely don't do any favors, but lots of people don't have taste. The shoes get you every time."

"You've got an expert hold on your weapons," the director said, ignoring her criticism. "I'm guessing you know how to use them."

"Let's stop guessing so much. You tell me why you're here, and I'll tell you how things are going to go down." She couldn't understand why the Feds were here when she'd expected the Marconis' cronies.

"I can see why you like her." Director Spandy looked behind Bridge to Cowen.

The ground unraveled beneath Bridge's feet. "You know Cowen?"

A grin slid over the man's lips. "I'm his boss. He always brings me the bad guys."

Bridge fought to stay upright, to keep from doubling over. Her heart stuttered. Pressure built in her throat. She'd been certain Cowen wasn't capable of betraying her, but she'd been wrong. Again.

Her reaction disarmed her for a single second, but it was enough for the closest agent to encroach into her space and grab both wrists, torquing them down. She could fight. It would be bloody, maybe even deadly with so many people so close, but she could do it.

But why bother? Why resist when her heart was gone? She'd done it again, trusting someone who didn't deserve it. Who was willing to abuse it. There was clearly something wrong with Bridge to keep falling for losers. For men who lacked a backbone and an ounce of decency. How could Cowen lie to her face when he'd acted like he wouldn't turn her in?

"Great job leading us here," Director Spandy said to Cowen as she allowed the agents to strip her of the weapons in her hands.

What mattered now? She'd let her guard down and Cowen deceived her. Fool her once, and she'd try again. But twice? There was no trusting anyone ever again after Mason *and* Cowen. And without trust, there was nothing to look forward to. No dreams of living a normal life with the people she loved in it.

She couldn't look at Cowen as someone slapped cuffs on her wrists. "What are you going to do with me?" Did it really matter if she didn't have hope? Her determination to protect herself disappeared. Liam could pull off the plan without her and she could go to prison where she wouldn't hurt anyone ever again. And where no one could hurt her.

"We're taking you in for questioning." Director Spandy glanced her over for a moment before resting his eyes on the bandage on her arm. Without mercy, he ripped it off, her tattoo visible for all to see. "You're too young to be the Foxfoot Thief, but maybe you knew her. Or maybe you know something about who murdered her killer?" He stepped away from Bridge. "Put her in the van."

A brute of an agent pulled her toward the edge of the porch, but she slid a leg around the beam holding up the roof, using it as a brake.

"You can always tell by their shoes," Bridge said, waiting for Cowen to meet her gaze, but he refused to look at her. All the years of practicing everything paid off as she aimed her spit and hit him perfectly on the lips.

"What do you want me to do?" he asked as he wiped it off, his focus on the director.

"Stay and watch over things until this is all sorted out," the director said. "It'll be best for both of you."

The agent holding Bridge tugged, and she let go of the beam, letting him cart her away.

Best for both of you? What did that mean? Was Cowen in trouble for getting too close to her? She hoped so, but whatever punishment the agency dished out wouldn't do justice. He needed to pay.

Regrets pooled in her eyes. She should have followed her brother's plan to leave town immediately, maybe then she wouldn't be in this mess. But maybe things were better this way. While she waited her days in prison, Bridge would petition the universe to make sure Cowen Amaratti got everything he deserved for betraying her.

chapter seventeen

Ransom

Pretending. That's what Cowen did for the next five minutes as the agents asked him questions on the road next to the van. There were no windows, but he could feel Bridge's glares on him. His emotions were climbing toward out-of-control, and he had to swallow often to keep himself from throwing up.

He should have warned Bridge sooner about the director. And he'd been so caught off guard by the team's arrival that he'd failed to refute Director Spandy's claims and insinuations that Cowen was involved. Failed…that seemed to be a reoccurring theme in his book.

He'd always believed in justice, that crimes had to be paid for. That amends had to be made. But he'd seen Bridge's ledger. She was already doing that without being forced. It didn't seem right for the FBI to take her now. Especially when her capture was his fault. If justice needed to be served, then he should also pay for giving her up. And what better way than risking his freedom. His honor. She didn't think twice about diving in to help someone else. It was his turn to rescue her.

The only way to help Bridge was to make it seem like he was playing on the FBI's side. "Did you search her before you put her in the van?" he asked as they were finishing up. If he could, he'd find a way to let Bridge know he was on her side without tipping anyone else off. After that, he didn't have a plan. But he would figure one out. He had to.

One of the other guys shook his head, not able to meet his eyes. They'd all been at Noah's funeral, and his partner's absence was still fresh for everyone.

"Want me to do it? I bet she's got another knife." He had no idea if they would believe him.

Agent Solis opened the back door, and the heat from Bridge's loathing stare grew.

"Are you going to kiss her again?" Agent Martinez asked with a laugh. He was a short, scrawny looking guy, but looks were often deceiving. "Benny got it on his scope."

Cowen had to shove down the violated feelings surging through him. "I had a feeling you all were coming today, so I had to do something to stall." He flashed around a cocky grin and waited for Agent Solis to unlock Bridge's chains and coax her out.

"I'll frisk her." Cowen started at Bridge's shoulders like she had with him, feeling everywhere covered by fabric. He tried to meet her gaze, but she refused to look at him. "Arms up." He waited for her to lift her cuffed hands high and then checked her armpits before reaching her side, tapping out Morse code for *no*. It was the easiest thing he could think of that might tip her in his favor.

He'd expected at least one more knife, had felt it along her back when they'd kissed, but didn't anticipate the strap under her chest. He reached under her shirt, ripping the Velcro and discovering ten thin blades.

"Good work," Director Spandy said, gripping Cowen's shoulder as he put his phone away. "Any more?"

He could only imagine what else he'd find under her skirt and how that could incriminate her. But if it didn't happen here, they would search her in Portland, possibly without him around.

Hate rolled off Bridge's body, slowing down Cowen's fingers as he pulled out two more knives from behind her back. Several waistbands hugged her skin, so he pulled off the skirt over her leggings and took a step back. Almost every inch of her fabric covered legs held weapons and equipment. Two guns. A lighter. Six clips of ammo. A bunch of tools. And a grenade. He should have left Bridge in the van. This search was the opposite of helping her.

Director Spandy ran a hand over his bald head. "Why didn't anyone else think to search her?"

"Is this live?" Cowen asked, unclipping the grenade and handing it to another agent. "What were you preparing for?" His question was soft. Too soft.

She looked away, refusing to answer.

"There's more in her pockets," Agent Martinez said.

Cowen had to fight the scowl he felt, not wanting anyone else to look at her so closely. "These are nothing," he said as he fished the casing and ledger out of her tight side pockets. "This belonged to an old boyfriend. And the casing," he said, holding it up, "was a gift from her dad before he died." He dropped it into Agent Solis's hands. "You might be able to use it as a bargaining chip. It means that much to her."

He walked away then, hoping Bridge saw through his lie and that no one else did.

"Amaratti," Director Spandy said.

Cowen halted, turning back. "Yeah?"

The director searched his face. "Good work."

"Thanks. It feels good to be back." He turned, draped his shoes over his shoulder, and walked off toward his car where he'd left it, feeling Bridge's glare pelt at his back.

The sun was about four hours away from the horizon when Cowen parked in front of his house. He'd searched everywhere for "Daryl," though he was positive the guy's name was Lee or something that started with that sound. Leo. Leopold. Liam.

The camera out front was still watching, and he again questioned if Alex or someone else had placed it. Bridge had so many weapons on her that something was definitely off. He wasn't about to take any chances, so he shot out all of the security cameras surrounding their houses before searching her place. He found the small stack of cash in the floorboard under her bed, plus her driver's license and passport—her real passport without a single stamp.

Bridget O'Niall. The name explained the fair skin and flaming red hair. He left the cash and removed her forms of identity, storing them in the glove compartment of his Jeep. He parked in the alley behind their restaurants, shooting out the camera before approaching the door. A single piece of folded paper was taped above the handle.

He glanced all directions again before snatching it off and reading.

We've got your brother. Bring the Pouncing Feline Over Koi to the beachfront in Oceanside at 11:00 p.m. on Sunday or his life is forfeit.

"Brother…" Cowen would bet good money that Daryl was Bridge's sibling. It made sense why she wouldn't give up any information about him. But what was the Pouncing Feline Over Koi, and who had her brother? He needed to talk to Bridge, needed to find out who kidnapped her brother so they could save him. Eleven p.m. on Sunday was less than seventy-two hours away.

"Where is she?" asked a voice behind him.

Cowen spun, his fingers inching toward the handle of his gun. A man with short red hair in a gray, tailored suit leaned against his Jeep. "Who are you?" Cowen asked, his skin connecting with the weapon. Everything about the man conveyed a rich air, but other than that, he wasn't sure of anything.

"I'd give you a six-point-two for your performance at the house. That was a nice shot to knock out the cameras, but you left the door wide open while you searched. I walked in, and you didn't even notice me. The only reason you get any points is because you found Bridge's stash. For that, I'm impressed."

"Who are you?" Cowen asked again, pulling out his gun and pointing it at him. He didn't need this man's approval on anything.

"Rory O'Niall. Are you going to help me save my daughter and my son or not?"

Bridge's father? She hadn't said anything about him. "You know who I am?"

The man nodded. "FBI. Baker. Love interest of my daughter."

Cowen kept the gun trained on him. "How can I be sure you are who you say you are? She's never mentioned you."

"She hasn't, huh?" He pushed off from the car, rubbing the scruff on his chin. "Well, does it help my claim that I know she uses actor names as her curses."

The references to Chris Pratt and Ryan Gosling now made sense. "Go on."

"And I can show you this." He pulled up the sleeve of his button-down shirt, revealing the same spider eating spider ink.

"Maybe you're a cult or gang, all with the same tattoo." Cowen circled the man, searching for a way to prove who he was.

"It's our family's crest."

Cowen still didn't have enough information. "If you had to describe Bridge's mom by listing two famous people, who would they be?"

Rory pointed at him. "I like you." It took him a moment longer to think. "Jackie Chan..." He shook his head. "No, Chuck Norris and Martha Stewart."

With limited time, Cowen was as sure as he was going to get. He returned his gun and extended his hand. "I wish we were meeting under different circumstances, Mr. O'Niall."

Rory eyed him for a moment before shaking. "Aye. Me too."

"The FBI took Bridge in for questioning." Cowen folded his arms. Maybe if he explained the ransom note to the director, he could get resources to help them track down the brother. "I have no idea who has your son."

"The Marconis," Rory said, his expression souring. "Ever heard of them?"

Cowen gagged. He was going to be sick. It was one thing to know Bridge had stolen a Degas from them, but it was entirely another to have them playing a game and holding all the cards. Every agent in the entire country knew of the Marconis. Almost half of the FBI's cold cases had suspected ties to the family or their crew. They were merciless. "How do we save him?"

"Bridge is the only one who can steal the jade cat." Rory shifted his shoulder and winced. "I'm recovering from a parting gift, compliments of the Marconis. I need her."

Cowen swallowed. "Steal? I'm not sure she wants—"

"If the FBI has any intel about her mom or the evidence about her killer, Bridge will take responsibility for all of it. I know my daughter, and she'd rather take the blame than see anyone else suffer. Stealing something is far better."

"My boss asked about the Foxfoot Thief and who murdered her. Was she your wife?" Cowen didn't even want to consider that Bridge had told him she'd watched her mother die. He'd pictured a hospital room. But murder was something else.

"Yes, she was." Rory massaged his temples. "You have to break Bridge out. She'll take the fall for something she didn't do."

"You want *me* to break her out of federal custody?" Cowen understood the need to bend rules occasionally, but breaking her out? "I um…I imagine you've lived a different life than me, but if I go down this road—"

"You might be on the run for the rest of your life. It's a little scary at first, but you get used to it. Trust me." Rory flashed him a smile. "And you'll still get to see your mom if you play your cards right. Dialysis is a few hours a couple times a week. I can teach you how to get in and out without being seen."

His mama. How could he have forgotten about her in all of this? And how did this man know so much? "You know about—"

"Look, do you want to be with Bridge or go back to your dog that isn't really your dog?" Rory waited for him to process. What was he going to say next? That he knew Cowen's boxer size? "Don't worry, Jasper is with a neighbor. And I know so much because I keep tabs on my little girl." He adjusted the sleeves of his suit. "Choice is yours, but the clock is ticking. I'm driving away in that Jeep in five seconds whether you're with me or not. Cool ride by the way."

Cowen struggled to process everything. How could this man expect him to make a decision that would impact the rest of his life in a few seconds. "I don't—"

"Five," Rory started. "Four. Three."

"I don't want you to drive." Cowen pulled out his keys, making his choice. He'd joined the FBI to protect people like his dad had done. If the agency wouldn't help, he'd take matters into his own hands, but he prayed that they would. "Get in. I'll get the director to help us."

Rory shook his head as he slid into the passenger seat. "Not this time. I need you to break her out. Then we'll steal the statue, get my boy back, and collect a few bodies."

"Bodies?" Cowen turned the key in the ignition, his heart racing and expression souring. Cowen planned to ask the director to release Bridge in exchange for the O'Nialls' help in taking down a few Marconis. Rory's plan meant there was no coming back from this. "I fail to understand why we need bodies."

"To stage our deaths. Unless you don't want a future with my daughter."

Cowen pressed the gas. "Are you going to keep holding that over my head?"

Rory crossed his arms over his chest and gave him a challenging look in response.

"Fine. Break Bridge out. Steal the statue. Rescue your son. And visit the morgue. Do you want me to rob a bank too?"

Rory grinned, covering the tiniest trace of fear. "I like you." The man was clearly trying to stay cool when he was probably as worried as Cowen.

Setting his jaw, Cowen sped toward Portland, keeping his focus on saving Bridge and her brother, not the fact that he was probably throwing his entire life away.

chapter eighteen
Mr. Polygraph

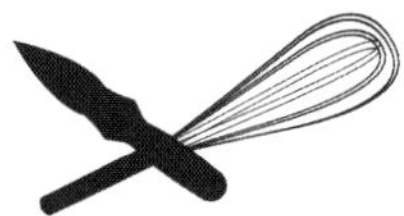

The single light in the interrogation room cast shadows on Agent Zamby's makeup-covered cheeks. Bridge sat cuffed to the chair, one hand free so she could drink the soda they'd given her. They still didn't know her real name, which confused the heck out of her. Cowen would have given it to them if he was on their side. And of course he was. Once a Fed, always a Fed.

She should have been smarter than to trust him. Should have locked away her heart. He couldn't even admit that the shell casing was from him, making up some stupid story about her dad that he had no idea about. And then there was the lie about her ledger. What did it mean?

Her brain spun, but kept returning to one question. Why hadn't he told them her name? She'd planned to take whatever punishment the authorities dealt, her emotions too fragile to return to the real world. But something within told her to not give up, to look for a way to escape. *Mom? Virgin Mary? Is that you?*

"Jane Doe," the woman said again, her voice biting and sharp as if hoping to annoy Bridge enough to correct her. "Tell me how you scrubbed our database of the image of your tattoo?"

Bridge slammed her fist on the table, and at the same time yanked on the chair with her cuff, testing for weakness. "What am I doing here?"

"What were you doing with all of those weapons?" Agent Zamby asked.

Bridge ran her hand through her hair. "I already told you. There's this reenactment happening at Fort Stevens later. And I didn't know the grenade was real. The guy who sold it to me on Facebook Marketplace listed it as a prop. Did you know that the Japanese attacked Fort Stevens during the Second World War? Most people don't realize anything happened in the contiguous United—"

"Yes, I know. And how did you hear about this reenactment?"

"TikTok. Where else? I'm guessing you're not finding anything on it online or when you call, huh? Social media is a fickle thing."

The woman gave the tiniest groan. Bridge was slowly chinking away at her armor.

"Let's switch topics," the woman said. "How do you know the Foxfoot Thief? We might not have an image of it still, but we have descriptions of a tattoo found on the body of an unidentified woman ten years ago. It matches yours. Was she the Foxfoot Thief?"

"Can I get a pen and paper?" Bridge asked nicely as if she were complying.

The woman snapped her fingers, and a moment later, a man with glasses and a collared shirt entered the room, placing the items in front of her.

"Thanks," Bridge said, eyeing him for anything useful, but there was nothing to steal. "Can you tell me the description of this tattoo you say matches some thief?"

The woman groaned again, but there was a single tap on the glass, and she turned her focus to the folder in her hands. "Two spiders. One is on the other's back, eating its head, with a knife sticking through both."

"Okay. Let's take that for a spin." Bridge got to work sketching out four different variations. "Which one does it look like? Because these all seem plenty different to me, but they match your description. These are black widows. This is a brown recluse attacking a wolf spider and—"

"Enough," the woman snapped, having to adjust her hair back in place. "How do you—"

"How do you sleep at night knowing you're questioning innocent people?" Bridge gave her a hard stare. "I drew this tattoo after a friend betrayed me by going after my boyfriend. And then he cheated on both of us. The only thing you have on me is that I got caught with weapons, but you should check every other hick in this state. I bet they've got plenty more. And you say you don't believe my name is Esty Ryan. Look at my driver's license. Search my record. Do you think I faked all of that?"

Liam was a pro when it came to backstories. They'd never find anything.

Bridge continued. "You've got a class A misdemeanor on me at most, though good luck trying to prove intent to commit a criminal offense."

The woman palmed the desk and leaned toward Bridge. "You pulled weapons on an FBI agent. And you seem to know a lot about our legal system."

"Yeah, it's called defending myself." Bridge shifted closer too, not letting the woman intimidate her. "He pulled a gun first. And is it a crime to be knowledgeable?"

"You're a very good liar, Ms. Doe. But I see through your elaborate stories and diversions. Were you there when the Foxfoot Thief's killer was murdered?"

"Time out. Do you not know the thief's name?"

"Of course we do." The woman bit the inside of her cheek, showing the tiniest indent on the outside. Lie. After all these years, they still didn't know anything about her mom. A double tap sounded on the glass. "I'll be right back." The woman exited, leaving Bridge alone.

What options did she have for escape? She could fake a seizure and hope to snatch something off a medical professional. More than likely, she'd hurt herself pulling it off. Throwing up had less painful consequences, but cameras watched her every move. It would be obvious if she shoved her fingers down her throat. And plus, vomit reminded her of Cowen.

The door swung open, and two agents rolled in a lie detector machine with squeaky wheels. They parked it just out of reach and began untangling the wires. The shorter man stepped close and Bridge fished his phone from his pocket with her free hand, tucking it under the sweatshirt she'd requested earlier when she said she was cold. But he had a fingerprint password and the drawing lock had thousands of combinations. Still, she started trying variations by touch, anything to get a call out to her dad or brother for help.

"It looks like Agent Amaratti is continuing to assist us. He just called to say that your brother is in custody, and he matches some of the evidence at the scene of the murder. Let's see what you have to say to Mr. Polygraph."

No. Not Liam. What horrible game was Cowen playing, and how had she failed to see his deception? Bridge held up the phone. "I just stole this off that guy who set up the machine. I'm a thief, and I'll talk if you release my brother."

"That's not how this goes," the woman said, grinning from ear to ear. "We release the innocent and prosecute the guilty."

"Good." Bridge met her grin. "Then let him go. I'm the one you want. I murdered my mother's killer."

chapter nineteen

Breakout

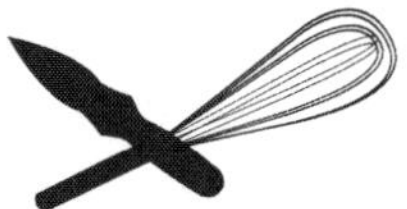

The straps around Bridge's chest moved with each breath.

"Repeat your name again." Agent Zamby crossed her hands on the table.

"Malya Collins." It was an alias Bridge had used and burned a long time before. She wasn't sure what they knew about Liam, so until she understood the stakes, she wouldn't give her real name away.

The polygraph technician nodded that she'd passed.

"Did you kill Mason Rossi?"

"Yes." When other kids played Monopoly or Clue, Liam and Bridge had played How Many Lies Can You Get Away With? The technician nodded again that she'd passed.

"Can you describe what happened?"

"Mason joined my crew a year before my mother's death. He had an in with the Boston Art Museum where the Valdez Family's Van Gogh collection would be on display. The plan was to split the profit fifty-fifty on the *View of the Sea at Scheveningen*, but he double crossed us after an alarm was triggered, shooting my mom in the back so he could ensure his escape. She died on the floor of the museum she'd worked at as a teen. That's where she fell in love with art."

Most of that was true except the part about Mason being on Bridge's crew. Her dad had always been in charge. And the bit about her mom working at that museum was false. She'd started in New York.

"So what happened next?" Agent Zamby asked.

Bridge understood she was burying herself with each word, each lie, but she'd do anything to save Liam. "Mason disappeared off the grid." Bridge didn't mention she'd taught him how. "I watched and waited for him to slip up, and when he did, I confronted him with a bullet to the head."

Agent Zamby glanced at the readout. "It looks like you're getting emotional. Let's break this down. Describe the setting."

"Warm." Bridge could picture herself on the rooftop like it was happening right now. Her skin turned clammy. Her stomach writhed. "The wind is blowing. But the birds aren't chirping. It's like they know what's about to go down."

"Did you plan to kill him?"

"No." That was definitely true. She hadn't even searched for him. As far as Mason Rossi was concerned, she'd never wanted to see him again. He'd used her. He'd killed her mom. She hadn't been sure she could control herself and not harm him. But she'd followed Liam on a hunch. For weeks, he'd been distracted. Irritable.

"What happened when you saw Mason?"

Bridge had to focus her thoughts, creating a lie from the truths. "I screamed."

"You screamed?" Agent Zamby lifted one perfectly plucked eyebrow. "Why?"

"Because I didn't want him to die." Bridge struggled to control her breathing, her body reliving the nightmare.

"But you killed him?"

She focused on Agent Zamby, pushing her memories out. "Everyone has to pay for what they've done."

The woman shifted her focus to the printout. "But did you—"

The door swung open, and Cowen entered the room carrying two Cokes. Bridge had to fight the urge to charge him, chair and all. She was already presumed guilty, she didn't need to get herself confined to the insane wing in prison. But maybe that would be worth it to knock him out. Make him bleed a little. Hurting her was one thing, but threatening her family—that was unforgivable.

Carefully, he placed one Coke in front of Bridge, his fingers fumbling as he absorbed her glares. He glanced down at the can and moved around the polygraph machine, inspecting the report. "The director suggested I come in to distract her. She's an expert liar. I'm sure your readouts aren't making much sense." He tilted his head, staring at her. "What's your name?"

"Malya Collins," she said through gritted teeth, focusing on the lie and not the memories of their kiss, of her former attraction to him.

"See, right here?" Cowen said, pointing at the results. "She spiked. That's not her name." He flipped a chair, sitting on it backward with his forearms resting on the top. "Mind if I try some more?"

Agent Zamby motioned for him to have a go.

"What's your favorite thing to bake?" he asked, his expression casual like this was just another day at the office.

Bridge threw all of her rage into a glare directed at him. "This is irrelevant."

Agent Zamby straightened. "Answer the question."

"I don't have a favorite."

"See," Cowen said, pointing to the readout. "That was true." He leaned closer. "Next question. Were you falling in love with me?"

Bridge yanked against the cuffs again, her wrist screaming. "What kind of a sick dishrag are you?"

Agent Zamby winced as if agreeing with Bridge but still having to do her job. "Answer the question."

Bridge focused, fixing him with every ounce of hate she could. "No."

Cowen watched the readout, a smile growing on his stupid lips. "See, now we're getting somewhere."

What did it say? She got the answer correct, right? She was definitely not in love with him. The emotion she felt toward Cowen Amaratti was twelve levels below hate. Maybe abominate or execrate.

"Did you pull the trigger that killed Mason Rossi?" he asked.

Focus. Focus. If Bridge took the blame, they would never look for anyone else. "Yes."

"Did you kill Mason Rossi?" he repeated.

Her jaw tightened. "I already said, yes." How could Cowen sit there and talk to her like she hadn't meant everything to him? He was an incredible actor. A devious liar. And he made her heart hurt.

Cowen leaned across the table. "Are you covering for your brother?"

Her legs shook. She hadn't expected that question.

"Answer it now," Agent Zamby said.

Bridge systematically relaxed the muscles in her body from her neck down to her toes. "No. I don't have a brother."

Cowen glanced at her Coke can again as he opened his and took a long sip. "I told you she was lying. She's covering for someone. But my guess, it's a sister not a brother. We booked the wrong guy."

Why on earth would he think she had a sister? Bridge had no idea what was going on, but maybe there was a way out of this after all. She took a moment to steady her breaths and used his misconception against him. "You're right. Her name was Sarah." If they released Bridge, her family could fabricate a sister, pointing to someone who'd already died. That way no one would have to suffer. Or they could go through with their original plan. Blame didn't matter if they were all presumed dead.

"See. That was the truth." Cowen pointed to the readout, but he focused on her Coke can. "Let's let her cool off for a bit. I'm starving." He took another drink, this time using his ring finger to tap the bottom of the can as he stood. "She let something slip about her sister once," he said as he walked out. "I bet she's regretting that."

What game was Cowen playing? She'd never said anything about a sister. And what was going on with his drink? She waited for everyone to leave, then picked up her own can. It was distinctly heavier than a normal soda.

Carefully, she opened the tab and took a drink, angling the bottom away from the cameras. And when she finished, she brought it to her lap, using two fingers to swipe three small rods off the bottom. They were probably too short for most people to work with, but Bridge was certain she could pick almost any lock with the pieces. So why did Cowen give them to her? He'd clearly sent signals—his fingers fumbling when he'd set the can down. Glancing at it. Tapping the bottom of his. And then there was his comment about her mentioning a sister. And he'd said that her dad had died in front of the director. Plus, there was that bit about some ex-boyfriend. Was he actually *helping* her?

She casually slipped the metal pieces into her pocket as the door opened again.

"That's enough for today." Agent Zamby said, shaking her head as if she was just as confused as Bridge. "Let's get you to your cell."

Two men entered with full tactical gear, and one unlocked her cuff from the chair. They walked beside her, escorting her through a hallway with a security camera and down the next one with a dead end, unmonitored for prisoner's privacy. She counted her steps, measuring off distances in her head. Four closed doors took up one side and four holding cells were on the other, all of them empty. Each had a toilet, sink, and a single mattress.

"Would you like a change of clothes?" Agent Zamby asked as she pointed Bridge into the cell and removed her cuffs. "I don't condone what you've done, but I respect you for being willing to take the heat for your sister."

Bridge dipped her head. "I'm fine with these. Thank you." She sat on the lumpy mattress and waited for the guards to lock her in.

Once everyone left the hallway, Bridge got to work. The cell lock took about six seconds, mostly because the picks were so short. She flushed the toilet and used it to cover the squeak of the door. Quietly, she edged it open and slipped out, noting the sounds coming from the next hallway. Though she couldn't see them, the guards were busy talking about the recent game between the Seattle Mariners and the San Francisco Giants. Either she needed to create a distraction or fight her way out.

The doors opposite the cells were all locked, and she quickly unpicked one in the middle, opening it to find a storage closet with linens, drawstring pants, and blocky orange shirts. But it also had a shelf of miscellaneous items. A few screwdrivers. A bouncy ball. Some toothbrushes, floss, and a bar of soap.

She returned to her cell with a few items, using the tools to remove the screws on the air vent. No human could fit through it, but that didn't matter. Cons were like magic, allowing the artist to control reactions by distracting people's minds. When people get stumped, they'll believe anything. At least she hoped it would work in this case.

Bridge left the grate on the floor with the screws strewn about then set her plan in motion, her heart beating fast. Her sweaty hand struggled to hold the ball, but she managed to chuck it into the air vent, the sound eliciting a comment from a guard.

"Did you hear that?"

It was time to move. Quietly, Bridge closed the door, ran back toward the storage closet, and slipped inside, locking the door as feet pounded past.

"How did she open that?" one of them asked, his voice high and squeaky.

"How did she fit through it?" the other asked, each word slow and drawn out. Either they would buy the ruse, or they'd start unlocking the storage room doors. Bridge's heart pounded in her throat.

A beep sounded from a radio, and the first man spoke. "Code ten-thirty-three. We've got an escaped prisoner in the ductwork. I repeat, the prisoner has escaped."

Bridge listened with her ear to the door as the guards ran past, her shoulders somewhat relaxing. Once she was positive they were clear, she exited with the soap, searching her surroundings to make sure she was still alone. A quick glance down the hall showed it was empty except for the security camera. She only had one chance at this. "Mom, Virgin Mary," she whispered. "Help." She aimed and launched the bar at the security camera, making contact and shattering the glass. Bells sounded overhead as the fire alarm went off. Fire alarm? The next second, the sprinklers in the ceiling started spraying.

That was unexpected.

Shouts and screams sounded, doors opened, and people rushed out. Everyone was too busy hurrying to notice Bridge as she joined them, working her way down a set of stairs and to the exit where armed guards were requiring everyone to show a badge.

Scanning the crowded hallway, she found another redhead up ahead with glasses. The woman's hair was straight, not wild like hers, but they were both wet, so they could pass for each other—at least that's what Bridge hoped. She slipped next to her, and faked a trip, using the woman as support and simultaneously snagging her ID. Next, she used one hand to release the clasp on a neck string holding a pair of glasses around a shorter gentleman's shoulders. Then she rushed ahead so she'd escape before the redhead knew her badge was missing.

Bridge put the glasses on, flashed the ID, and rushed outside to a darkened sky, the clouds so thick no stars or satellites shone through. She wasn't more than ten steps away before a hand slipped into hers.

"Keep walking."

"Dad." Bridge's heart pounded with relief. She was a little girl again, gripping her daddy's hand, feeling perfectly safe in his care. "What are you—"

"I'll give answers after a boost. I already unlocked this one." He pointed to an older Kia hatchback, handed her a Swiss Army knife, and

Bridge slipped into the driver's seat, tugging at the wires while he got in on the other side.

Pull. Strip. Connect. The engine roared to life, and she backed the car up.

"If it comes to a chase, this car was the worst choice," Bridge said, still relieved to have her dad beside her.

"Everything else required more tech to boost. I didn't suspect you had tools on you."

She gripped his hand. "Thanks for breaking me out."

He squeezed back, his expression still tight.

"How are you here?" she asked.

"Like I'd let my girl suffer in there. You took the blame for Mason's death, didn't you?"

Bridge shrugged, edging the nose of the car into the line of cars waiting to exit. "They have Liam in custody. I couldn't let him—"

"Yes, you can. Liam shot Mason. You don't have to pay for it. And he's not in custody."

That was a relief to know. "But he was still a kid." She struggled to stay in the present, to not revert back to the scene on the roof. "He didn't know what he was doing."

"Maybe. Maybe not. But he shouldn't have gone. He was too emotional." Rory gripped his knees, the veins on his hands swelling. "I wanted Mason to pay more than anyone. He took my wife. He took everything that mattered most to me besides you kids."

The line moved up and freedom was three cars ahead. Unlike a real prison, there were no entry or exit points at the FBI headquarters, just a regular, glorious parking lot.

"But I wasn't going to resort to revenge," Rory said. "I didn't want his blood on my hands."

"But it's on mine." Bridge gripped the steering wheel tight. "I was responsible for Liam. I should have paid more attention to what he was doing. I should have stopped—"

"If anyone is taking the blame for what Liam did, it's me," he said. "I'm his father, and I've been too soft on him. Look where we are because of it."

Bridge was positive Liam had nothing to do with this. "No, this is Cowen's fault." At least she'd thought it was. Her mind was so confused. "He's this guy I met, and he led the FBI—"

"Love," Rory said, squeezing her hand. "I've met Cowen. There's a lot going on that you don't know about."

"What are you saying?" she asked as she left the parking lot, scanning the cars around her for potential tails.

"How about we just drive for a bit. Turn right in three blocks, then follow the 205 to the airport."

She turned on the windshield wipers to take care of the mist and gripped the steering wheel tight, watching the road ahead and the cars around them, waiting for one to follow. "Why are we going to the airport?"

Rory patted her hand. "Don't freak out."

Bridge's heart thrummed in her chest. "Why would I freak out?"

"Because we have one last job."

So much had happened that she'd almost forgotten about the plan. "Right. We need to fake our deaths."

"No, love." Rory heaved a sigh. "First, we've got to re-steal the Pouncing Feline Over Koi."

chapter twenty
Takeoff

"Re-steal?" Bridge asked through gritted teeth as she drove, her foot practically flooring the gas of their ridiculously slow getaway car. That name—Pouncing Feline Over Koi—was so familiar. How did she know it? She strained and the image of a jade cat came to mind. "What are you talking about, Dad?"

"It's one last job to make things right." He kept his focus on the road. "Maybe you should slow down to avoid attention."

She made a face and switched lanes, keeping the same pace. Her anger controlled her. "That's what you said in Milwaukee. What's going on?"

"We'll talk once we're on the plane."

Bridge slammed on her brakes, causing the car behind her to swerve. "No, we'll talk now. You stole that jade cat once before, didn't you?"

Rory groaned. "Sometimes I curse that you're just like your mother." He pulled his gun out, cocked it, and aimed it at his own head. "But two can play this game. Drive."

She let off the brake and pressed the gas. "We've got a tail."

Rory glanced in the mirror, putting his gun away. "The Corolla is with us. Keep driving."

Liam. Relief swirled through Bridge's chest, knowing he was behind them. But the reprieve was short lived, her mind racing. How did her dad know Cowen? Why had he helped her escape? Why did he say he had her brother in custody if he wasn't?

"If you're not going to fess up to what you've done, then at least tell me why the jade cat?" Her eyes grew as she remembered something. "Did you know the lady in town has a replica of it?"

Rory turned toward her, his face uneasy. "What lady?"

"Gertie. She's a bit psycho. Owns a hair salon, and inside is this creepy wall of cat figurines. Sometimes, she carries them around and uses them to hiss at people."

"It's probably a coincidence," he said with a shrug that wouldn't fool anyone. "The replicas were popular in the seventies."

"Yeah, a coincidence." She got off the freeway, heading toward the airport. "Which terminal?" she asked.

"Hangar thirteen."

Bridge gave him a hard look. "Dad, we both know how much a private jet costs."

"Yeah, well, keep tallying up each of my sins. You can blame me later."

She pulled up next to the building, the Toyota following suit. A new wave of rain started as Bridge jumped out, expecting Liam. Her face fell as Cowen got out of the car.

"What are you doing here?" she asked, her feet as unsteady as her heart. Which side was he on? And did that change anything? For hours, she'd hated Cowen. Could that fade if he'd rescued her?

"I came to help." His eyes pleaded with hers.

Too much pain had already wormed its way into her heart to have room for him. "Help with what? You got me arrested. You—"

Rory pulled her back by the shoulder. "Cowen stalled the investigation to give me time to prep this," he said, pointing at the plane. "He slipped you the tools, and he was the one who started the fire. Breaking you out was all him."

Bridge wasn't ready to believe his intentions could be in their favor. "How do you two know each other?"

Her dad sighed like this wasn't important. "We met in town. Let him come."

Cowen took a step forward and she put her hand up, warning him not to get closer. She needed to think, and like the polygraph showed, he muddled everything.

"I am *not* getting on that plane without answers." Bridge faced her dad. "If you want my help, I need the truth. Now."

The wind roared past as Rory dropped his head. "That last job I mentioned at the airport—it was to clean up your brother's mess."

Bridge took a step back, disbelief rushing through her.

"He was doing jobs on the side to pad his bank account and cheating his way through school," Rory said.

"What?" She could feel her face flame. "No. He was getting straight A's. He was going to be a dentist. He had no need to steal anything."

Rory tilted his head to the side, giving her a look that told her to question everything.

All she could think about was Liam's schooling—the schooling she'd sacrificed everything to pay for. "He wouldn't fake his grades," she said, the mist turning to rain, her world crashing down. How could her own brother betray her? "He's smart. He can pass anything."

Rory motioned her and Cowen toward the plane. "You wanted him to make something more of his life, but he had other plans."

"So, this is my fault?" she asked, staying put. Blaming her would not get him anywhere. She was already doing enough of that herself.

"No, love." Rory's voice was soft. "But we can't choose anything for anyone else. He wanted a big score to prove to himself he could do jobs alone, and he screwed up. I picked up the pieces with the Marconis."

"So that's why they were watching me?" She still struggled to believe Liam went behind her back. That he'd used her.

Despite her earlier protests, Cowen inched closer as if to comfort her.

"I have no idea why they were watching you." Rory kept glancing at their plane. "But a flag went up on our family crest that weekend and—"

"Wait." Bridge rubbed her temples. "That old lady saw my tattoo."

"What old lady?" Cowen asked as if he were part of the conversation.

She glared at him, not wanting him here. He created too many unknowns. "Gertie. She came over my first morning at the cottage, and my bandage had fallen off while I slept. I changed the subject fast."

"You need to steal a jade cat, and the lady who saw your tattoo has a cat wall? That seems like more than a coincidence to me," Cowen said.

Bridge nodded because he'd made a good point, not because she wanted to agree with him. "Why don't you go check that out while we—"

Cowen stepped forward until they were close enough to touch. "I'm not leaving you."

"You can't come." She tried to look away, but the weight of what he'd sacrificed finally registered. Cowen had helped her escape. He'd torched his life and would face prison time for what he'd done. But he'd also handed her over to the Feds. She glanced around, needing something else to focus on and instantly found a reason to make her panic. "Wait, where's Liam?"

Rory's gaze drifted over her face before finally settling on her eyes. "The Marconis are holding him for ransom. They want the jade cat in sixty-eight hours."

Bridge's knees gave out, and she dropped to the ground, her hands palming the tarmac for support. "Why didn't you tell me earlier?" Spittle flew with her words. "We can find him and break him free."

Her dad softly touched her shoulder. "Without the cat, we don't have leverage."

"We don't need it." In a swift motion, she stood and pulled Cowen's gun for the second time that day. "I'll kill all of them."

Rory slowly approached her, his hands extended until he reached the gun. Carefully, he took it out of her shaking hands and gave it back to Cowen. "And then what? Keep running? Keep blaming yourself for everything that's happened?"

Rain dripped down her face in angry streaks. "If that's what it takes." She'd suffered too many emotions in too little time. Her mind was shutting down rational thoughts.

Cowen touched her arm. "Let's just get on the plane and make a plan."

She jerked away. "You are not going anywhere with us. You can't throw your life away." That wasn't the cutting remark she'd planned in her head. Against her will, she kept picturing him behind bars for rescuing her. But then her thoughts intertwined, the cords tightly kinked with the knowledge that he'd betrayed her. He'd led the FBI to her. Like all of her own mistakes, she couldn't let his go.

He stepped closer. "It's *my* life, Bridge. And I've already done enough damage. Helping your brother is the only way for me to look at myself in the mirror again. I hate what I've done. I let you down. I didn't protect my partner. I took a life. You of all people should understand wanting to make amends."

She crossed her arms over her chest, her wrist still aching from the handcuffs. "You don't get to."

Pain sank into the creases next to his eyes. "Won't you let me explain? The FBI tracked me with my phone. I had no idea they were coming today. The director learned about you after your *boyfriend* showed up. I was upset, and I'm sorry. Your brother was never in custody, I lied about that to stall them, but I redirected the conversation so they would think you have a sister and never look for your brother. Yes, I screwed some things up, but—"

"I'm sorry you risked everything for nothing." No amount of apologies or explanations could heal the betrayal she felt. That was the way things had to be, because she literally couldn't process any more. She needed to rescue her brother, and she couldn't do it with Cowen around. They were wasting precious time.

"I don't care about anything I've given up." He stepped forward, rain dripping off his hair. "I care about you."

"That's a mistake you shouldn't have made. C'mon, Dad." Bridge gripped her dad's arm and yanked him away.

"How do I prove myself to you?" Cowen jogged to keep up with her hurried steps.

"You can't."

He stretched for her hand as she reached the stairs to the plane, but she pulled away.

"You knew the Feds were coming, and you didn't say. That is betrayal. And it's something I can never forgive."

Cowen dipped his head, keeping his expressions to himself. "I'm sorry, Bridge. For everything." He pulled her ledger out of his pocket and slipped it into her hands.

His apology was so sincere, she felt herself drifting toward him, but emotions were stupid complications she couldn't entertain. Her brother needed her help. "Good, now get out of our way."

Bridge stormed up the stairs, shoving the book into her pocket. She fell into a seat on the plane, her body slumping, her muscles caving in as raindrops pelted the windows.

"He could have helped us," Rory said as he sat across from her, wet streaks staining his suit pants.

"Can we just not?" Bridge placed her folded arms onto the table and buried her head in them. There was one task at hand, and she needed to focus on it. *Save Liam.* "Where are we going?"

"Texas."

She groaned, partly because of the location and partly because her mind kept foolishly drifting back to Cowen. "Please tell me we're not going to steal from a gun-happy right-winged republican."

Rory winced. "Jackson Sloan is all of those things, plus, he has a thing for precious stones in his art collection. He thinks there's some sort of healing property in crystals, especially jade."

"Great, even better." She flung her arms in the air as the plane took off. "Is everyone we're dealing with crazy?"

Rory ignored her question. "I've got the plans for his house. It looks like he's got an underground art wing. The walls, floors, and ceiling are four-feet thick concrete. The only way in is a…"

"Let me guess, it's a Garber-Redding safe door?" She waited for her dad to nod. This day kept getting worse. "He built the freaking Fort Knox in his basement?"

Rory ground his teeth. "And the hallway leading to it is pressure, heat, and sound sensitive."

This was impossible. "You want to pull this off in sixty-eight hours? The equipment list alone is a mile—"

"Make a shopping list. I'll have someone pick everything up."

Bridge let out a sigh. Her brother's life depended on her stealing the statue. "Fine." She pulled out her phone and began typing in needed items.

"How's your Texas Dip?" he asked.

"Dad!" Bridge laced her voice with every weapon possible. "I told you I'd never play the part of a debutante again."

He took no notice of her complaints. "Sloan loves redheads. Especially ones with curly hair. And there's a ball tomorrow night at his estate. Steal his heart. Get him to show you his collection. Knock him out. Easy."

"Easy, says the guy who's never had to wear heels and a corset."

"Remember the Drag Princess Runway show?" He shifted uncomfortably in his seat. "I wore heels to protect your mom. She got a little too close to the mark on that one."

"Well, she had to get that diamond off his neck." Bridge put her head in her hands as the plane took off. "I can't let anything happen to Liam." That's what she said, but her mind was picturing Cowen. Even though she couldn't stand what he'd done, he didn't deserve whatever fallout was coming. If they had time—if they survived this—maybe they could help him.

"I know. That's why there will be a wardrobe and limo waiting when we land. Get some sleep, you can memorize your backstory when we arrive."

The plane leveled off, reaching altitude, but Bridge was anything but level-headed. "Did I make things worse for Cowen by not letting him come?"

Rory shook his head, his eyes soft and concerned. "There's probably no coming back from what he's done. It would be best for us to kill off his identity when we end ours."

"We can't take him with us." If all went to plan, they'd find a private island for sale with no extradition and live out their days. "I can't be near him."

"I know that's what you're telling yourself." Rory leaned back and closed his eyes. "Maybe this job will change your mind."

Nothing could change how Bridge saw the world. No matter what she'd felt for Cowen, it couldn't cover the mistake he'd made.

chapter twenty-one
Alarm

The clock read 1:04 a.m. when Cowen made it back to Pilpil Bay. More than likely, someone was looking for him—the director, field agents, maybe even the Marconi family. He was nowhere near as skilled as Bridge in eluding danger.

He'd come back to town to scratch an itch to find Liam. The double mention of Gertie with her replica of the jade cat and her seeing Bridge's tattoo meant something. Maybe she was an innocent old woman on the salty and…special side. Or maybe there was more. Either way, he was about to find out.

His plan had been to grab the fake Pouncing Feline Over Koi to use as a bargaining chip, pretending it was the real deal, but when he noticed the alarm system wires outside of Gertie's salon, everything changed. He crouched in front of her store, and it took him about twenty seconds to pick the lock. As soon as he did, he triggered the alarm, grabbed the jade cat amongst hundreds of creepy ones, and jumped into his Jeep, driving away with his lights off.

Gertie lived above everyone on a single hill a mile north, dotted with pine trees. His heart stuttered as a light flipped on in her house, illuminating one of her windows that was visible to the entire town. He parked on a side road, killing the engine, and waited.

Cowen half expected Gertie to call someone to check the salon out for her, but three minutes later, her car flew past. His countdown began as he sped up her private drive. If she were hiding something, he had to discover it quickly. There was only one way down the mountain.

A light mist fell, and his shoes left footprints on the driveway. It took him thirty-two seconds to pick the lock, his nerves fighting to take over. And when he entered with his flashlight on, instead of finding another alarm, he found floor-to-ceiling shelves in the hallway full of organized sections of porcelain dolls, gold plates, tea sets, comic books, vinyl records, stamps, and coins. He walked further in, the hallway expanding into a combined living room and kitchen decked out in seventies retro curves. Each wall was lined with art crammed so tight that all the frames touched the others. He hurried down the hall, trying each closed door. A linen closet. A room with mirrors and costumes. Another with a bunch of wires and tech. A master full of art and naked men statues.

There was no sign of Bridge's brother on the main floor. Cowen glanced outside for signs of Gertie before descending the floating stairs to the basement. Rugs hung along the walls in an open room, and they covered the floor. And that was it. Just rugs. A single hallway ran to the left and Cowen entered the first door, his nose wrinkling at the acidic smell of a darkroom. The second and third doors were locked. He didn't have time to pick them both.

"Liam?" Cowen whispered, knocking on the wall. "Liam," he said louder as he crouched down and got to work on the first lock. Time was running out. He knew it. There was nothing incriminating in this house, other than hoarded junk. If he were caught…well, he didn't want to finish that thought. His fingers fumbled as he worked. Why was he doing this? He had no idea if he could ever convince Bridge to forgive him, but here he was for the second time that night, scorching his future.

The lock released, and he swung the door open. His heart shuddered as his flashlight gleamed on the metal barrels of a gun lined room. Weapon collecting wasn't a crime, but among several Lugers and a sea of Glocks were three illegal machine guns and a pile of short-barreled shotguns. The evidence was enough for Gertie to serve jail time—if he'd had a warrant. Cowen snapped some pictures and turned to inspect the last room.

"Yours was a pretty face," a gravely woman's voice sounded through the dark before something hard slammed into his forehead, knocking him out.

chapter twenty-two

The Texas Dip

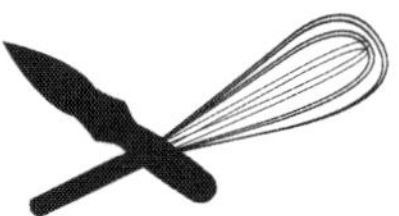

Crystal chandeliers hung with Texan pride as Bridge entered the hill-country styled Sloan Mansion wearing a froofy gown with elbow length gloves. "My dress is clearly not peach," Bridge whispered, her earpiece able to pick up her voice as she passed another girl, their skirts swishing in the tight space of the crowded entrance hall.

Every other debutante ball Bridge had attended, the required dress color was white. This one was peach. Traditions everywhere, in every culture, seemed to be disappearing. Except for amongst thieves. The Marconis had given them seventy-two hours. That was honorable.

"Pink. Peach. Close enough," Rory said, his voice sounding inside her ear.

"Not when everyone else is matching." Bridge drifted to the side of the hall so she could get her bearings. If this were real life, she'd love to be dolled up. But Liam's fate was on the line. And stupid Cowen wouldn't get out of her head. "I swear, they have the same Pantone."

"*Peach Fuzz* is the Pantone name and tonight's required color. There wasn't enough time to build an entirely new dress."

"Build? You mean stitch," Bridge said under her breath before flashing a smile to a young man across the way. "I'm going to stand out."

"It's just a shade off," Rory said without seeming to share Bridge's worries.

Bridge eyed the other girls, finding one about her height. If she followed this girl to the bathroom, she could knock her out, tie her to the toilet, and steal her dress. She took two steps before her dad interrupted.

"Don't even think about it," he said, his voice already annoying. "Jackson is a guy. He won't notice. And stand straighter. You're supposed to look graceful."

Bridge looked ahead in the hall and spotted her dad carrying a tray of champagne flutes in a server's uniform. "How about *you* line your body with tools, and then try to walk like a porcelain doll?"

That shut him up for a while as she entered a ballroom with lavishly draped tables, the linens stitched with gold threads. Lanterns sat on top, surrounded by fresh greenery, and servers kept the wine and champagne glasses full.

"I should have asked this earlier," her dad said, "but can you do the Texas Dip with all of that?"

"I don't know." The last time she'd done the bow in public, she'd had a private coach for two weeks. That was six years ago. "Target acquired," Bridge said, spotting Jackson Sloan across the room dancing with a brunette. But his eyes were on a woman in the center of a sea of men, each of them eyeing the redhead like a vulture would a carcass.

"Get his attention first. Make him want—"

"I know what I'm doing." Bridge strolled the perimeter with her head high, each footstep perfectly placed. She passed the redhead and her entourage, distracting more than half the men. Soon, she had several following on each side, talking her ear off, each one upping the others about his accomplishments. It made her miss those quiet moments in Cowen's arms on the swing or on a couch, watching a movie.

She cleared her voice loudly, banishing those thoughts. "Sorry, boys. I'm a bit out of sorts until I get some dancing in. Would one of you mind doing the honors?" She grabbed the man to her left, a broad chested blond with too white teeth, and let him lead her onto the dance floor.

"There's a kiss later if you can get me to laugh." Bridge gave him a flirty grin. A woman's laughter was Aphrodite's nectar to men, and she needed to lure Jackson Sloan in. Liam's life depended on him falling for her. At least enough to get him to show her his vault. But each time she looked his way, he was glancing at that other redhead.

"I never lose a challenge," her dance partner said as he launched into a waltz and his personal tales, some of which were marginally funny. Bridge leaned into each one, letting her laughter grow and carry across the room.

The song ended, and they were instantly surrounded by men, each vying for a turn.

Her dance partner bowed, kissing the back of her hand. It did nothing for her compared to the kiss Cowen had placed on the inside of her wrist. "It looks like I won your challenge," he said. "I'll meet you at ten for my kiss?"

Bridge gave him a flirty grin. "Ten is already full, but I'll see you at ten twenty-five. Who wants ten thirty?"

Another man whisked her away. Another laugh. Another promised kiss on her calendar.

By the time she'd endured a dozen songs, Jackson Sloan made his way toward her. He was tall and husky with the straightest teeth money could buy. The men parted, letting him have the next turn. He pulled Bridge close, his expensive Dior cologne unmistakable.

"We haven't met yet." He moved her around the floor with ease. "I'm Jackson Sloan."

Bridge blinked once, slowly. "Victoria Hunt. Pleased to meet you."

Usually men's heart rates quickened with her demure look, but not his.

"So what do I do to make you laugh?" he asked. "Every other guy had you giggling within the first twenty seconds. I'm already at twenty-two."

Why wasn't he falling for her? Bridge shifted her lips into a scandalous smile. "I bribed each one with a kiss to tell me something funny."

Jackson's gaze traveled all over her face, but he didn't pause at her lips. "Why is that?"

Rory spoke. "Ease up."

Exactly her thoughts. She averted her gaze, seeing if Jackson preferred his women to be hard to get, but he still seemed disinterested. "I was trying to win your attention."

"Why? You're already in love with someone else."

"Tom Holland," Bridge choked out, her thoughts drifting to Cowen. His arms around her. His lips against hers.

"Keep your character," Rory hissed in her ear. "Find a different angle." Easy for him to say. He was serving drinks without a memorized backstory and the weight of everything on his shoulders. Or rather, his legs.

Jackson watched her, his expression calculated but curious.

"How can you say that about me when you're clearly in love with someone else too?" Bridge flashed her eyes at the redhead glancing their way. The woman's ears were practically smoking.

Jackson glided forward. "Is it that obvious?"

"I'm very observant," Bridge said. "Did you just meet her?"

Red crept up his cheeks. "I've known her my whole life. We actually used to hate each other, but that's a long story."

Bridge tilted her head, making herself appear interested. "We have at least a minute left of this dance. Three if we take another spin. What's the CliffsNotes version?"

Jackson laughed. "If I was keeping a list of the women I wanted to pursue, you'd definitely make number two."

Two didn't get the Pouncing Feline Over Koi. "The story?" she asked.

"Annie rigged the scale at the county fair so my hog weighed less than her brother's."

Pigs? Where else could anyone combine ball gowns, Stetsons, and talk of livestock? Only Texas.

"Turns out, her brother was dying of cancer and she'd done it to make sure he won. I guess it was one of his dreams." Jackson pushed Bridge away in a spin before rolling her back into his arms.

She tried to make the moment last, to cast a spell as she batted her eyes, but he was never going to bite with this tactic.

Jackson eased her back into the waltz. "I'm now a firm believer that intentions outweigh wrong deeds."

The con was afoot, albeit struggling, and all Bridge could think of was Cowen after that comment. He'd helped her, risking his career, his future, and the freedom to visit his mom. But still, she wasn't able to forgive him—not even close. Intents couldn't outweigh deeds in her book, but if Jackson believed that, she would exploit it to save Liam.

"So, what if someone were to steal the Pouncing Feline Over Koi from your vault because they need it to free their brother from kidnappers?"

Rory cursed in her ear. "You better know what you're doing."

Jackson stumbled only once as he searched her eyes. "You're here to rob me, Ms. Victoria?"

She shrugged her bare shoulders, giving him a playful look that morphed into her deadliest challenging stare. "What if I was?"

He tipped his head back and laughed. "What will everyone think? You got me to laugh, but I didn't get you."

"Maybe we need to extend our dance with a trip to the vault. What do you say? Once the statue is in my possession, I'm willing to pee my pants at one of your jokes."

His lips twitched as he considered her. "Your brother?"

Bridge nodded. "Four years younger. I practically raised him, so when someone threatens him—"

"The mama bear comes out." He nodded. "If you were to get your hands on the statue, I'd say you need to steal it back and return it in two weeks when my mom visits again. She swears it's keeping her vertigo at bay." The dance ended, and he took her hand and bowed low and deep.

"Deal." Bridge followed suit, crossing her heels, back straight, arms extended, and lowered herself like a pretzel to the ground until her butt touched the back of her heels. It was the perfect, painful Texas Dip.

Jackson helped her up.

"Just like that, you'll let me have it?" she asked.

He tucked her hand around his forearm. "I've learned that a woman who can do the Texas Dip will stop at nothing to get what she wants. And plus, Annie is so flaming jealous right now because of you, she's going to stop dragging her boots and accept my proposal."

"So win-win for both of us?"

His teeth gleamed. "I reckon so."

Everyone watched as Jackson led Bridge toward the elevator blocked by a sentry carrying at least two guns under his suit coat. Bridge suspected he had a few more. She certainly did under all of this froufrou.

When the elevator doors closed, Jackson kept his grip on her. "So… who's the guy in your life?"

Bridge wrinkled her eyebrows. "There's no one."

Jackson leaned into her space, and she flinched. "Sorry sweetheart, but I'm calling your bluff. Girls whose minds are elsewhere can't receive a man's gestures, and when I pulled you close at the beginning of our dance, you shied away. It's the only thing us men know for certain about women."

This was not supposed to get personal. Bridge could work under every kind of pressure, but this…talking about herself was not her strong suit. She let out a sigh, owning the truth. "He's not in the picture anymore."

The elevator stopped and Jackson breathed into the sensor to get the door to open. "Maybe, but he still has your heart." He placed his palm on the scanner of a glass door, leading to the sensitive hallway, and it opened. "This way." Jackson led her to the vault, releasing her hand to punch the keypad.

"Biometric. Nice." She'd expected that and carried a kit to pull his fingerprints off her skin—though they had a short shelf-life. Fifteen minutes at most.

He spun his finger, waiting for her to turn around and punched the code.

"You'll have to change the password when we're done." She faced him with a smirk. "It's seven, two, four, nine, nine, nine, eight."

"How did you—"

"The tones. They're distinct."

Jackson shook his head, grinning as he spun the wheel, and the two-foot thick door opened into a brightly lit room big enough to house a large corral. The shiny granite floors paired perfectly with paintings lining the perimeter and pedestals holding sculptures.

Bridge instantly saw the Pouncing Feline Over Koi on the opposite side, but she took her time weaving between the art. "You have interesting taste," she said, pausing at a sprocket and gear contraption, no doubt the art of Cyrus Kabiru.

"Most of it was acquired from my pa. He didn't really care what he had, as long as he owned what someone else wanted." Jackson led her to a bench in the middle. "Wait here, and I'll get it for you."

She sat, and he unexpectedly joined her, slipping his hands around her waist. Bridge could hardly get a breath in before he approached her lips for a kiss. "What are you—"

Cold metal clamped around both wrists, and when she yanked, it dug into her wrists.

Jackson stepped away with a condescending smirk. "Sorry sugar, but thieves can never be trusted."

chapter twenty-three

Bombs

Pain forced Cowen's eyes open, but his vision was blurry, blending together rug patterns in the faint light. His thoughts were hazy. Guns. Danger. Bridge. Was she safe? He should have been focused on his own neck, but his mind kept spinning around her.

He wasn't fully cognizant when a cruel, scratchy voice sounded near him.

"If you weren't snooping through my house, I'd maybe be sorry about the goose egg on your head." The old woman pointed a forty-five at him, her legs crossed beneath her on the floor across from him, her body covered with a silk robe.

"Gertie," he said, picking his words carefully and feeling his surroundings. His hands were zip tied behind his back. "I can explain. There was a kidnapping, and I've been searching all the homes nearby for—"

"You're not nearly as good a liar as your girlfriend. Why don't you tell me the truth?" She cocked the gun.

What if he died right here in this psycho woman's house without ever getting to see Bridge again? Cowen's demons whispered that's what he deserved. He'd taken a life. His should be forfeit.

But what about Liam's? The question came out of nowhere, as if his mind was trying to prove a point. If Cowen thought his own life was worth nothing for shooting someone in defense, what did that make Liam's worth? Hadn't Cowen already risked everything to rescue a murdering thief?

"I *am* looking for someone who was kidnapped, but I was drawn to your house because the ransom is a jade cat statue, and you have a replica in your shop. I thought there was maybe a connection. But I was wrong."

Gertie's eyes narrowed. "Who knows you're here?"

Cowen knew the odds of both answers. If he said no one, she could easily kill him—if she were that sort, and chances were with her gun collection, she was. But if he mentioned that Rory or Bridge suspected he was here, she might go after them.

"No one."

"For being FBI, you're pretty dumb. But just in case I need you later, you can stay as my houseguest. Breakfast is in an hour, bathroom privileges are revoked, and there's a trip wire tied to your zip tie. Move and you'll blow yourself up." She stood effortlessly, her robe billowing. "Enjoy your stay."

"So," Gertie said as she placed a tray of food in front of Cowen on the rug an hour later. "Where's your girlfriend?" A bowl of oatmeal steamed beside a plate of fresh blueberries and raspberries. "I picked those myself," she said when he didn't answer.

Cowen just stared straight at her, refusing to respond. Where was Bridge? Was she safe? Even if she never forgave him, how could he protect her when he was stuck here?

"Hopefully for you," Gertie said, "she's on her way back with my cat."

He shrugged. "I honestly don't know what she's doing right now. If you haven't noticed, I'm a bit tied up. And my phone appears to be missing—"

"And you don't have any other communication devices. I know. I already searched you." She gandered at him like a cougar inspecting a meal.

The contents of Cowen's stomach sloshed. "If you've got sick plans, please shoot me first."

She glanced at the gun in her hand before placing it on the floor beside her. "I'll think about it. *If* you help me."

"Why would I help you? Where's Liam? Why are you—"

"Oh doll, this isn't the movies. I'm not going to confess to you. But I can honestly say that I don't know where Liam is. The Italian mob legitimately has him. I *will* give you one of my secrets though, seeing as I'll need to relocate. The hoarding is fake. I just use it to hide my original pieces. Who would believe I have millions of dollars of art hidden amongst so much junk?"

The woman was certifiable.

"What part do you play in the kidnapping?" More than likely, Cowen was going to die. If that's how his story ended, he wanted to do anything possible to get help to Liam. The more he knew, the better.

Gertie laughed, her ridiculously tall hair swaying. "I'm just here to get my cat back."

His stomach rose. At any moment, he might puke. "You intercepted the ransom note?"

A demonic grin spread across her lips. "Maybe I did. Maybe I didn't."

Cowen's shoulders sank, the joints grinding with the sudden movement after sitting still too long. Coming here had brought him no closer to helping. "But if Esty shows up with your cat and not what the mob wants, they'll kill her brother."

Gertie shrugged like it wasn't her problem. "Aren't you going to eat your food?"

He gagged, but somehow held it in. "I can't. You've got me hooked up to a bomb."

She laughed again, her shrill maniacal voice absorbing into the rug-lined room. "There's no bomb connected to your hands, silly. But eat up so you can drive your filthy Jeep off my property. I'll let you park it in the ocean where the high tide will barely cover your nose." She stood, pointing her gun at him. "If you're smart enough, you can live. If not, well, goodbye chum." She waved the gun above her head as she climbed the stairs. "But I should probably mention there *is* a wire attaching your feet to the bomb on the south wall. See you after breakfast."

Cowen glanced around, finding a device on the other side of the room with the number fifteen glowing in red. Fifteen seconds. The next time Gertie came down, he could blow them both up. That would be a fitting end for him since he'd royally ruined everything. If he was gone though, how would Bridge know the ransom note had been altered? How would he ever beg her for forgiveness? He left the food untouched, trying again and again to bust the zip tie behind his back—but without proper leverage, he couldn't get the bands to break.

Music sounded from upstairs, along with footsteps as if Gertie was dancing. She was seriously messed up. Cowen bent at the waist, searching his shoes for the clear thread. It ran around one of his ankles. Carefully, he scooted forward to give himself some slack and brought his legs in like a frog to use his teeth to remove the string, but he couldn't bend far enough. It took him a few more tries before he realized his stupidity, forced himself to his feet, and walked over to the bomb, which looked an awful lot like a CD player. Cowen crouched down, his head throbbing, and inspected it. It definitely was a CD player, and when he followed the end of the thread, it was simply tied around the player's handle.

He could strangle her.

The footsteps continued overhead, the music something Latin. With his arms still behind his back, Cowen tried the door to the weapons. Locked. But the darkroom wasn't, and he found a paper cutter on the counter. He backed up and sawed the zip tie, slicing the flesh on his left palm only once. As soon as the plastic snapped, he grabbed a bottle of Phenidone developer with eye and skin irritant warnings on the side and sneaked back into the room with blood dripping from his hand. Quickly, he tied the string she'd used to trick him across the bottom two stairs at shin level, glancing up the whole time, expecting her to catch him. He emptied the bowl of oatmeal under one of the rugs and refilled the bowl with the chemical before returning the bottle to the darkroom, resuming his earlier position with hands behind his back, and waited.

The woman didn't return for a few hours—at least she hadn't stolen his watch. She took her time on the stairs, her hair bobbing. "That looks uncomfortable. And to think, I've got a nice, soft bed up—"

Gertie tripped on the thread, her body catapulting toward Cowen. He grabbed hold of the bowl and splashed her face as she fell. The robe splayed open, revealing more wrinkly skin than he ever wanted to see. Screaming, her body hit the ground with a thud.

"How does that taste?" he asked as he stole the gun from her. She whipped around as if ready to kick it from him, but he cocked the trigger, pointing it at her stupid hair.

"You're smarter than I thought," she said, one hand covering her eyes, preventing her from seeing his shaking limbs.

Cowen never wanted to shoot anyone again, but if he had to, he'd take out her fingers or a knee. Slowly, he crept toward his escape, keeping the gun trained on her.

"Good thing I put a bomb in your car," she said with a sadistic smile, the rest of her face wincing.

Like he was going to fall for that again. Cowen aimed far above her head and shot. Gertie rolled out of the way, and he darted up the stairs and out the door. He was one step closer to helping Liam. One step closer to Bridge.

His keys were in the cupholder like he'd left them, but as he got ready to start the engine, he couldn't shrug an uneasy feeling. He got out and crouched down to see a red light flashing on a pack of C-4 attached to the four-wheel drive transfer case. Fear weighed his steps as he ran toward the woods, making it ten feet before a beep sounded.

His Jeep exploded.

chapter twenty-four

Pressure

Bridge yanked on the handcuffs, her eyes staring disbelievingly at Jackson.

He laughed, glancing her over as if she wasn't capable of doing anything to him while cuffed to the bench. "Do you think you're the first debutante to try and steal from me?" he asked, circling her.

"I told you, I just need to borrow the statue for a few days. Let me get my brother—"

"You're a fool to think I'd let you walk away with a four million dollar piece of art."

"And you're a fool to think I don't have backup. Have you developed a resistance to chloroform?" she asked as her dad approached from behind and smothered Jackson's face with a soaked handkerchief. Really, it wasn't straight chloroform—the amount needed to actually make someone pass out was more lethal than useful—but she'd perfected her own chemical blend over the years, even infusing it with lavender and melatonin so their victims slept peacefully.

"I guess it's a good thing I don't trust anyone." She bent, using her lips to grip a thin piece of metal from the tool belt around her calf and drop it on her dress. "A little help?"

Rory considered her a moment before grabbing the tool and slipping it into her hands. "If we weren't pressed for time, I'd rather watch you get out of it yourself. It's entertaining."

Bridge released the cuffs and stood. "Remember that the next time you need me. Is the hallway still disabled?"

"Aye, for now. I placed some stoppers, so even if we set off the alarm, we should still be able to slip out." He waved an electrical meter along the pedestal holding up the statue. "It's got a pressure sensor under the plate." He felt around the back to open the maintenance hatch and winced.

Bridge could thwart the mechanism in her sleep—if she had the correct tools. "What's the matter?"

He shifted. "Old wound. What do you need?"

She inspected the mechanics. "If the mass changes, a clamp tightens around a hose with the sole job of dispensing a gas—most likely oxygen— that spins a dial that connects to the sensor. If I touch the dial, it'll sound the alarm. But if we apply our own air, we can fool the system while I adjust the required weight." Bridge would have preferred using a concentrator to provide a buffer while she recalibrated the sensor, but they could only pack so much. "Give me your meter."

Rory handed it over, and she slipped him a clear plastic tube about the width of her pinky that she'd pulled off one of the straps around her leg.

"You can still do that weird, circular breathing thing, right?" she asked.

"Just call me Kenny G." Rory pulled items from his pocket and attached a ball inflator needle with a modified tip to the end of the tube, using some adhesive tape to make an airtight seal.

"What are we going to swap the cat with?" Bridge continued to fiddle with the wires in the electrical housing until she understood the purpose of each one.

"I've got an idea." Rory slipped away for a moment and returned with Jackson's shoe filled with the man's keys, wallet, and phone.

"Not bad." Bridge pulled a digital luggage scale off her leg and used it to calculate the weight. According to the reading on the pedestal, the new "statue" was four ounces lighter than the cat. "Give me a second. On my count, stab the hose and apply steady airflow while I adjust the weight. When I nod, swap the items as you blow, and I'll make sure this works on my end."

Rory gave her a sideways glance. "You don't sound positive."

"It's been a while, okay?"

He touched her arm. "This has wires and moving parts. You can fix anything with moving parts."

Bridge tried to smile, but her dry teeth prevented her lips from budging. The pressure of the situation gnawed at her. If they didn't get this right, escaping could end in catastrophe. And then who would save Liam? "Three. Two. One. Go."

Rory stabbed while Bridge tapped into the sensor, connecting the wiring to her meter.

"Good. Keep going," she said. "I can spoof the reading by half a second. That's all you'll have to make the switch before the new weight is entered."

Rory lifted the shoe toward the pedestal, his lips around the tube, but he tapped Bridge's knee, the whites of his eyes growing.

"You can't reach the cat," she said, tipping her head back as she gritted her teeth. They needed a longer tube, but without one, without any other option, they'd failed.

Rory pleaded with his eyes for her to question everything.

"Fine, you'll have to enter the weight while I swap." Bridge was good at many things, but quick moves were her dad's specialty. And he wasn't great at anything with buttons. This plan definitely had flaws.

He gave her knee a squeeze as if to say she could do this.

"I hope you're right." Bridge took the filled shoe, handed him the meter, and showed him what to push. "On three." She stood, staring at the stupid cat. She'd never understood why art was worth so much that people could value it over a life. It was just another status symbol, a way to show superiority. Sure, there were pieces she liked, but they were never worth the prices people were willing to pay. World hunger could be eradicated if people donated that money instead.

"One." Bridge stretched her fingers. "Two." She focused on her breath, and for some reason, that brought a memory of Cowen searching for her underwater in the boat's cabin. He'd risked his life to save hers. Didn't that count for anything? She pushed the thought away and said, "Three." The shoe left one hand and the cat entered her other. She handed it to her dad and took the meter, checking everything over and disconnecting as he continued to blow. They'd done it. "You can stop now."

He pulled out the inflating needle from the hose and took a deep breath. "Nice job, kid."

"Nice job, yourself," she said as she strapped everything back onto her legs.

"While you're at it…" Rory handed Bridge the nine by six inch statue.

"Seriously?" She glared at him for being a man with only pockets and not a place to hide anything big as she secured the cat around the back of her right calf. "This doesn't make my walking look awkward at all." At least the skirt was massive and hid everything.

He laughed and held out his arm for her. "Let's go save Liam."

Bridge followed her dad onto the elevator, and he boosted her through the grate in the ceiling. As soon as he pressed the button for the second floor, she lowered a rope down to him and held it as he climbed up, groaning.

"Old wound, huh?" She didn't buy his excuse for a second. His injury was recent.

"Add it to my list of sins."

They slid the grate in place while the elevator rose. The doors opened, and the security guard got in, his weight shifting the cabin.

A beep sounded, followed by his frantic voice as they watched him through the grate. "Sir, is everything okay?" he asked. When no answer followed, he tried one more time before switching channels. "All units, code 10-33 in the vault."

The elevator jolted down, and once low enough, Bridge and Rory stepped onto the narrow ledge of the first floor, barely big enough for the tips of their shoes. Bridge lifted her left leg, and her dad unstrapped a remote. Two presses tricked the doors into opening, and they stepped back into the party. He turned toward the kitchens while she headed into the ballroom, having to dance and promise another kiss for a laugh as her partner circled her around the room.

They neared the veranda and Bridge stopped, gripping her head. "I think I drank too much. I need some fresh air."

The young Texan escorted her outside and she feigned dizziness, leaning against the balcony, the statue digging into her calf. "Could you get me a glass of water? Maybe a piece of cheese too? Bacon gouda if possible. If not, some gruyère."

"Cheese?" Rory asked through her ear.

As soon as the guy disappeared, Bridge walked along the edge of the porch, waiting for an opening to hop the railing. "I wanted him to have to search long enough that I'll be long gone when he returns." She glanced both ways, making sure no one could see her, hefted the dress, and jumped into a bed of purple verbena. Her heels dug into the soft soil, but she quickly walked away as if she were out for an evening stroll. Rory joined her, his waiter uniform replaced with a fitted tux, and offered her his arm.

"I love dressing up with you. Maybe we should do it more often," he said.

She bumped his hip with hers as an alarm sounded behind them. "Find a legitimate reason, and I'll be there."

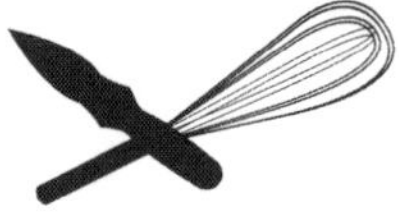

Bridge woke as their plane descended toward Portland.

Her dad was sitting across from her, sipping from a mug. "When you told Jackson you don't trust *anyone*," Rory said, his forehead wrinkled, "does that include me, your dear old da?"

The pressure in her ear shifted, and Bridge yawned, stretching. She pointed to the interior of the jet. "When we disbanded, you said you were going to donate your money to charity."

"Fair point," he said with a shrug. "But what about Cowen? Shouldn't his intent figure in to whether or not you can trust—"

"Why are you so insistent about him?"

Rory took a long sip before leaning closer, pointing the mug at her. "Because of the way he looks at you." He settled back, staring at his empty cup. "I see myself in his shoes, chasing after the girl he loves, being willing to do *anything* to keep her." He gave her another one of his looks that meant to dig deeper.

"What does that mean?"

He spun his mug on the table between them as if debating what to say. "It means I was in medical school when I met your mother."

Medical school? That made zero sense. "No. You met her following the same mark on a con."

Several moments flew by before her dad spoke. "The mark was my dad."

Bridge's head thrummed with too little sleep and illogical information. "You told us…"

"We told you wrong. This was the life we chose, and it did no one any good to consider otherwise."

"So what, you found her trailing him, and you thought that a life of crime sounded like more fun than being a doctor?"

He gave Bridge a sheepish shrug. "I saw her and knew I couldn't ever let her go, even if it meant dipping into the dark side."

Bridge planted her hands on the table. "Dad, you plunged. And did it ever occur to you to convince Mom to join *your* side?"

"If you knew your mother then, you'd know it never would have worked. Look, I'm not trying to get into a moral argument here. I'm just trying to explain to you that Cowen has already jumped for you. Either you can let him fall and suffer the consequences, or you can catch him."

"I don't want him to fall, but even if I could help—which I'm not sure about at this point—I don't even know how to reach him."

Rory grinned. "I guess it's a good thing I told him how to contact us."

"You didn't," Bridge said, her jaw dropping in disbelief.

"I did."

She didn't know how to process her dad's actions. Their family's communication system was intended only for them. No one had ever been given access. Not even Mason Rossi. It was…sacred. "But how can you trust—"

"I never trusted Mason, but you wanted to give him a chance. This time, I'm listening to my own gut. I'm certain Cowen won't let us down."

chapter twenty-five

Pillbox

Cowen glanced both ways before hopping the fence to Karen's tree-lined backyard and knocking on the back door. His skin and muscles hurt from shrapnel and being flung into brush from the blast, but otherwise, he was unharmed. His thoughts kept drifting to Bridge. Was she safe? Could he help save her brother? Would she forgive him?

Footsteps sounded and he expected Virgil, but the man's wife answered, wearing a Def Leppard shirt.

"What on earth happened to you?" Karen said loud enough to alert anyone nearby. "And who was that man who dropped off your dog?"

Cowen brought a finger to his lips. If she said more, he'd have to cover her mouth with his hand. "Can I come inside? It's not safe out here."

She nodded up and down, but her feet barely moved. No doubt Cowen looked alarming with the gash and bump on his forehead and the cuts on his face and arms. He'd been lucky to escape the blast, even luckier to flee down the hill and through town undetected. Gertie was a chocolate chip cookie missing eggs, sugar, butter, and flour. Probably the chocolate chips too.

"I just need a place to regroup for a bit," he said, slipping past Karen and entering the kitchen. "I thought you'd be working."

She closed the door, turning toward him with sullen eyes. "I called in sick. Jasper…" Her hands trembled. "He's not doing too well. Virg went to Tillamook to get him some medicine, but I don't know if it will help." She led the way into the living room where Jasper lay between the two nursing mothers.

"Hey, ol' boy," Cowen said, crouching next to Noah's dog, now *his* dog, and scratching him behind the ears. "I'm sorry for leaving you, buddy. And I'm sorry you're not feeling well. I'll try and come for you soon." Cowen turned to Karen so he didn't have to keep watching Jasper's sufferings. So he didn't fixate on the guilt for letting him down too. "I don't know what's going to happen. I—"

"Were you near that blast? It shook the house."

He nodded. The debris had shaken him—cut into him—and the boom had made his eardrums ring, taking minutes before he could hear again.

"What's going on, Cowen?" Her skin lost its color. "Some stranger drops off your dog. I can't get a hold of Esty. Then there's this big boom. And now you show up looking like this. I need answers." She put both fists on her hips. "Now."

Bridge's confidence was the last thing Cowen wanted to upset, but she needed help, whether or not she knew it. "Esty's brother is in trouble, and I need to warn her. Can I use your phone?"

"In trouble with who? How did you get hurt?" She handed him her flip phone with texting only capabilities.

"There was a bomb." The less she knew, the better. "Do you have something with the internet?"

"Sure." She led him to a back room and sat down in front of a CRT monitor the size of a large microwave. It took a moment for the computer to start up, and she initiated the dial up sequence. Screeches sounded in the room.

"You don't have cable or fiber?" he asked, seriously regretting this plan.

She glanced him up and down. "You don't have any room to criticize right now. I still want to know about this bomb. Was anyone hurt?"

He shook his head. "Just me."

"I don't understand. Who was involved? Why was there a bomb?"

Cowen recognized her concerns, but he didn't have time to soothe them. "Let's just say that not everyone in this town is as they seem."

Karen tugged at the bottom of her shirt's hem, wringing it with her hands. "Are we in danger?"

"I don't think so." He desperately hoped Gertie thought he was dead and wouldn't retaliate. "Do you mind shutting the door? There are some things about Esty that she might not want you to know. I'll tell you everything about me when I know help is on the way."

Karen nodded, her face still ashen as she closed the door.

Cowen got to work on the computer, following the directions Rory had given to contact them while dialing Director Spandy's number on the phone, his hands shaking. Bridge might not ever forgive him. Actually, he was sure she wouldn't, but he would rather make sure she was safe and alive to hate him than be disposed of by the mob. Still, it took him a moment to hit the call button, and he questioned his decision over and over as the phone rang.

"This is Cowen," he said as soon as the director answered. "I took a civilian's phone, so don't even think about implicating them. I admit to helping Bridge O'Niall escape. And I'm telling you this because far more is going on than you realize. The Marconis kidnapped her brother, and this psycho lady in town knocked me out and tried to blow me up. She hijacked the ransom note, making her own demands so there's no way to get Bridge's brother back."

"Bridge O'Niall, huh?" The director said her name slow, dissecting it. "Is this another alias?"

"It's an olive branch." Cowen momentarily squeezed his eyes shut. "Please treat it carefully."

"I don't know what you're expecting. She's a criminal and—"

"Sometimes we enlist less-threatening targets to take down dangerous ones. We could do that now. Will you help or not?"

The second hand on Cowen's watch made a full circle before the director spoke.

"What do you need?"

Cowen kept in a sigh, grateful his plan had worked. "Bridge and her companion need a ride from the airport."

"When?"

"I don't know when they're flying in. Hopefully they'll respond soon, but it will probably be a private jet from Austin, Texas."

"What else?" the director asked.

"We need to find out where the mob is holding her brother. He was abducted from Pilpil Bay on Thursday. We have until Sunday night to exchange." Unless Gertie changed that detail too. "But we don't know what they want." *We.* Cowen was inserting himself in the situation whether or not Bridge wanted him to.

Director Spandy sighed as if he was unable to help. "That's not a lot to go off of. I don't know—"

"You'll figure it out." Cowen hesitated for a moment before he plowed forward. "Because if you don't, I could let slip the college admissions bribe you made for your son to get into Cornell. You really should be more careful about the documents you leave on your desk." Cowen had never made a threat before, but he was desperate and willing to do anything.

"I didn't know you had it in you to blackmail."

What was left to lose when he'd already destroyed everything? And if it meant helping Bridge, he was willing to go to the end of the earth. Or was he? Could he pull a trigger to save her? "Whatever it takes to get the job done," he said, infusing confidence in his words, even if he didn't fully believe them yet. "Report back in an hour with an update on this phone. I'll share this information with a select few so even if you take me out, it can still leak into the open." He hung up and typed a message into the decoder program.

Problems. Gertie wants the jade cat and hijacked the mob's demands so you would steal it for her. Hate me if you want, but I enlisted the FBI to help find your brother. I blackmailed the director with something sensitive. He's willing to help you in exchange for taking down some of the Marconis. Agents will pick you up at the airport. Let them help.

He closed the program and removed all traces of his activity off the computer, doing anything to avoid the gnawing in his chest. At some point, he would run into the mob or Gertie again. And then what? Would he take another life to save one? Or would he freeze and let people die?

Bridge could die.

Cowen grabbed some scratch paper and wrote the details he remembered from the forms he'd seen on the director's desk and sealed them in an envelope he found in a stacked pile on a shelf. He labeled it with a message to open if something happened to him and left it on the desk. Time was ticking down. He opened the door, ready to go search for Liam, but Karen stood there in an all-black, poufy dress like the one she waitressed in, combat boots, and a dark beanie. She handed him a 9mm gun with five extra rounds of ammunition.

"Sorry, the walls are paper thin. How can I help?" She pulled at the skirt of her dress when he failed to speak. "I figured this outfit is good for reconnaissance. I wear it during Halloween week at the restaurant."

If Cowen could find any humor in the situation, he might laugh at her get-up. But he'd already involved Karen and her husband enough. "If anyone asks, I stole this gun and your phone. I can't let you get hurt."

Karen shook her head. "That's not how we do things here. We call in the calvary."

"Yeah, well, there's a traitor in this town. We need to—"

A pounding sounded at the door, and Cowen shoved Karen to the floor behind him, readying the gun. He maneuvered to the other side of the room. "Who's there?" If it was Gertie and she was tracking his voice and had one of her machine guns, he wanted Karen out of the line of fire—if that were even possible. Oh, why had he come? He wasn't thinking things through enough. If anything happened to Karen or Virgil, it would be as if he pulled the trigger himself. The contents of his stomach started to climb.

"It's Alex. Cowen, is that you?"

He inched toward the window, peering through the slats of the blinds. Alex stood alone in a summery dress, holding a paper. "Why are you here?" he asked, scanning the street. Other than Alex, it was empty—the norm for Pilpil Bay during the day. He wished she *was* the one running surveillance, even if that made her a creepy stalker. Then Bridge would still be here and not on a mission to steal anything. She'd still trust him.

Alex's hands shook as she lifted the paper. "I think I found a ransom note."

Cowen kept the safety on as he cracked the door and pointed the gun at her. "Where did you find it?"

Her expression twisted as she looked over his mutilated face. "On the back door of Esty's bakery. What happened to you? Were you in that blast?"

He motioned her in with the gun, widening the opening.

She slipped inside, and lifted the note with both hands so he could see. Written in black charcoal like the first note were the words:

You missed the deadline. We'll give one more chance. Meet at the Oceanside shoreline tomorrow. Eleven p.m. Bring the Monet.

A picture was attached of Liam bound and gagged with a printout of today's news in his hand. That's what he'd been afraid of—that Gertie had tampered with the original ransom note for her own gain. Stupid woman. How could one old lady be so selfish?

"What's going on, Cowen?" Tears streamed down Alex's cheeks as she noticed Karen crouched on the ground. "Are you going to shoot us? Did you kidnap Esty's boyfriend?"

"It's her brother, not boyfriend," Karen said and winced when Cowen gave her a reprimanding look. She really had heard everything through the closed door. "Sorry," she said. "I'm not the best with secrets."

Secrets. Hadn't Alex asked Karen to keep one? He pointed the gun at Alex. "Who put the mud in Esty's bakery?"

Alex backed away with both hands up, but her feet quickly hit the kiddie pool holding one of the mama dogs and her babies. "It wasn't me, I swear. Gertie said she'd help me win you over, and I trusted her. So I got the keys to the bakery while she distracted Sydney. I had no idea she'd go to the lengths she did."

Karen stood up, gripping a baseball bat. If she'd heard his whole conversation with the director, she probably had reservations about Alex's association with Gertie too. "Are you still working with her?"

"No." Alex bit her bottom lip as she shook her head from side to side, her eyes wet. "Why was there an explosion at her house?"

Cowen didn't have time for all of their questions, and he'd already made everything worse by including more civilians. Bridge's brother was somewhere out there, and Cowen needed to get to him. "Gertie tried to kill me. There's a mob family that kidnapped Esty's brother. The FBI is going to lock me away forever. Does that answer enough questions? I need to go and find Liam."

"Who's Liam?" Alex asked, glancing between them.

Karen groaned. "Esty's brother. But her name is really…"

Cowen gave Karen another sharp look and returned his gun behind his back.

"Never mind." Karen lowered the bat. "I'll try and hold that one in."

"Good. If you want to help, you can both canvas the town, asking if anyone saw something suspicious on Thursday night."

"Suspicious? Like a light in the pillbox off Highway 101?" Alex asked.

Cowen stepped toward her. "Tell me everything."

"I went to Tillamook for supplies." Alex struggled to meet his eyes. "I was pretty down that you've repeatedly chosen Esty over me. So I pulled off the road and went for a jog along the coast. That's when I saw the light coming from the pillbox. I figured it was some teens, but there weren't any cars nearby. It's pretty far from everything else."

"It's a good place to start. Karen," he turned to her. "Keep an eye on Alex to make sure she doesn't contact anyone. I don't want to be led into a trap in case she's working with Gertie."

Alex threw her hands to her side like a toddler starting a tantrum. "I'm telling the truth."

"Yeah, well. I don't know who to trust these days." Hopefully he could trust the director and Karen. "Can I borrow your car?" he asked Karen.

She winced. "We only have the one and Virg has it."

"You can take mine," Alex said, pointing to her purse. "Keys are in there. I'll even go with you."

"Fine." He slipped the purse off her shoulder. It would be easier to keep an eye on her if she was with him. "You can show me where to go." He pocketed the extra ammo before leading the way to her car. It was unlocked, and he slid into the driver's seat. It didn't take long for him to navigate to the pillbox in silence, parking a few hundred yards away to keep anyone inside from noticing.

"Wait here," he said as he got out, flipping the gun's safety off. His mind raced. What would he do if there was a shootout? How could he protect anyone anymore? Noah's blood. Antoine's blood…he could see both. Smell and taste both. The urge to vomit hit his throat, but he had to keep moving, had to try. Once he got within twenty feet, he took six steps at a time then paused to listen to the silence. Hopefully, the lack of noise meant only one guard. He could incapacitate a single person without killing them. But if there were more…

Cowen reached the edge of the building and pressed his back against it, scanning the area. There were zero clues about what he'd find inside. "For Bridge," he said to himself, not knowing if he'd still be alive in five minutes. Quietly, he crept around to the opening, edging his head out until he could see inside. His shoulders dropped as he stepped into the opening of the empty bunker. They were too late. He crouched down to inspect a candy wrapper when a shadow swallowed his own.

"Thanks for making a call with an unsecured line," Alex said, her voice unmistakable. "Now we know where to pick up the cat."

Cowen knew what was coming next—another blow to the head—or worse. So he dropped to the ground, rolled onto his back, and kicked, catching Alex's stomach. She groaned and stumbled, dropping the tire iron she must have grabbed from the car. By the time he was up, she'd straightened, blocking the exit.

There was no way out without a fight.

"Why couldn't you have just chosen me?" She swung a fist at him, missing. "Then you wouldn't have gotten involved in Esty's mess and you never would have known—"

"Known what?" He faked a swing with his right, and caught her ribs with an uppercut. "That you're a liar? A criminal?"

"I prefer con artist." She rushed him, punching and jabbing. Several of her shots hit him in the chest and face. "Didn't your mom teach you to never hurt a girl?" She shifted away so he couldn't retaliate.

Pain screamed from his open wounds from the bomb, from the new ones from Alex, and he panted to catch his breath. "Yeah. But it's a good thing for me that I only see you as a threat." The words came out of his mouth, but he didn't know if he believed them. What if he hit her too hard and she had permanent damage for the rest of her life? What if he accidentally killed her? "How about let's negotiate. I'll make sure you get the cat. Just let me go so I can save Esty's brother."

"How about no. We can't have any loose ends lying around. You already told that waitress about Aunt Gertie. Now I've got to kill her too."

Another shadow crowded onto the floor. "The name is Karen. And I'm here to speak to your manager." Karen stepped into the opening in her all black outfit and swung a baseball bat, smacking Alex in the back of the head. Limp, Alex flew forward, her eyes rolling back before she hit the floor.

Cowen crouched beside her unmoving body, panic rippling through him. "What did you do?"

Karen stomped her boot on Alex's back. "What had to be done. I figured you were too soft to attack, so I followed on the moped. Sorry she got in a few blows before I arrived. These boots are really heavy."

Cowen checked Alex's wrist and found a pulse. "You could have killed her."

"She was about to kill you," she said, pointing to the gun in Alex's hand.

He pocketed the weapon and scooped Alex into his arms. "We need to get her to the hospital."

Karen blocked the entrance. "No, we need to tie her sorry butt up. I'll call the sheriff."

That was probably the smartest thing to do, but his conscience wouldn't allow it. "I'm not letting someone else die when I could do something. Bad or not, she's still a human."

"A pathetic one." Karen let him pass, following him to the car.

Cowen placed Alex in the trunk, his thoughts growing into a complicated knot. What if this detour to save her cost another life?

chapter twenty-six

The Solution

Bridge tightened her seatbelt, refusing to get off the plane. The men waiting outside were clearly government agents, just like Cowen had said in the single message he'd sent. She would have preferred a lengthy apology, even though it wouldn't have done any good. "He told the FBI where to find us. How could he?" There was no way she could trust him. Ever.

Rory crouched next to her in the aisle. "Because he's trying to help."

"And I said I didn't want him to be involved. Now he's in too deep, and—"

"You care about him. Don't deny it. Let's use these agents as an asset, and after we save Liam, we can save Cowen."

"Fine. But just so you know, I won't ever love him. Your eyes say you're hoping for that."

Rory extended his hand. "I think you're seeing your own reflection."

Bridge unclipped her seatbelt, swatting him away. "I want no talk of forgiving Cowen."

He shrugged as if agreeing. "Until we've got Liam and we're all safe, my lips are sealed."

It was as good as she was going to get. Every ounce of stubbornness she possessed came from him. "I'm scared, Dad. We're unprepared. We don't know where Liam is, and—"

"We've got each other. You know my strengths. I know yours. If anyone can pull this off, it's us."

Rory was right, except he was slightly wounded. She'd asked to see his shoulder, but he wouldn't let her, telling her he was fine. Hopefully, he wouldn't be a liability. Bridge slipped her hand along the ledger in her pocket. Items she'd used at the debutante ball were strapped to her waist, legs, and arms. By the end of this, she would have more sins and wounds to make up for. But it was the only way. Family was family, even if they were annoying and stupid at times.

She stood and led the way out the open door of the plane. A black SUV sat parked near their hangar, and two FBI agents—their suits and shoes distinct—waited with their guns in the holsters.

"Bridge O'Niall?" The short one asked. He stood at the front, his stance wide. "We've been directed to assist you and your companion. We have intel that your brother—"

Shots rang out from two o'clock, the sound of a machine gun unmistakable. Bullets flew at the SUV, dropping the short man as the other scurried behind. The gunman was hiding somewhere in the hangar, out of sight. Bridge pushed her dad back into the plane, ripped the guns off at her side and slid down the stair rail, throwing her body into an unprotected sprint, her mind creating an order of attack: take out the gun then help the downed agent. Her eyes followed the line of fire as it pummeled the exact same spot on the vehicle. Something wasn't right.

She got close enough to draw the attention of the gunman even though she couldn't see one, but still, the machine gun fired in an undeviating direction. The weapon had to be rigged. Bridge turned back to find her dad on the stairs with Gertie holding a shotgun against his back.

"Thanks for being a doll and getting this for me." Gertie shouted to be heard over the roar of the machine gun. She held the jade cat in her other arm with some sort of remote in her hand. "And sorry about Cowen. He stuck his nose in the wrong place at the wrong time. I'm sure they'll be finding bits of him around town for the next few weeks. Bombs'll do that to ya."

Bridge's knees gave out and she fell in a crouch, her bottom connecting with her heels. She gripped the shirt on her chest, tightening it in her fist. Her emotions brimmed to the surface, ready to pour out of control. "No. You're lying."

"Oh, honey, why would I need to do that? I've got what I want." She clicked a button on the remote, and the machine gun stopped.

Cowen…How could he be gone? Bridge squeezed back tears as her limbs lost strength. She'd been stupid to be so upset with him. If she could turn back time, she'd forgive him instantly. Then he would have come with them, and he'd still be here. The pain in her head, in her chest, grew to be unbearable. She probably wasn't breathing. Her heart might have stopped. This was all her fault, and no amount of service or donations could atone for this mistake.

"Everything will be fine as long as you all let me go." Gertie nudged Rory down the stairs with the barrel of her gun. "Though I'm sorry to hear about your brother. The mob wants a missing Monet by tonight. Too bad." She kept pushing Rory down the steps. "You seem like a smart girl. Drop your weapon. Get the FBI to do the same, and let me leave peacefully. Or, I'll press one of these buttons, and my favorite gun will start shooting again, but this time, it won't be stationary. Do I make myself clear?"

Bridge set her guns on the ground, her chest empty. Before, Cowen's betrayal had consumed her mind, but now, with no more possibilities, it seemed so trivial. Her limbs refused to work. She couldn't even pick a gun up to fire if it meant saving her life. "Where is my brother?"

Gertie shrugged. "Don't know. Don't care."

"What did we do to you?" Bridge screamed. "Why are you being like this?"

"What? You don't like the taste of your own medicine?" She laughed and pushed Rory off the bottom step, joining him on the tarmac and backing away. "Your family stole this statue from me. I had it in my hands, but your mom swooped down in her fancy harness, flashing that stupid tattoo and yanked it away, taking a chunk off the ear. And you all pushed me out of my market back east, getting to every single heist first. Because of all of you, I lost my credibility as a thief, and I've been reduced to living in that stupid town. I've had to enjoy my art amongst garbage. Do you know how hard that is?"

Bridge had no idea what the woman was saying. Honestly, she wasn't sure if Gertie had a fully functioning brain. "Were you behind the sabotage of my bakery?"

Gertie grinned in response.

"Why?" Bridge couldn't understand her maliciousness.

"That was just to keep you distracted. It's the oldest trick in the book."

"I'm sorry for whatever we did to you," Bridge said, but her apology was useless, falling on deaf ears. And they had more pressing matters. "We'll let you go."

"Smart girl." Gertie stepped away from Rory and slipped inside a Range Rover, her tall hair probably hitting the roof.

Bridge put up a hand, waving to the hiding agent. "Let her go."

Gertie's car started, and as she drove off, she rolled down her window with the remote in her hand. She laughed maniacally, and then the machine gun came to life.

"Hit the deck!" The agent shouted.

Bullets whizzed past Bridge, and she threw herself to the ground, glancing over at her dad. He was face down, army-crawling toward her, but she was already on the move in the direction of the injured agent as shots spread overhead in a back and forth motion.

"Please don't be dead," Bridge pleaded when she reached him. She visually scanned his wounds, wishing she could have been there for Cowen. Maybe she could have saved him. Maybe being there to comfort him could have kept him alive. But no, she had to push him away because her feelings were hurt, and she'd stolen again to make up for a host of other wrongs. When would her punishment stop? When would she ever be even with all the bad she'd done? Cowen hadn't deserved to die. He hadn't deserved anything, and Bridge couldn't keep living with the pain. It was too much.

The scene in front of her begged her attention. The agent had one bullet in his left side a little above the hip, but it was the one in his thigh that worried her most.

"It hit your artery. I'm going to apply pressure." As soon as she said it, the bullets ceased. A glance back showed her dad had disabled the machine gun, but his shoulder was sagging more than before.

The other agent finally came out of his hiding place, gun pointed in case of another threat.

"You," Bridge said, nodding at the agent as he approached. "Take off your shirt." She turned back to the injured man. "I'm so sorry you got hurt. I'll do everything I can to help you and your family through the recovery. You're going to be just fine." She had no idea if he would make it. Already, he'd lost so much blood. If he died, she would take care of his family. She would right every wrong. Except she couldn't alter his fate. And she couldn't bring Cowen back.

Rory rushed beside her, kneeling. "Doing good, kid. Just like I showed you."

Once the agent had his shirt off, her dad used it as a tourniquet. "Check his other wound."

Bridge waved the man over, showing him where to apply pressure until the ambulance came. "What do you know about my brother?" she asked him.

"There are some abandoned warehouses on the west side of Bay City.

We think he's being held somewhere in there, but our team hasn't found him yet. It's a lot of area to cover."

"Keep applying pressure no matter what. He's going to make it," Rory said with a twitch of his jaw, the tell he struggled to hide when he lied.

Bridge stood, her emotions surfacing. This man might die. How much more did she have to pay for her past sins? Didn't it matter that she wanted to make amends? That she was trying? Why did the universe hate her so much? Why did it have to take Cowen?

"We've got to go," her dad said as the sound of sirens approached. He urged Bridge toward a Honda Accord parked near the hangar. The doors were locked, so he shot the back door window. He opened up the driver's side, waiting for Bridge to hotwire it, his shoulder limp.

But she could barely breathe. Cowen was gone. She crouched next to the car, unable to move, unable to help. Rory slipped inside, managed to strip the wires despite his injury, and got the car to start. "C'mon," he said.

"When is this going to end?"

"When everyone thinks we're dead." He motioned for her to get in. "Or when we actually die."

Death. The word took root in her chest, creeping and crawling through her veins. That was the answer. The only way to stop hurting people was to die.

She didn't move, couldn't, so Rory helped her into the passenger side and drove them away. Bridge knew she shouldn't, but she pulled out her phone and searched *Bomb in Pilpil Bay*, her stomach caving with the results.

"There was an explosion…" Bridge shook her head. Hot tears streamed down her cheeks. "They say a Jeep exploded, killing the driver."

Rory touched her knee, giving her an ounce of comfort, as he drove out of the airport. "I'm so sorry."

"After this, I'm done." Her body shook as she said the words, but they were more true than any others she'd ever spoken. "We save Liam. We fake our deaths. And then I never want to see either of you again. I'm not stealing for you or him. If you screw up, it's on you. I'm done."

She would make sure of it herself.

chapter twenty-seven

Surrender

By the time Rory pulled into the warehouse district of Bay City, the sky was as dark as Bridge's mood, the air thick with a strangling fog. They were unprepared to meet the Marconis. No defensive gear, no night vision—only the items they'd collected for the heist in Texas. And with her dad's injury… she didn't want to focus on that.

They both got out as soon as he killed the engine, quietly closing their doors to not attract attention. If they used flashlights, anyone on patrol could pick them off. They had to rely on their instincts, and hers were clouded over.

"We don't have much time," Rory said, grabbing her hand so they could feel the way forward together. "We should split—" A thud sounded, followed by his gasps for air. Her dad bent at the waist, holding his head.

"Matt Damon." Bridge crouched. "What happened?" She struggled to see in the dark, trying to pry his hands away and feeling warm, sticky blood. She reached above them and felt the end of a metal beam, the edge rusted and jagged. Somehow, someone had had the idea to place it on the top of a dumpster, creating the worst possible safety hazard.

"We've got to take care of this injury," she said.

Rory shook his head. "There isn't time. Lead me." He extended his hand, waiting for her to guide him.

"Can't you see?" she asked, worried about the seriousness of his injury.

"I don't know if it's too dark or…" He didn't finish that sentence. "Everything is spinning."

He was right. Everything had spun out of control.

Cowen. The downed agent. Liam's unknown location and predicament. Now this. Bridge wanted to tip her head back and scream to the universe that she understood they were being punished. But she'd been wrong all along, thinking she could fix things. She was now positive the suffering would never end for someone with her past. She was certain she was forever cursed, tossed aside, not worthy of happiness or a life without constant pain, constant torture. If she had some time to think, maybe she could sort through these thoughts, maybe double-check if they were true. But she didn't have a chance—she had a mission.

The sound of the crashing waves in the distance failed to cover their heavy breathing or a voice. It was low and distant, but she could swear that someone spoke. "I think we're close. Wait here." She leaned her dad up against the wall and rushed ahead, quieting her breaths, focusing on using her oxygen efficiently as she glided along the alley between buildings, her senses sharp. Another voice. This time, she zeroed in on a location to her right. At the end of the next building she peered out, seeing movement ahead in the dark. This had to be it. She went back for her dad, searching for a door as she went, finding one a hundred yards later.

"This way," Bridge said, dragging him to it. Quickly, she picked the lock and ushered them inside. A sea of empty crates provided cover as they navigated the expansive, windowless room, lit somewhere in the middle. More voices bounced off the walls with the unmistakable sound of cards shuffling. She paused to check out her dad. He was blinking, and the blood was still flowing from the gash on his head.

"Follow me." She weaved in and out of the crated aisles stacked taller than she was until she caught sight of her brother, bound and gagged in a chair with two men standing guard a dozen paces away and four more men playing cards at a makeshift table of crates.

"Ryan Reynolds," she swore. Six guards…In order to walk away without her family getting more hurt required three people with six total guns. She could only count on her own two weapons because her dad kept stumbling with his steps.

They needed a diversion. Bridge scanned, making calculations in her head. The pallets could easily start on fire. If she lit several sections around the room, it could provide enough of a distraction. And at this point, it was the best idea she had.

"I'm going to smoke them out. Give me some fabric." Bridge got to work, ripping her leggings while her dad tore the bottoms of his dress pants. Once they had enough, she left him, scurrying around the room, looking for the best spots to start the flames. There was so much dry wood—a code violation for sure—that the chance of dying by smoke inhalation was very probable. Once she set the fires, they would have to work fast.

Bridge returned to her dad without lighting any piles, needing confirmation that this was the best play and that he was ready to leave once the smoke got thick. She couldn't worry about him *and* getting Liam.

She placed a hand on his leg. "Are you able to get yourself out of—"

The front door swung open, and a new player entered the warehouse in stilettos, wielding a Glock. "It's a good thing they didn't kill you yesterday," the woman said as her heels clicked on the concrete floor. "I didn't want to miss this, but there was somewhere I had to be." She stopped in front of Liam, her dress short and bright red. "Do you know who I am?" she asked, running the tip of the gun up his neck.

He muffled a response through his gag.

"Nah, you probably don't. My name is Harley Rossi, and I was a kid when you shot and killed my brother."

Bridge covered her mouth to quiet her gasp. This was why she'd wanted to find Harley—to keep her from the vengeful life Liam had lived—the same life of crime Bridge couldn't escape without taking matters into her own hands.

Harley cocked the gun. "And now you're going to pay."

Before Bridge or Rory could do anything, Harley fired her weapon, hitting Liam in the kneecap, the shot sounding like an explosion in the massive room. Bridge lurched forward, her desire to help her brother outweighing her instincts, but Rory held her back.

Bridge could only imagine the pain her brother felt. She aimed her gun, lining up with a clear shot—at least as clear as she could with this distance and a 9mm.

"Take her out." Rory whispered to her as he texted 911, the urgency in his voice so thick, she could slice it with a knife. She'd never killed anyone, though she'd always blamed herself for Mason's death. Now she knew the pain Cowen had felt without even completing the deed. She already had too much in her ledger, the weight so heavy she hadn't allowed herself to live. Hadn't given herself room to be happy. But taking a life would add so much more. Justified or not, killing Harley was more than she could ever process, ever heal from, and even with a suicide plan swirling in her head, she couldn't do it.

Another shot rang out, taking Liam's toes on the opposite foot. He'd be useless escaping now.

"Take her out," Rory repeated.

Even if Bridge shot Harley, there were too many armed men. Their chances of rescuing Liam weren't good enough.

"I'm sorry, Dad," she said, squeezing his hand one last time. "Do what you have to, but I'm going to find another way."

Bridge handed him her guns and walked out into the clearing with her hands up, her heart pounding in her throat. There had been no time to concoct an actual plan. From here on, she was winging it. "Excuse me. I'm the one you want. *And* I can find the Monet."

chapter twenty-eight
Pulling the Trigger

Bridge stopped twenty feet away from Liam with half the guards pointing weapons at her, the others canvasing him.

"Well, if it isn't Bridge O'Niall," Harley said, her lips turning up into a snide grin. "Do you know how hard I've looked for you?"

"Not nearly as hard as I've searched for *you*."

The woman took a step back, clearly not expecting that answer.

"Your brother told me about you," Bridge said. "I've been looking ever since his death, wanting to make sure you're okay."

Harley laughed, using her gun to point around the room. "Look at me. I'm better than okay. But what's this talk of a Monet?"

Bridge frowned. "You didn't request that in your ransom note?"

"No, but I should have. I told you to show your face or your brother would die." She watched Bridge's confused expression. "Imagine my surprise when an anonymous package arrived with instructions on how to tap into surveillance, and the video feed showed you. Once we knew where you were, we wanted the whole family together. But now, I'm curious about this brilliant pirate who tried to piggyback off our kidnapping. Maybe they're the one who sent us the feed."

Gertie. That women seriously had zero morals. She would probably sacrifice her own mother for a hideous piece of art. "I'll tell you all about it, once you release my brother."

Harley laughed. "Nah, that isn't how this works. You all need to die because you won't stop causing us problems. I found your brother stealing from our clients."

If Liam had just focused on dental school like he was supposed to, none of this would have happened. But it was foolish to think about the *what-ifs*. Bridge knew better than anyone that the past was already set. Cowen was gone forever.

"You could turn us over to the Feds," Bridge said, forcing her tone to stay steady even though she was ready to break. "We can rot in—"

"And risk you escaping?" Harley shook her head. "I heard chatter that a redhead escaped federal custody recently. Know anything about that?"

Bridge pressed her lips. "It sounds like she had help."

"Who's to say you won't have help next time?" Harley alternated pointing the gun at Bridge then Liam. "Nah, here's what I'll do. I'll give you options. You decide how you die, and we'll take care of it for you. It's the least one thief can do for another."

Getting to decide her end sounded a lot better than doing it on her own, but Bridge couldn't agree to the terms. "Fine, but let it just be me. Liam is young and an idiot, but he's incredibly smart." Her descriptions contradicted each other, but it was the best she had. "And it seems he can't get this way of life out of his system, so why don't you recruit him?" Bridge wished there was some other way, but clearly, she couldn't change him. At least this would keep him alive. "And my dad—" She let her feelings about Cowen rise to the surface, using the emotions to convey what she needed. "There was a bomb." Her chest caved as she met Liam's eyes. "He didn't make it."

Harley laughed again. "You mean this dad?" She pointed behind Bridge as one of the lugs pushed Rory into the middle of the room. "Maybe there *was* a bomb," she said, glancing at his bloody wound. "So? How do you want him to die? Since you feel like talking and lying so much, it's your choice, sweetie. 'Cause none of you are getting out of this room."

"Please," Rory said. "Take me. Save my kids. Bridge is more talented than my wife and I combined. If you throw in Liam, you'll be unstoppable."

Harley considered him. "No dice."

"What can I give you?" Bridge held her empty hands out. "What can I do for you? There has to be something you want? You can shoot me yourself, or give me a slow, painful death if you let them go."

"No, take me." Rory fought against his guard, but the man held him firm.

"Both of you shut up. Someone, gag him." Harley tapped the gun to her chin. "I wouldn't mind a Monet. How about I'll let you and your brother join us, if I kill your dad. It's been twenty-two hours since I've finished someone off, and I'm needing my fix." She gave Bridge a sadistic grin. "I'll even let you hug goodbye. It's more than you got with your mom. More than I got with my brother. So what do you say? Someone has to die."

Rory nodded, his eyes pleading with Bridge to accept. She knew he was willing to protect his kids and ready to see his wife again. And if it meant she could save Liam, she would. It was the best option under the circumstances. But her life as a thief was over. She'd make sure of it. No one would get to exploit her skills. No one had the right to use her.

"Let him drown in the sea," Bridge said as she wiped her eyes. "Then his body can find our motherland again." With the gash on his head, Rory might not be able to think too clearly, but if anyone could escape between here and the water, it was her dad.

Sirens sounded in the distance, and Bridge seized upon the panic on Harley's face. "We called an ambulance. If you let my brother leave for the hospital, I'll go with you right now. You can pick him up after they remove the bullets." She gave her dad a hug, the type she would give if she might not ever see him again—because she wouldn't. These were her last moments. Her ledger would have to accept her blood as payment. She couldn't handle the guilt anymore.

The ambulance sirens screeched as the vehicle pulled up in front of the warehouse. "Don't worry," Bridge said to Harley. "You can hand Liam over to the paramedics in exchange for no questions asked. And we'll clear out before anyone else can come. We can destroy all of the evidence with a single match." She approached Liam and leaned down.

"What are you doing?" Harley shoved the gun against Bridge's spine.

"Giving him a hug. Look, my hands are empty, and you can watch my mouth, so I don't whisper something to him. It's not like anything we try would work. You've got us surrounded."

Harley removed her weapon from Bridge's back. "You're right. We do." She motioned to two goons to escort her dad out the back door and for the other two to untie Liam's hands and unbind his mouth.

He wiggled his jaw back and forth. "Thank you," he said, giving Harley a curt nod.

Bridge bent more and folded him into her arms as she silently pleaded for the Virgin Mary, her mother, or anyone to listen and save her dad. Her fingers tapped out Morse code on Liam's shoulder to spell *Run. Hide.* She stayed back as Harley's men carried her brother away.

Harley kept her gun pointed at Bridge's chest. It took some convincing, but the thugs finally got the paramedics to take Liam without calling in backup. Two guards followed them in an SUV. Bridge had no idea how her brother would escape with his kneecap and toes shot, but he got himself into this mess, and he could get himself out. She was no longer able to help him.

This was the end of the line for Bridge. The weight of hurting people was too much to bear, and she couldn't live this life anymore. The agent at the airport might already be dead—because of her. She'd wanted to help Harley for all of these years, but she'd failed. Her skills were dangerous in the wrong hands, and there were too many evil people who could exploit her.

Her life would end now. On her terms. No one would ever get to use her again. She just needed to get close enough to Harley to steal her gun. "I'm sorry about Mason. I really am."

The two remaining guards kept watch as Harley circled Bridge. "Yeah, well, *sorries* don't bring people back. And they don't make up for the time when I had no one. I was lucky the Marconis adopted me like one of their own." She paused. "For the record, I blame you and your family for everything that happened to me. We'll work together, but I'll never forget."

Had Bridge sounded this unforgiving with Cowen? It took all of her focus to swallow and get her next words out. "You know Mason killed my mom, right?"

Harley shrugged. "Yeah, well it was your fault for trusting him."

"You're right," Bridge said with a renewed determination. "Thieves can never be trusted." She lunged at Harley, her fingers connecting with the gun. The woman shoved Bridge with her hip, but Bridge pulled Harley with her, the two crashing to the ground. Bridge's elbow caught her fall, shooting a soul-sucking pain up her arm and through her body.

Wildly, she clawed, wrenching the gun free from Harley's hands. She shoved the woman away with a kick to the stomach and scrambled to her feet as the guards watched, their faces entertained by the brawl. Their reaction disturbed her. So did the thoughts of what was coming next.

"Blessed Virgin Mary," she whispered. "Please help everyone I've ever wronged."

The warehouse doors flew open as Bridge pointed the gun at her own head.

"FBI. You're surrounded," a familiar voice yelled as a gunshot sounded and Bridge closed her eyes, pulling the trigger.

chapter twenty-nine
Heaven or Hell?

Bridge's eyes flew open and she yelped, her wrist spraining as her gun flew out of her hand. The motion torqued her injured elbow, sending her backward. She was dead. She had to be because Cowen stood in the entrance with his gun aimed at her, his shoulders heaving.

How was he here? How was he alive? Bridge wanted nothing more than to run to him, to jump into his arms. But how? If he were really here, how would they escape? He'd shot her weapon away, and they were outgunned. And any minute, the guards in charge of finishing off her dad could return.

Cowen shifted, turning his aim toward Harley and the two remaining guards. "Drop your weapons."

Bridge kept blinking. Was this real? It couldn't be. Cowen's face was covered in too many cuts and gashes to be in Heaven. Clearly, she was dead and sent to hell, the universe making her live out her nightmares forever.

Cowen took a step closer. "I said, drop your weapons."

Harley slowly lifted her empty hands, but when she reached waist level, her arms darted behind her back, pulling out two more guns, aiming one at Bridge, the other at Cowen.

"Look out!" Bridge screamed as multiple shots fired. Reality seemed to pause. Time slowed. Which guns went off? Was Bridge hit? She couldn't differentiate her own body from the thought of someone hurting Cowen. Was she falling? Upright? She couldn't even tell. And then in an instant the corporeal world hit her hard and fast as the gun Harley had aimed at Bridge flew out of Harley's hand, and a second bullet hit the woman in the forehead. But not before she got a shot off, piercing Cowen's left chest. As he went down, he shot twice more, and the guards collapsed.

Bridge rushed to Cowen, pulling him into her arms. She'd expected, hoped for a bulletproof vest, but blood was seeping through the front of his shirt and onto her lap. Her eyes kept trying to drift, to look at the other bodies on the ground. Harley…how could she be gone?

"I should…tell you…" Cowen said, gasping for breath.

She shook her head, shushing him. He maybe had seconds left. Minutes if they were incredibly lucky. Sure, a heart had moving parts, and she could fix anything with moving parts, but not this. Not with zero equipment and no prep or experience. "I love you too."

His lips formed a weak smile. "Dextro…cardia."

Dextrocardia. Dextrocardia. Where had she heard that before? "Brad Pitt!" It was from *World War Z* when a patient received an infected zombie heart—on the wrong side of his chest. "That's the condition where your heart is on the right side?"

He blinked once, the universal answer for yes.

Bridge grinned big despite the scene around them, her cheeks wet. She grabbed the tube she'd used to steal the Pouncing Feline Over Koi off her leg. "A punctured lung is something I can stabilize."

Hopefully, that would be enough.

chapter thirty

Thieves

Cowen woke to beeping. An itchy throat. And something warm along his right side. The lights were dim, and his eyes adjusted slowly to an empty hospital room. Empty except for Bridge on the bed next to him, snuggled close.

"Hey." It took him three tries to produce the word, his brain fuzzy. He knew he should remember what happened, but all he could think about was Bridge saying she loved him as she'd held him tight. He wanted to say it back.

Bridge shot off the bed and plopped onto the closest chair, running a hand through her matted hair. Her wrist was bandaged. So was her elbow. "Human touch…" She couldn't seem to look at him. "It's supposed to help you heal faster."

"Is there something wrong with my face?" Each word came out slow and labored, his chest aching.

She shifted, and the light caught on the crusted streaks on her cheeks. "No. Just some scratches." Bridge fiddled with her fingers. Why wasn't she looking at him? "Karen told me about the blast. And about Alex."

"It's a good thing I was never interested in her." He reached for Bridge's fingers, but she was too far away. "I've only been interested in—"

"So…dextrocardia is rare."

Why was she changing the subject? Cowen scanned the room for danger. "Is there a bug?" he whispered.

Bridge stood, her hand drifting toward his before abruptly pulling back. "The director will want to know you're awake."

His arms were connected to cords and his chest throbbed. With no way for him to stop her, she disappeared out the door, returning a nap or two later with his former boss.

"Good work, Agent Amaratti," Director Spandy said as he stood over Cowen, his height casting shadows on the blanket.

Bridge leaned against the door, her focus on the floor.

"I…I don't remember…" Cowen's eyes drifted closed. His last few minutes of consciousness before the gunfight were hazy. He'd found Rory evading two attackers and sent agents to pursue. He'd already gotten word that Liam was safe enough in the ambulance, and when he entered the warehouse and saw Bridge with that hollow look in her eyes, the gun aimed at her head, he knew what she was about to do. He'd blasted her gun away, right before she pulled the trigger, her bullet piercing the side of the building. And then when Harley Rossi wouldn't back down, her gun trained on Bridge, he'd acted instantly, shooting the woman's hand and hitting her in the head also. He'd taken out the two guards, knowing each shot would be lethal.

He expected the pain to hit, the guilt and grief to be unbearable for taking three more lives, but the feelings stirring in his chest didn't make sense. Somehow, he was at peace. And that's when he understood. Bridge was safe because he'd done his job—done the one thing he *could* do. And that was shooting with perfect aim. He hadn't hesitated in protecting her, unlike with his partner. He'd painfully learned his lesson.

"Any survivors?" he asked, even though he already knew the answer to the question.

Director Spandy shook his head. "Did Ms. O'Niall explain your new assignment?"

Cowen winced. "Assignment? I was hoping to go back to Pilpil—"

"According to the news, the mob and everyone you know think that you and Bridge, Liam, and Rory O'Niall are all dead. We made some arrangements with Ms. O'Niall and her family. In exchange for expunging their past, they'll now work with you on a…let's just say an unofficial team. Alex and her aunt Gertie have disappeared. Their list of crimes is a mile long, and we need help finding them. Plus, there's a whole country full of other criminals who need to be caught using skill sets we don't condone."

The weight of the director's words came crashing down. Everyone thought they were dead? "What about my mom?"

"She'll understand," Director Spandy said without any emotion. "Her husband died serving his country, and so did you."

The pain in Cowen's chest grew. "But—"

"Just so you know, that little bit you have over me is all cleared up. No trail. You can either take this *opportunity* or you can run. If you do, I'll have to alert the officials. Plus, the mob that was chasing the O'Nialls is aware of who you are. If you were to show up on the radar again after they believed you to be dead, well…I don't have to explain how angry they'd be for how many of their people you killed. And you'll be wanted for aiding and abetting a known criminal, murder, and as many other charges as I can tack on. The same goes for Bridge and her family."

Cowen searched her face, but she wouldn't look at him. He addressed the director. "You can't—"

"Oh, I can. We've needed a new off-the-books crew for a while. I don't care how you earn the funds to operate, but when we need you…when this country and the citizens need you, you'll be here to help."

Cowen gripped the bed rail. "You can't expect an operation like this to work."

Director Spandy laughed, his voice anything but jovial. "I can because it has. Do you think your own government is above breaking the rules?" He let that sit as he buttoned his suit coat. "We'll be in touch. Ms. O'Niall will fill you in on the rest." He tipped his head to her as she stepped aside for him to exit.

Cowen held out his hand, and Bridge looked at it but stayed next to the door. "I'll explain more when you're well enough to leave. But for now, you need to understand the stakes. Karen and Virgil are being watched as collateral, making sure we do what we agreed to."

"But I haven't agreed."

There was more she wasn't telling him.

"What is it?" he asked her.

Pain crossed Bridge's face so tangibly he could touch it—if she'd get close enough. "Your mom is being watched too."

"Oh." He sank into the pillow, the stuffing threatening to suffocate him.

"We won't let anything happen to them," she said, her face a determined stone.

He held his hand out again, this time higher so there was no mistaking his intention.

Bridge shook her head. "We're coworkers now. Our mission is to protect other people."

"Please," Cowen said, his hand still extended. "I should have told you about the director coming. And I'm sorry for asking for the Feds help, but I thought it was the only way to keep you and your family safe. Ever since I met you, you've been trying to make up for your mistakes." He didn't know what he'd do if she didn't forgive him. "Won't you let me make up for mine?"

Bridge looked away, her chest heaving. "You should get some rest."

She slipped out, closing the door and taking all hopes of happiness with her.

Cowen collected the blanket into a pile and heaved.

The heat of the day swirled through the automatic doors as Bridge pushed Cowen out of the hospital in a wheelchair.

"Security cameras are everywhere," he said, shrinking down in the seat. "How is anyone going to believe I'm dead? That we all are?" He couldn't let anything happen to his mama.

"You'll see." Bridge pushed him toward the far end of the parking lot where a dark gray full-sized, windowless van sat waiting.

The back door swung open revealing Liam in a knee brace, working at a computer. "They'll believe whatever I want them to believe." He tilted a screen that showed no one in front of the hospital, but when Cowen looked back, there were at least a handful of people walking in and out.

"Nice job. How did you hear what I said?" Cowen asked.

Bridge showed him the tip of her finger. On the end was a translucent dot, barely a millimeter thick. "It's a microphone that uses thermal energy from your body and transmits to these." She pulled a com-unit from her pocket and slipped it into his ear.

"Does it make those horrible scratching noises when—"

She pressed the mic against the armrest of the wheelchair. "It only activates when it's not being touched."

A car door opened and Rory appeared, his forehead wounded but healing. "Let's get you in." He hoisted Cowen up, and together with Bridge, they got him into the van.

"Why are you doing this?" Cowen asked as he settled on a bench seat near the back door, the stitches in his chest aching.

"To protect your mom." Bridge gave him a quick look, then darted her gaze away. She eased his chair into a reclining position before she shuffled to the front of the van and took the passenger seat.

Rory pulled the doors closed and placed his hand on Cowen's shoulder. "And it's the only way to keep my girl safe."

"What's that supposed to mean?" he asked, but Rory ignored him, settling into the captain's seat and driving off.

Bridge roused as the van pulled to a stop. Her wrist and elbow still ached, but the pain was manageable. Ocean, or rather the Gulf of California, waved back, the sun high overhead. They'd cleared the border easily, passing through with a generous tip.

"We made it?" she asked.

Rory yawned as he stretched. "Welcome to San Felipe. Our new headquarters." They were close enough to the US to assist when needed, and far enough from Director Spandy's constant attention. "I'll help your brother if you can get Cowen."

Bridge didn't know if she could handle touching Cowen again, but this was the life she had to get used to. Until she began to forgive herself, Cowen was just a guy that worked with her and lived in the same house. Too much was at stake to have emotions.

"He needs more answers," Rory said, giving her a pointed look.

Her dad had spent the entire trip feeding her messages of hope. Telling her she was needed in this world. That her goodness outweighed any bad they'd done. It was so hard to believe she mattered when the narrative in her head had focused on all of the wrongs, weaving its way through her sense of identity, taking root and growing thorns. And the trauma from pulling the trigger on herself wasn't something that could be fixed on a single road trip.

"Let's do this." Bridge unbuckled her seatbelt and stretched, putting on a show that things were normal. But in her head, the original plan was still floating around. She didn't want to end her life, but she struggled to see a way around it. For the moment, she clung to her dad's hope. It was all she could do to put one foot in front of the other.

Liam was still busy on his computer in the back, expanding and building their aliases to the point where they had electronic dental records, elementary through college grades, and certificates for music lessons, karate classes, and everything else under the sun. Rory helped Liam out of the car and they hobbled to their "vacation home" on the water. That's what they'd told the realtor when they transferred over an extra thousand to get the place stocked before their arrival.

Drool dripped down Cowen's chin. Bridge had given him something to knock him out. Blood covered the inside of his hands. His pain had been so intense during the drive from Oregon, that his fingernails had cut into his palms.

Bridge hated seeing anyone in pain. That's why she didn't want to keep living. She couldn't be responsible for any more deaths. Any more suffering. She steeled her breaths and wiped up his drool with the hem of her shirt. "Hey, sleepy head."

Cowen's head rolled to the side as he blinked his eyes open. A grin slid across his face at the sight of her. "Where are we?"

She helped him up and out of the van, careful not to disturb the stitches holding him together. Her own heart was stapled shut. "The Villa de Retiro."

"Is that Spanish for retirement?" His steps were heavy and slow.

"No, retreat from our enemies."

Cowen paused to catch his breath. "That sounds inviting."

It sounded better than the war in Bridge's head. She helped him into the house and stopped at the kitchen sink near the great room with floor-to-ceiling windows. "You should drink." She filled a glass for him from the tap and waited until he was done. "You should rest."

"I'm hearing a lot of *shoulds*. What about you? Shouldn't you tell me why you're putting distance between us?"

Bridge slipped her arm around Cowen's waist and helped him to one of the two bedrooms on the main floor. With his body pressed against hers, she didn't need these questions. What she needed was for him to heal so they could spend their time helping people to ensure the safety of the ones they loved. And after that…well, she still didn't want to be used. Ever. She didn't want to cause harm. Ever.

"Why did your dad say we're doing this to keep you safe? What's going on?"

She helped him onto the bed, stuffing pillows behind his back to reduce the strain on the stitches in his chest.

"We can talk when you're better." She turned to go.

Cowen grabbed her hand. "You said human touch makes people heal faster."

Bridge swallowed, knowing he was right. "Yeah, I did say that." She slipped off her shoes and climbed next to him on the king bed, laying her head on his shoulder. "I'm only doing this to help you."

Cowen caressed her bare arm. "I don't buy that."

Many days later, Cowen found Bridge on the beach, her toes in the sand, her focus on the sky overhead. She wore white shorts and a baggy green t-shirt, and he knew the color would make her eyes pop. An evening storm was rolling in, and soon, it would hit. He walked gingerly in a pair of loose shorts and a Henley, his body still sore, but the constant pain was gone. His wounds were slowly healing. Once Rory gave him the okay in a few days, he'd start with some simple exercises to regain his strength. They'd be painful—he was certain of that—but what could hurt worse than Bridge's avoidance?

He opened his mouth to say something before he would scare her with his presence, but she beat him to it.

"You should be resting," Bridge said with her back to him.

"How did you know I was here?" Cowen resisted the urge to touch her.

She turned to him, her long hair flying with the wind. "I'm always aware of my surroundings."

Cowen stepped closer, wishing Bridge would let him hold her. "Did you notice the weather today looks like the day we met?"

She angled away from him. "I can see some similarities."

If she hadn't kissed him so hard that day at the rental or told him those three words, maybe he'd believe that her heart would never be his. But he knew Bridge O'Niall loved him. He just had to help her remember. "We could recreate how we met on the porch swing. I'll even let you frisk me."

"You should sit down," she said without any playfulness in her voice.

Cowen wasn't about to give up. "I will if you join me." He slipped his hand inside of hers and held it tight enough that if she tugged, it would hurt him.

"I know what you're doing," she said, glancing at their hands before zapping him with a glare.

"That's fine, as long as it works." He led her to the swing on the porch as the hot wind whipped past.

She waited for him to sit, then positioned herself on the other end, the gap between them a raging ocean.

"I don't get why you're pushing me away," he said.

Carefully, she tugged her hand free. "Nothing is ever going to work between us."

"Why?" he asked, not understanding. "Because you can't forgive me?"

She shook her head.

"Because we have to do some jobs together?" he asked. "People can be in a relationship and still work—"

She swallowed, staring straight ahead. "I can't do this forever."

He scooted closer, feeling like they were getting near the root of the problem. "Do what?"

Bridge dropped her head into her hands. "I can't let people use me. I can't hurt anyone."

The wind settled for a moment, and Cowen dared to place his fingers on her back. When he spoke, his voice was a whisper. "Is that why you tried to kill yourself?"

It took Bridge minutes before she could respond. "I don't want anyone to abuse my skills like the director is doing. Or to fall in the hands of someone worse. Until we can find a way to release Karen, Virg, and your mom from their watches, I'm going to help, but after that—"

Cowen softly touched Bridge's face, pulling her focus toward him. "I respect your plan to help others, and we can talk about that soon. But we can't gloss over what you did. You pulled the trigger on yourself. If I wasn't there to shoot your gun, you wouldn't be here. You can't give up."

Bridge tensed and shifted away like he'd said the wrong thing.

"Help me understand." He was willing to admit he didn't get it, but he'd listen until he did. "Walk me through what you were feeling." His own suicidal thoughts had been born of grief. He imagined everyone who suffered with these demons had varying reasons for how they'd started.

Her throat caught. "I wasn't giving up. I was doing it to protect everyone. I'm capable of too many dangerous things, and if someone exploited that—"

Cowen pulled his gun from behind his back and shot a rock the size of his fist on the beach, making it fly. "I am too." He let her process his actions, let her recover from the shock of the gunshot. The sound had made him wince too. "So if having these skills is reason for suicide, then I'll have to end my—"

"No," she said, pulling his gun away and setting it on the porch's floor. "You can't."

He crossed his arms. "Then neither can you."

Bridge shook her head. "There's still a risk that someone will find us, and when they do—"

"I'll stop them." He meant it. He could still see Noah's lifeless body, plus the four others he'd killed whenever he closed his eyes, but he would do it again to save anyone. To save her.

Bridge put her hand on the right side of his chest, covering his heart. "I can't let you do that. You're too gentle, too—"

He slipped his hand over hers. "I'll do whatever it takes to protect you."

"But those people…" she didn't have to say more. He knew she was talking about the ones he'd shot in the warehouse. The guilt had come once the pain killers wore off, and it ebbed and flowed. Even if it never went away, he'd still make the same choice to save her.

"They were going to kill you. I wasn't sure beforehand, but in that moment I made my choice. I *will* protect you. Always. You're my Bridge Over Troubled Water."

"That's cheesy," she said, but her defenses were visibly crumbling. "I don't want you to hurt anyone."

"Then put tranquilizer darts in my gun."

It took a moment for Bridge to mull over his suggestion before she softly placed her head on his shoulder. "I'll think about it."

His lungs filled as if he hadn't had a full breath since he'd been shot. He slipped his arm around her waist, pulling her tight. "Will you try something with me?"

She stiffened. "Maybe."

"Will you tell me five good things about yourself?"

She pulled away. "I uh…I don't know…"

"This part of healing is going to be hard. You're going to have to rewrite how you think about yourself. Tell me five things. Five qualities. What do you like about yourself?"

Her gaze bounced around, settling on the floor. "This is so hard."

Cowen gripped her hand. "I know. But it's essential. You might struggle to name any, but I could list dozens. Probably hundreds." He waited, but she remained silent. "I'll start you off. You're amazing at caring about others."

She shrugged like she struggled to believe it.

"Repeat after me, I'm amazing at caring about others." Again, he waited. "If you don't start coming up with your own, I'm going to start talking about how you're the most incredible kisser. And the shape of your—"

"Fine." She flashed him a fiery look, dropping her focus back to the ground. "I'm amazing at caring about others." Her chest heaved. "I'm good with dogs…I've got a decent sense of humor. I want other people to be happy."

"Good. That's four." Cowen squeezed her hand. "You've got this. And when you believe these things, you'll realize that you deserve happiness too. I think people who struggle with suicidal thoughts have a hard time accepting this. I know I did."

Bridge finally looked at him, her lip quivering. "I'm willing to sacrifice myself to protect other people."

Cowen loved her willingness to be so selfless, but he worried about that notion driving her. "Promise me you'll never consider taking your life again." The wind picked up, and he waited for it to settle. "Maybe there are a few extreme instances of sacrifice to save others when it's okay, but other than that, there is no reason *ever* to take your own life. Even if you think things will be better with you gone, they won't. Nothing has ever filled the hole from my dad's death. I'm sure you can say the same about your mom. Suicide is never better." He stared into her eyes. "I can't lose you."

The shudder in Bridge's chest rippled through his arms. "I can't lose you either."

"Do you believe me?" he asked.

She bit her lip as she nodded.

"Do you believe in yourself?"

It took Bridge a moment to find her voice. "I'm beginning to." She seemed to move closer.

Was Cowen imagining the distance between them shrinking? He glanced at her lips. "You know, this moment is almost perfect."

"Almost?" she asked as an alarm sounded from his phone.

He sighed. "I guess we need some dessert. And from what I understand from a baking competition I was in, my chocolate chip cookies in the oven are award-winning."

Bridge pulled away, narrowing her eyes. "Did you just diss my cookies with yours?"

"Only if it gets you to punch my arm," he said, trying to keep a straight face. "I'll do anything for your touch."

Bridge dropped her head into her hands again, not the playful reaction he'd hoped for.

"Hey," he said, rubbing her back. "I'm sorry. I'm just trying anything to get you to come back to me."

"But why?" Bridge turned toward him, her gaze blazing through his. "What happens if I can't protect you? Or you can't protect me? What good are these nice things we tell ourselves if we lose each other?"

Cowen took both of her hands in his. "We're all going to die someday. There's nothing we can do about that fact. And our tomorrows are limited. We can live them all alone, or together." He rubbed the backs of her hands with his thumbs, trying to get his point across. "I would rather lose you tomorrow if I got to hold you today."

She angled an eyebrow. "Is this your way of saying my fear is irrational?"

"No." Why was she so difficult? Though, he wouldn't have her any other way. "The dangers in our future are on my mind too. But I hope you see how I've already given everything up to be here. To be with you. I could have gone to prison and still had visits from my mama, but I chose to be here. I *want* to be here."

"About that…" Bridge stood and held up a finger for him to wait. "I'll be right back."

"Are you getting the cookies? Or are you leaving because of something I said?"

She paused. "I'll take care of them while I'm up." She conveniently didn't mention why she was going.

"Don't forget to sprinkle the kosher salt." Cowen tipped his head back as the wind picked up. All the angles he'd played weren't working, not that this was some game. He was opening up his heart over and over again. Couldn't she see that? Or had she truly moved on? Maybe Bridge would never be able to forgive him for the mess they were in or accept his love.

At least she was learning to forgive and accept herself. That was most important.

Cowen shook his head and closed his eyes against the incoming storm. Regardless of what Bridge chose about him today, he wouldn't give up unless she asked him to.

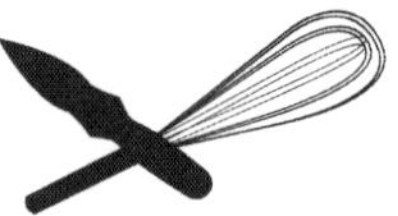

Bridge held the papers that would give a Mr. Bradley Damon an all-expenses-paid vacation to The Virgin Islands for a week. His absence from work would require someone to fill his position at the East Portland Dialysis Center. It was a good thing Bridge's dad still remembered enough in the medical field that he could train Cowen how to do the job. It might be a while before the mother and son could celebrate holiday dinners, but Cowen could at least spend some hours with his mom, explaining what happened in person. She'd already received a secure phone in some funeral flowers with pictures showing her son was still alive along with messages that he would contact her shortly.

The cookies cooled beside Bridge while she watched the wind tousle Cowen's hair. He was right. In so many ways, he was right about not giving up on each other for fear of the future. He'd already proved that he would protect her and that it wasn't ripping him apart. But she was still unsettled. Her skill set was so dangerous.

And even though she'd started to think more positive things about herself, it was hard to remember them minute after minute. She'd barely left Cowen on the porch and her negative thoughts were already weighing on her.

She knelt on the floor and closed her eyes tight. "Virgin Mary. Mom? What should I do? I want to make things right. I want to do good. And I want to feel worthy of happiness. But how can I guarantee that no one will ever use me again?"

A high-pitched voice answered back. "You help your brother Liam steal lots of money and then retire on a deserted island in the Bahamas."

Bridge swung her fist back, connecting to Liam's stomach, and he doubled over laughing.

"Seriously, sis. Relax. You don't have to have everything planned out. And you don't have to fix everything for everyone. You're so focused on repairing the past that you're ruining your future. Trying is what counts. So keep going and accept yourself. You're doing better than you think." He extended his hand to her.

She glared at it before letting him pull her up. "Why, of all people, would it be you that gives me good advice?"

Liam shrugged. "I've got to be good at something to stay on the team." He gave her a wink and motioned outside. "Are you going to leave him out there? He's waiting for you in a hurricane." He pointed to the window before disappearing out of the kitchen.

The weather wasn't that bad, but the outdoor curtains *were* flying horizontally. Before Bridge could decide whether to go to Cowen or not, her dad entered, folding her into his arms.

"I received word that the agent from the airport made it home. He's recovering fine."

Bridge's throat hitched as she pulled her dad tighter. "Thanks for letting me know." She couldn't bring Harley back, couldn't even begin to fully mourn her loss or the deaths of the other mob members, but knowing one person was going to make it lifted an enormous weight off her shoulders.

"You are so important to me." Her dad wrapped her tighter. "And that's why I'm going to tell you this. Ever since you were little, you've taken things apart to learn how they work and then you fixed them. You've always said that if anything has moving pieces, you can repair it. Aren't you and Cowen made of moving parts?" He let that sit as he let go and slipped away, leaving Bridge to make her own decisions.

But she needed more time. Days passed as she thought everything through. Happiness sounded a lot better than the opposite, and every day, she told herself she deserved it. She was on her way to believing those words because deep down, she felt that every person in this universe deserves second chances and joy. Those notions had to be true for her too.

On an overcast afternoon, she found Cowen sitting on the porch.

"Why are you smiling?" He scooted over to make room for her, giving her plenty of space.

"What?" She bit her lip and settled beside him, her hips touching his. "No smiles here."

Hope shone from his expression. He inched his fingers toward hers, letting a few of them touch. "I don't believe it. Do I need to kiss it out of you?"

Bridge shook her head, fighting nerves that lit up like neon signs.

He traced the family crest tattoo on her wrist. There was no point in hiding it now. Liam had leaked the design on the web, creating fake hype on TikTok. Already, dozens of other people had it. "Now that I'm part of the team, does this mean I get one?"

"Sorry, you have to be family," she said.

"Does marrying in count?" he asked with a delicious smile. "Your mom had it."

Flutters erupted in Bridge's stomach. "Marriage *does* count."

Cowen's shoulders slumped. "Man, I was set on getting one. Do you think Liam could be interested in me?"

Bridge softly punched his leg.

"Hmm…I guess I'll have to find another way. Maybe you…and me…" His gaze lowered, settling on her lips.

Electricity zinged up and down Bridge's spine. "I have some conditions."

"I'm pretty sure I'll accept them all."

She swatted his shoulder, not knowing how else to respond to his flirting. "The first is that we only steal from bad guys and only when necessary."

Cowen nodded. "I'm down with that, though these are weird marriage terms."

She ignored him and his use of the "M" word. "We work on repaying all the wrongs in the ledger."

A slight groan came from Cowen's throat, his expression falling.

Bridge understood his disapproval. She'd let her focus on atoning for everyone's sins control her life. And that had been miserable. She wanted happiness. No, she deserved it. "But we can do it slowly because I *want* to fix things, not because I have to. Some stupid person told me that intent makes a difference, and I'm ruining my life by focusing on the past."

Cowen laughed. "That seems like pretty good advice from someone who's dumb."

She rolled her eyes. "Are you in or not?"

"Still in."

Bridge let his acceptance seep into her beliefs about herself. Little by little, she was healing. "We have to create the perfect plan to catch Gertie and Alex. Jasper needs rescuing, though I'm sure he's loving all the puppy action at Karen's. I hear he's better, by the way. And of course freeing Karen, Virgil, and your mom from the director's grasp is the priority." Bridge paused, remembering another thing she'd hoped to fix. "And I want to take down a corrupt online waitressing school."

He nodded. "This is sounding better and better, though I have no idea what an online waitressing school is."

Bridge took a steadying breath and reached for Cowen's hand. "And you have to bake something every day to process your grief. I know it's still there."

He swallowed and intertwined his fingers with hers. "I can do that. But what about you?"

"If I bake, we'll have too many sweets. I can't fit through ductwork if I'm three hundred pounds."

Cowen shook his head as if not believing she could put on that kind of weight. "What if we sell what we make?" He rubbed the back of her hand with his thumb. "I already checked. This side of San Felipe doesn't have a bakery. We could start a business. A legitimate one." He lifted her hand and kissed the inside of her wrist, his lips lingering. "What do you say to opening A Pinch of This here? You and me…working side by side… making things sweet?"

Bridge choked on her breath, his kiss scrambling her body's normal functions. "How do we know which desserts to sell? I don't want to hurt your feelings if mine are better than yours."

He laughed again. "We'll have a bake war. Our customers will decide, and the winner takes all." He tenderly kissed her wrist again. And again. "What do you say?"

"Cowen Amaratti," she swore.

"What?" he asked, clearly confused at her tone.

Bridge couldn't keep the grin off her face. "You made the list."

"What list?"

"Your name is officially a swear word," she said, "mixed in with all of my movie star gods."

"I guess I should be flattered?" he asked with another laugh. "Why did you curse?"

"Because you're a thief." She bit her lip. "I always figured I'd end up with one."

His expression danced, clearly amused. "How am I a thief?"

Bridge tugged him in for the deepest, longest kiss of her life, more decadent than the gooiest chocolate chip cookie. Creamier than the fluffiest whipped cream. Breathless, she pulled away. "You're a thief because you stole my heart."

"You know that sounds cheesy, right?" he asked, leaning in for another kiss.

She jerked away. "Are you sure you want to make fun of my word choices? I'm always carrying a knife, you know."

"Okay, okay." He pulled her close. "It's not cheesy if we both say it. You stole my heart too."

acknowledgments

Here's a peak into the life of a writer. I thought this book was done, and I sent it off to readers, but deep down I knew I hadn't given everything yet. Frankly, I didn't want to. In my last book, The Lonely Mortician, I was very vulnerable. If you know me, you know my heart was the ink that bled on each page. Bake Wars was supposed to be a fun, quick read (The Lonely Mortician was supposed to be that too…ahem), but Bake Wars took a turn I wasn't expecting. I tried to let it run its course, to let the story go where it wanted to go, but in order to make it work, to not fall flat (maybe for some of you it still did), I had to put a piece of me in it.

Some of the feelings hit so close to home. Hopefully, I did them justice for you. And hopefully, you had fun reading this.

There are some interesting moral topics in this book, and I've grown in considering the different perspectives of these characters. I love how literature not only gives us an escape, but it can help us become more empathetic to others and their beliefs and opinions.

If you've ever struggled with suicidal thoughts, know that you're not alone. Know that you matter. You are wanted and needed. We all are.

I'm grateful you're here, reading my works and sharing this journey with me. I'm also very grateful to several people who made this book come to life.

Acknowledgements

To my editor, Faralee Pozo, I'm so glad I could work into your schedule. Your knowledge inspires me, and I learned a lot. Plus, I think you're one of the coolest humans. Ever.

Taylor Christianson, you rescued this book multiple times from the scrap pile when I stopped believing in it. You convinced me to go that extra mile and leave a piece of myself on the page. You absolutely deserve the dedication for this work.

Thank you to Kate Ryskamp for always being my biggest cheerleader. Someday we're going to grow old, wear purple, and get censured from town hall meetings.

Teira Wilson, you get an award for sticking with me through so many novels. Your insights are always exactly what I need.

Thank you to Ali Biorn, Brittany Frary, Bryce Christianson, and Daniel Thurston for sharing so many insights into what you were feeling and thinking while you read. You all kept this book going, helping me to believe in it.

Thank you to Melinda Barker, Kim Golding, Leandra Carter, Maren Sommer, Kelsy Hinton, and Lisa Sandlin, for reading some or all and providing feedback.

To Richard, you are always my favorite person. Thanks for listening to countless hours of my ramblings about my books, being the first to read them, and supporting me at every step. I'm holding you to your promise to take me to Switzerland once I hit five thousand followers.

To my kids, thank you for letting me be an author mom. I know it's not easy. I'm proud of who each of you are becoming, just don't get too lost along the way. You are not alone. You matter. You are wanted and needed.

And thank you to my Heavenly Father. You make everything possible, give me the best ideas, and haven't given up on me. Rumor has it You never will.

<h1 style="text-align:center">sneak peek</h1>

scenes from D.M. Tregaskis' next book, a romantic comedy:

<h1 style="text-align:center">Definitely NOT Cruising for Love</h1>

<h2 style="text-align:center">Coming Spring 2025</h2>

*Words, thoughts, plot, and characters are subject to change.

Indie Clizby tugged at the furry Chewbacca head again as she paced in the costume shop near her research lab in Cambridge, Massachusetts. Like the first time she'd pulled, the strap snagged her fine, caramel hair and refused to budge without balding her scalp. If her brain was wired for physics instead of biology, maybe she could think her way out of her rubbery prison that grew sweatier by the second. And if her family were slightly more normal, she wouldn't be here, picking out a vacation gift for her brother-in-law.

"Just a friendly reminder," came an annoyed male voice over the intercom. "Do not try on the masks."

Too late now. Indie tugged repeatedly as she paced, but no dice. Her hair seemed bent on trapping her.

"Can't you read?" the same male voice sounded behind her, but it had moved past annoyed, settling on perturbed.

"Yes, I can." Indie turned, facing a guy around her age in his late twenties. He had hotty-vibes hair and an adorable cleft in his chin.

Oof. Why did he have to be cute?

"I have a PhD in cancer biology from Harvard, so I can definitely read." Indie made a tight fist and counted to five before releasing it, a technique she'd practiced with her therapist. Her oversharing stopped—for now.

The disgruntled worker crossed his arms over his chest, staring her down. "A PhD? Thanks for proving that money can buy everything. Are you inept or bent on breaking the rules?"

"Neither." It was getting hard to breathe. She stripped off her winter coat, dropping it to the floor in a heap. "I didn't know you can't try—"

He pointed to a huge sign above the stack of Chewbacca heads that she'd overlooked.

"Clearly, I'm buying this mask," Indie said, her vision becoming spotty. Her lack of oxygen indicated the need to pick a different gift, even though her brother-in-law, Clay, hated Star Wars, making the Chewbacca mask perfect. She wanted him to be uncomfortable, not suffocate. "Can you help me get this off?"

The worker gave her a loathing look but motioned for her to turn around. The instant he stepped close, she breathed in his delicious scent through the sweaty mask.

"You smell amazing." Of course, these words should have stayed in her head, but Indie had a problem. "I'm sorry. I have logorrhea, or at least something similar, though we have no record of any trauma to my head." She would give anything to stop talking, but once on a roll, her rambling mouth was like a bad day that wouldn't end. The clench and release technique couldn't save her now. "Some people compare it to diarrhea, but it comes out the other end as words I don't want to say. I almost always have it under control, just not around hot guys, especially when they smell good."

The heat rising to Indie's face made the mask even more unbearable as she waited for him to process her info dump. Since puberty when her problems started, most people tried to get out of conversations with her. Some laughed. Others put on airs of revulsion. This guy was different.

"It's okay. I get it." He slipped his fingers gently around the mask's strap. "My cousin has Down syndrome."

Indie's problem was *not* comparable to a genetic disorder.

"Why are you buying a Chewbacca mask in February?" he asked, his fingers tugging and pulling at her hair.

What possessed him to ask her questions? Did he not understand that she had zero control around him? "I'm leaving for a cruise today." She had exactly one hour to get to the airport. "Every family trip has a theme and my mom and sister make matching items for us to wear, or *humiliations* as I like to call them." This wasn't answering his question directly—that's not how her mouth worked once activated. "Two years ago, they made patterned leggings with images of our family cat, Mr. Ruggles. I still have squeamish nightmares from seeing my six-foot, two-hundred-pound dad in skin-tight fabric."

The worker continued to pull and tug.

"For this trip, they've added a new level of embarrassment. Everyone has to bring a costume item for someone else to wear. I drew my brother-in-law's name, and though I love Clay because he's married to my sister Alice, we've got a past."

"Oh?" the worker asked, his tone slightly amused. At least one of them was enjoying this.

"He asked me out first, probably a sympathy date to get my sister's attention because no one wants to get stuck with this mouth." Her lips settled as if taking a break. Hopefully, she was that lucky.

"I'd get this costume for him too." The worker gave one more tug, lifted the mask off Indie's head, and shoved it into her hands.

The nearby mirror showed her shoulder-length hair pointing in a million different directions. "Here, hold this." She returned the mask and began smoothing each piece into place, but not before a sixty-something woman turned into their aisle and startled at Indie's appearance and her coat on the floor.

"It's not make-out hair," Indie said, her cheeks growing red. "I mean, it looks like it, but we haven't kissed yet." Yet? Why did her mouth hate her so?

The woman grimaced and backed away as if pretending she hadn't heard.

Indie slowly turned around, and the worker shoved the Chewbacca head back into her hands. "You're still buying this."

"Yeah, I know." She tucked it under one arm, the fur tickling her skin where her roaring twenties t-shirt didn't cover. "Do you have recommendations for something else to get my brother-in-law? I don't want him to suffocate. And I'm sorry for insinuating we might…kiss." She let the word linger, letting him know she wasn't opposed to exploring that option. This guy could be the one. He hadn't laughed or run away in fright. She'd just have to explain some things about how comparing her condition with Down syndrome wasn't appropriate, and—

The worker gave her a side-eye as if solidifying his conviction that a kiss between them was never going to happen. "Follow me, I have just the thing."

Indie walked out five minutes later with the Chewbacca head in one bag and a tiara in another. But not just any tiara. It had a disco ball that would light up when anyone clapped, and it produced a high squeaky voice that said "Call me princess," whenever anyone used the word *like* in the vicinity.

Best purchase ever.

Snowflakes fell as Indie inched along the ice-covered sidewalk toward her reliable Toyota 4Runner. She was *almost* excited to experience the sun, sand, and wind in her hair. But like usual, she had no one to share the experience with. Her family didn't count. Not when she was the only single adult. Plus, she would probably spend the entire vacation in her cabin, catching up on research. That didn't require sunscreen.

***

Rain. Sunny Florida greeted Indie with torrential rain. She stepped onto deck eighteen of the Ventura Royale cruise ship at 1:34 p.m., her shirt soaking in six-point-two seconds. Some women look even prettier with wet hair, but Indie was more of the drowned rat variety.

Her room onboard wasn't ready yet, and the text from her mom said for everyone to meet here. Indie had insisted on paying for a private cabin, not wanting to sleep in a drop-down bunk above her parents. Jeff Clizby snored like an overweight freight train on a worn track and Eloise Clizby preferred sleeping in the nude.

No, thank you.

The other option was to share with her niece and nephew, watching them all night instead of sleeping. Double no, thank you. This was supposed to be her vacation too, though she had a literal stack of research to go over in her suitcase.

The rain poured harder.

Was this really where she was supposed to meet her family? Indie found a seat alone under a shade umbrella by mini golf hole one, which wasn't hard to do seeing the entire deck was empty. She shot off another text to the group chat.

Guys, where are you?

Indie glanced up and saw the cute, chin-cleft guy from the costume shop in Massachusetts. What was he doing here, and why was he approaching her? She blinked repeatedly, and her world came into focus. This guy had zero clefts—not that people usually have more than one in their chins, but you never know. He *did* have a set of dimples, his hair was a messy tangle of delicious dark locks, and he had a swoon-worthy scar above his eyebrow. Her staring seemed to summon him.

"Do I know you?" He stopped in front of her under the umbrella, tilting his perfectly chiseled head to the side, releasing water droplets from his hair.

She felt her face flame, expecting the worst to come. "You look like someone I know." Except the chin-cleft guy was a stranger. "I mean, someone I annoyed this morning."

"I'm honored?" A laugh was hiding in his voice. "Will I get the same privilege if I sit next to you?"

"Possibly." A flutter set loose in Indie's stomach. He was considering sitting next to her? There was no hope now. "Fair warning, I have a condition where I say things that I shouldn't, like I didn't bring enough tampons if I start my period, and I haven't kissed a guy since I was twenty-two." This morning's conversation in the costume shop was a tease compared to this full-on strip show, divulging far more than Indie ever wanted to.

The cute, dimpled guy dropped his gaze. Her chances of ever kissing anyone again were so slim, they were in the negative.

"Did you know there's someone trapped in your bag?" He sat beside her, pointing to the packaged tiara as it finished saying, "I'm a princess."

She kept watching him, wondering why he hadn't run away screaming.

"I'm aware. It's a voice-activated gift that I bought because the first one I picked out was too mean." Indie shook her head, her brain clunkily shifting gears. "Is there something wrong with you?" She knew that wasn't polite to ask, but it came out anyway. "I'm struggling to understand why you would willingly sit next to me after hearing what I'm like."

One corner of his lips lifted, and he leaned toward her ever so slightly as the tiara continued its loop. "My only problem is that I don't know your name."

For once, Indie had nothing to say as a gust of wind blew a smattering of rain into her face. Maybe this guy liked her wet rat look. Maybe someone in this world could tolerate her. "My name is Indie, but do *not* confuse me with the fictional explorer. I'm not the adventurous type."

"That's fixable. You just need to be around the right people. I'm Ansel."

Fixable…was there something wrong with how she approached life? Indie tucked that thought away to address later. A hot guy was actually talking to her. "Like Ansel Adams? And can you prove that you're real, not a dream?"

Ansel wet his lips. "May I?" He pointed to her hand before gently picking it up and placing a soft kiss on the back.

Indie had to fight to keep her eyes from rolling back.

"My name is spelled exactly like the photographer's, but I don't take pictures," he said, placing her hand back in her lap. "At least not amazing ones. What do you do?"

"I study plants and organisms, looking for a cure for cancer." How had she said something normal? Maybe the right guy had a calming effect on her runaway mouth, and maybe he was it. If Indie could finally get married and have kids, her family would lay off the pressure. She might even settle for far less than Prince Charming if they'd stop pushing her.

"That sounds more intellectual than my acting. I'm performing in one of the shows onboard. What do you think the odds are that I'll see you after?" he asked.

His question didn't compute. Did he want to avoid her…or did he want to see her again? "The ship is huge. The odds are one in five thousand, six if you count the crew."

Ansel rubbed his kissable, cleft-free chin. "I don't think that'll do. We need a place to meet up. How about the aft lido deck, ten p.m. I'll be ready for a swim."

Words refused to form. Indie always had something to say—way too much—but she was officially tongue-tied.

He leaned closer. "This is the part where you accept. Or you crush my hopes."

Usually, Indie put her niece and nephew to bed on family vacations, but not tonight. She had a date with a stranger. "I'll be there."

Ansel stood and gave her a lingering stare. "I'll see you soon." A grin lifted his lips as he turned and walked away, his gait sprinkled with the tiniest inflection of a swagger.

The moment he disappeared from view, Indie's phone rang, and an image of her mom's face flashed on the screen.

"It's about time," Indie said, pressing the device to her ear to hear over the rain. "Why haven't any of you returned my messages?"

"I'm sorry." Eloise sounded confused. "I don't remember sending any of those texts about meeting now. Alice gave me something so I won't get sick when the boat moves, but it knocked me out. Your dad too. I'm on the observation deck to get a signal. Where are you?"

"Deck eighteen. You didn't message me to meet you here?" Indie watched a sailboat passing their docked cruise ship on the bay. They were scheduled to set sail for the Caribbean at six-thirty.

"I don't remember sending that." Eloise had an impeccably sharp mind at fifty-two, but she still forgot things now and again. "Plus we're meeting at dinner. Everyone else agreed to relax and rest before then. I probably butt-messaged you."

Meet near miniature golf hole one on deck eighteen seemed too specific to be a random message, but her mom wasn't one to lie.

"What's your room number?" Indie stood, readying to walk out into the rain.

"Twenty-three-nineteen," her mom said. "I'll meet you there."

Indie hung up, grabbed the gift bag and carry-on, and headed toward her parent's room, her feet barely touching the floor. She had a date!

As soon as she knocked, the door swung open.

Eloise gasped. "You waited in the rain?" She pulled her daughter in for a hug, even though Indie's wet clothes instantly soaked her own. Her short hair had long ago turned gray, but she wasn't one to act her age.

Indie hugged her back and pulled away. "Yeah, but this guy approached, and—"

The door across the hall opened and Alice, Indie's older sister stepped out. She was one of those perfectly polished types with straight, auburn-colored hair and naturally rosy cheeks. Plus, she had a genuinely nice personality that no one, not even Indie, could ever hate.

"A guy?" Alice's lips curved up in a gossip-hungry grin.

Indie's stomach fluttered as she grabbed her mom's and sister's hands and pulled them into the room. Her dad was snoring softly on the bed, oblivious to their presence, and they all sat around his feet.

"I met a handsome guy." Indie let that comment sink in.

"What did you say to him?" Eloise asked, confused. "Therapy must be working because you're smiling."

"I mentioned tampons, my period, and how long it's been since I kissed a guy."

Alice smacked her head with her palm. "That's the Holy Trinity of the worst things you could say."

Indie could hardly sit still. "I know. But he wants to meet me tonight."

Alice shrieked and bounced on the bed. "It's working!"

Indie and Eloise gave her confused stares.

"My, uh, prayers. My kids need cousins." Alice swiped a stray hair off her forehead. "What's his name?"

"Ansel." Indie's hands began to shake, her nerves kicking in because she didn't want to screw this up. "What do I do? I haven't gone out with a guy in so long." And usually, she only had sympathy dates like the one with Clay before he became her brother-in-law.

"Maybe this one is a keeper." Eloise gripped Indie's hands fiercely as if calling down some magical powers to seal the fate of her words. Apart from lying and murder, she'd do about anything to see her youngest daughter married off to spawn more grandkids.

Alice cleared her throat. "Or maybe he's a springboard to someone better."

Indie narrowed her eyes. "You're writing him off before you even meet him?" That was so Alice, not trusting that Indie knew best for her life.

"No, I just don't want your hopes to be crushed. Be careful, okay?" Alice waited for her sister to nod. "We need to get you ready. Your hair is Medusa meets Russell Brand."

***

Soft piano music played overhead as Indie got in line for the dining room where elegant chandeliers hung above tables with velvety slipper chairs. She wore a cocktail dress for dinner. It had a boat neck that accentuated her shapely collar, capped sleeves, and it hugged all the right places. The gold color made her hazel eyes shimmer.

Scents of cooked meats and garlicky sauces floated in the air, reminding Indie she should have stopped by the buffet line earlier for a snack. But like usual, she'd gotten sucked into her work, locking herself into her portless interior room after Alice had finished her hair and makeup. To justify a swim with Ansel, Indie needed to stuff as much research in as she could before ten. And study helped her to squelch the terrors bubbling in her throat. She was afraid of saying all the wrong things and scaring him off.

Indie's family was already seated somewhere inside the dining room, and she was running late, *also* as usual. Every second was an opportunity to find a cure for cancer. At any moment, she might discover something that could change the course of history. It made sense to her to spend each waking minute pursuing a solution. It was a sacrifice she was willing to make, though she wished dating the perfect man would easily fall into the equation somehow.

The line moved up, and Indie inched forward while her face was glued to the phone in her hand, the screen detailing the preliminary findings from the skin of the goblin shark. She was so absorbed that she failed to notice the man in front of her had stopped, and she bumped into him.

"I'm so sorry," Indie said without looking up. Like a whirlpool, she was completely sucked into her research. She had to know if this shark was the answer or a waste of time. And she had to focus on something other than her date tonight.

"No problem," the stranger said as the line moved forward. But he lingered.

Indie finally gave him some attention, and her lips started to twitch, itching to say something without her consent. He didn't have a cleft in his chin, at least she couldn't see one behind perfectly manicured facial hair, but he had ridiculously kind eyes, muscly arms, and his hair…it was thick and begging for her to run her hands through it. He was a mix between a younger version of Brad Pitt and an older Miles Morales if the character were real and not a cartoon. *And,* he was checking her out.

"You should know that my mouth literally can't be controlled when I'm around handsome men like you," she said, grateful her opening statement was so benign. "And I'm on a mission to save the world. No time for distractions."

His head tilted as he considered her. "The name is Elijah. I can get behind a mouthy heroine. Maybe I'll see you around?" He let his question linger as the hostess waited for his attention and then connected him to a server. He gave Indie one last look before he disappeared from view.

Indie touched her cheeks, knowing they were red. Maybe she should go on more cruises if this was how the men acted. None of them had run away yet.

"I can seat you now." A female worker approached and showed Indie to her family's large, round table. Everyone was there: her mom; her dad, Jeff; Alice and her husband Clay; Jolie age five, and Karson, age two, with the chubbiest thighs that Indie loved to squish. But there was also an unfamiliar fifty-something woman and a guy maybe around Indie's age. It was hard to tell with his face carpeted in hair.

"Who are you?" Indie asked as the host seated her between the male stranger and Alice. She had never understood the whole long, scraggly beard movement. It screamed *Do not disturb,* which was exactly the vibe this guy was giving off.

"The cruise line uses every seat in the dining room, regardless of people's preferences to eat alone, so we're stuck together for every meal," the guy said, clearly not happy about the arrangement.

Indie was so grateful she didn't find him attractive or else she'd fire off a retort like *I hope your vacation is as pleasant as you are.* But could she find him attractive with his attitude, even if he were a heartthrob? Not likely.

The woman shifted uncomfortably. "I'm sorry, we're not the best company right now. I'm Georgia. This is my son Decoy. We'll try not to bother you."

Eloise touched the woman's arm, their seats next to each other. "I hope we don't bother *you.* We can be a little much sometimes." She took the liberty of introducing each family member.

Indie snuck a peek on her phone at the molecular structure of the tissue sample from the goblin shark. Alice elbowed her, and Indie turned her phone off, sulking.

Eloise pulled out a gift bag from under the table and handed it to Alice. "I can't wait for you to rock this." She turned to Georgia and Decoy. "We always do silly things on our vacations, and this year, we're exchanging costumes or props that each person *has* to wear all night. If I knew we were sharing a table, I would have gotten something for you."

Indie shrank. It wasn't a mystery who she got her oversharing gene from. Eloise was never one to be *rude* by not including someone in a conversation.

Alice lifted an eyebrow as she pulled out a black, spiky, mullet wig from the bag. "Is this payback for the time I peed on the sofa when I was two?"

Eloise tilted her head five degrees and gave her oldest a half-smile that read *What do you think?*

Indie stole another peek at her research, but it was so hard to focus with Mr. Grumpy pants beside her. His vibe was messing with her head.

Alice donned the wig, raised her hand with the rocker symbol, and stuck out her tongue. "I've got Dad." She handed him a small box, tied with a curly bow.

"Should I be scared?" Jeff was tall and lanky except for his pantry-bandit stomach. His role in the family was going along with almost everything while keeping his spunky wife in check. He opened the package, revealing a set of ridiculously long, fake eyelashes. He grimaced but allowed his daughter to move around to his side of the table and put them on. Within three minutes, he was batting his eyes. "Am I hotter now?" He stole a kiss from his wife.

"You're…something." She laughed and pointed to Clay. "You have Indie."

Clay was a novelty. He was built like a basketball team's forward player, but he was a purely intellectual soul. He pulled out a box and handed it over, avoiding the water glasses on the table that had yet to be filled. "Alice says you used to love these."

Indie rarely liked traveling down memory lane, potholed with loss and regrets. Carefully, she steeled her heart and opened the box. Inside, sat an authentic, gold 1920s flapper turban hat. The sight of it transported Indie to freshman year at Harvard where she was vice president of the Vintage Preservation Committee. She'd organized a Charleston dance class that met weekly with a social at the end of the year. But she never got to go. Her eyes scanned the full table that felt incomplete.

"I hope it's okay," Clay said as everyone watched Indie, her silence building. Even Georgia and Decoy stole glances her way.

"It's really sweet. Thank you." Indie quickly wiped her eyes and placed the cap on her head. "I'm regretting your gift now." She handed Clay the bag, at least grateful she'd gone with the tiara instead of Chewbacca.

He pulled it out, and his young daughter reached for it, her golden curls trailing down her arms. "Sorry sis, tonight, Daddy gets this." He placed the crown on his head. "Do I want to know why it has batteries?"

"Like totally," Indie said, making the voice announce, "I'm a princess." His kids clapped, initiating the flashing lights.

"How long do we have to wear these?" Clay groaned.

Eloise grinned. "All through dinner and at the dance party tomorrow night."

"Great." He slumped in his seat. "What do *you* get to wear?"

Eloise drumrolled on the table as her husband slid over a box tied with a ribbon. She tugged it open and pulled out a Jack Sparrow braided beard and a bandana-clad dreadlock wig. "I've always wanted these!" She was entirely serious. Halloween was her favorite holiday, and she often dressed up in a different costume every day in October.

Eloise pulled up her phone's camera as a mirror and placed her beard. "Take me to treasure," she said, sticking out her hand and sweeping it across the table. Her fingers stopped as they pointed to each of her grandkids, making them giggle.

"Gran Gran, you look silly." Jolie clapped, making the tiara flash again.

Her little brother grunted and pointed out the window. All eyes followed his gaze to see the ship had started to move. Silently, they watched the scene outside as one waiter filled their water glasses and another placed a roll and a round scoop of butter on each person's plate.

Georgia lifted her purse onto her lap and dug through it, the sound of pill bottles and trinkets clanging together.

"Mom, we already took something." Decoy glanced around the table. "For motion sickness," he said as if needing to explain their conversation since the Clizbys were telling all about their lives.

His mom's movements became more frantic. "It's not working." She pulled out a multi-compartment pill box, inspected the handwritten labels, and gasped. "I'm so sorry Decoy."

His expression fell. "Mom?"

Georgia stared at her plate, avoiding Decoy's gaze. "I gave us my hormone replacement pills instead of Bonine."

Decoy managed to swallow. "You gave me estrogen pills?"

Alice cleared her throat, shifting her family's attention away from their uncomfortable dilemma. "I think Indie should be exempt from her costume tonight because it's messing up her hair for her date."

Their dad snapped his head up. "*You* have a date?"

Eloise backhanded Jeff's chest. "Don't act so surprised." She turned to Georgia and Decoy. "Indie has an unusual—"

Alice tossed a chunk of bread at her mom, hitting her square in the cheek and leaving a smidge of butter. The Clizbys clearly had excellent table manners. Maybe the cruise ship needed another act—a circus.

Jeff strangled his napkin, still backpedaling from his previous comment. "I…I'm not surprised," he said, focusing on Indie. "It's just… you met someone on the ship?"

Indies face grew hot. "Yes." Even though she wasn't attracted to Decoy, he was still a guy. This wasn't the type of conversation she wanted to have in public.

Eloise wiped the butter off her face. "Do we need to talk about manners?" she asked her oldest.

Alice nodded. "Yes, we can start with things we shouldn't tell strangers."

"And you're going out tonight?" Jeff asked Indie.

Indie could feel Decoy watching her. "I'm meeting him at the swimming pool." This cruise line would *not* get a good review. Why did they think strangers would want to sit together? Didn't people go on vacation to get away from everyone?

Clay rubbed his face, picking to jump into the dating conversation, not the fight brewing between his wife and mother-in-law. "Make sure you don't talk about your research tonight," he said, as if he were allowed to give her dating advice.

"Research?" The waiter with *Raoule from Portugal* on his name tag asked as he passed menus to each adult. Indie snatched hers, so ready for this dinner to be over.

Eloise smiled up at Raoule, ignoring Alice's warning look. "My husband had cancer when our daughter Indie was eight, and she became obsessed with finding a cure." Eloise turned her focus to Georgia and Decoy as Indie shrank further in her chair. "She asked for a microscope for her birthday the next year and when our son…" Eloise cleared her throat as if thinking twice about finishing that sentence. "Let's just say she's motivated to solve the world's problems."

"And you usually talk about your research?" Decoy asked, glancing between Indie and her phone that was currently dinging with the boring, basic ringtone she'd programmed, informing her an email had come in from the lab.

Alice leaned forward to look directly at him. "All the time, and she doesn't relax. I bet one of her suitcases is full of papers for work." Who was oversharing now?

"Wow, guys. *She* is right here." Indie loaded her roll with butter and drew her arm back, threatening her family with it. "Do we have to include strangers in our personal conversation?" Her cocked arm seemed to appease everyone, that and someone in an official-looking suit slowed as he passed their table, giving them each a warning look.

Decoy drummed his fingers along his menu. "Since we've been included in your conversation, can I ask a question?"

"No," Indie said while her mom said, "Of course."

He turned to Alice and Clay. "Do you suggest Indie should be someone else to impress her date?"

Georgia tugged on Decoy's sleeve as if warning him.

Alice frowned. "Well, no but—"

Decoy turned to Indie. "I think you should talk about your research. If a guy is going to like you, he'll like all of you."

Indie nodded along with his logic. She shouldn't have to pretend to be someone other than herself to make a guy like her. Maybe Decoy wasn't half bad—at least his advice didn't suck.

"Except she's not herself when she's talking about her work," Clay muttered barely loud enough for Indie to hear.

The ship picked up speed, and Indie could feel the almost imperceptible shift of the boat rolling side to side with the waves. Her mood shifted too, rocking between hurt and irritation.

Georgia placed a hand on her forehead. "I'm sorry to interrupt, but I need to lie down." She stood and dropped her napkin on her uneaten roll. "Excuse me."

Indie had no idea what the mother and son's dynamics were like, but Georgia's leaving seemed to ruffle Decoy's scraggly feathers. Having an extra dose of estrogen in his system probably didn't help his mood.

Their waiter came and glanced at the vacated seat. "Will she be returning?"

Decoy dropped his head. "I doubt it." He turned to Indie, his eyes searching hers with an unexpected intensity. "I think you should skip the date altogether because love is the biggest farce ever created." His brash words pushed Indie back against her chair. "All it brings is pain and misery, so why bother wasting your time?" He stood and tossed his napkin on his chair. "I'm sorry. I'm just going to get worse. I hope you all have a pleasant meal." He trudged away, leaving Indie unsettled. What was his story to have made him so bitter?

"Well, that was interesting," Eloise said as the waiter pointed at her to pick her selections.

Alice leaned close to Indie. "Don't listen to him. Go enjoy tonight, but leave out talk of research until the second…or third date."

Indie stared so hard at the menu that all the letters jumbled into one big black blob. Her family didn't understand that her research was part of her identity. She'd given up all of her interests, every ounce of her spare time, to seek a cure for cancer to prevent the suffering of others. She was proud of who she was. Why didn't her family feel the same?

The waiter turned to Alice, and she ordered the Secret Treasure, the only menu item that had zero descriptions except for a promise to thrill the adventurous person who picked it.

"Excellent choice, madam," the waiter said, his voice rich with his Portuguese accent. "And speaking of treasures, has anyone in your party signed up for the X Marks the Spot add-on? The prize is twenty-five thousand dollars."

Alice gripped Indie's hand under the table. "You should do it."

Indie had seen something about the extra package when she'd booked the room, something about a multi-port excursion treasure hunt. As fun as that sounded, she wasn't planning to get off at any stops unless her family made her. She had too much to do, and she didn't have an international plan, only the wifi she paid for on the ship. Working on excursions would be impossible.

"Going on this date tonight is enough adventure for the entire trip." And if history repeated itself, her night with Ansel would be a disaster like all of her other failed attempts. Decoy's words were souring all of Indie's hopes. She pointed to her menu, her nerves breaking past the walls she'd built all evening. Hiding behind her research was always easier than thinking about all she was missing in life. No husband. No kids. No dog. No house. "I'll have the chicken salad with ranch."

She pulled out her phone to check the email she'd received. Her eyes scanned the words once. Twice.

"What's going on?" Alice asked.

Half of Indie's lips smiled, and the other fell. "It looks like I'm not going on a date tonight." At least she could put her nerves to bed.

"Why?" Panic etched Eloise's voice. "What's wrong?"

Indie didn't want to explain something that her family wouldn't understand. "A new plant was discovered in Columbia. I have five days to study the preliminary findings and write a proposal so our lab can get it. Researchers could only smuggle one plant out of the country, and every scientist will claim they need it."

Her mom shook her head, reinforcing the action with three verbal *no's*. "This is vacation. Your work needs to wait."

"You don't get it." Indie felt like a broken record, always explaining her rationale for working so hard. "This plant could hold the cure for cancer."

"And Ansel could be the one." Alice grabbed Indie's phone and shoved it down her shirt. "You're not getting this back until you go on that date."

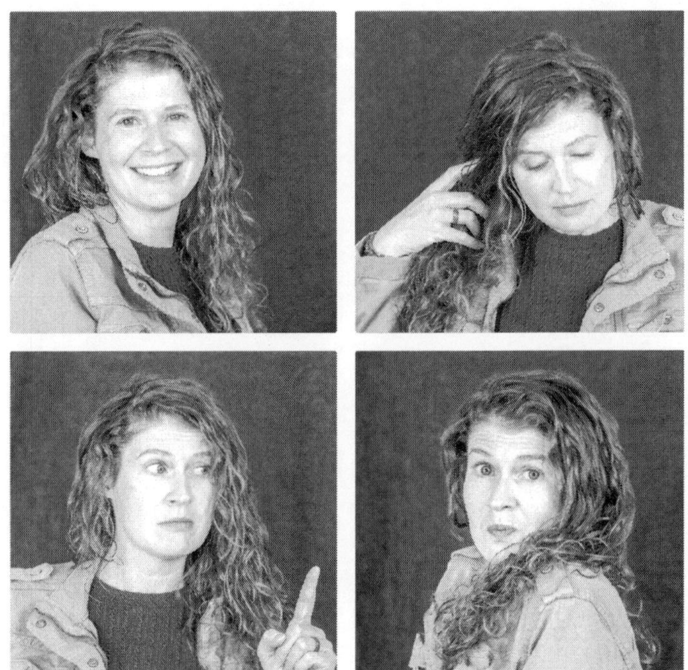

D.M. Tregaskis has a B.S. (the degree, not the expletive) from Brigham Young University. She enjoys traveling, making things pretty, and rarely being serious—at least with the people who understand her. Cookies and pie are her love languages, in case you want to get on her good side. She loves following Jesus Christ (at least she's trying to).

In her younger years, D.M. was kicked out of girls' camp for pulling pranks and now suffers payback from more daughters than she knows what to do with. She's got a doting, hunk of a husband, plus two felines. Could she be a legit author without cats?

Follow her journey and see other books at www.dmtregaskis.com. She's also on Instagram: authordmtregaskis, Facebook: Author D.M. Tregaskis: and TikTok: d.m..tregaskis (Yes there are two dots).

Made in the USA
Columbia, SC
28 July 2024

39140549R00176